THE
other
SISTER

MW01178899

Also by Lola Lemire Tostevin

Novels
Frog Moon
The Jasmine Man

Poetry
Color of Her Speech
Gyno-Text
Double Standards
'sophie
Cartouches
Site-Specific Poems
Punctum

Criticism
Subject to Criticism

THE other SISTER

a novel

Lola Lemire Tostevin

inanna poetry & fiction series

INANNA Publications and Education Inc.
Toronto, Canada

Copyright © 2008 Lola Lemire Tostevin

Except for the use of short passages for review purposes, no part of this book
may be reproduced, in part or in whole, or transmitted in any form or by any
means, electronically or mechanically, including photocopying, recording, or
any information or storage retrieval system, without prior permission in writing
from the publisher.

 Canada Council **Conseil des Arts**
for the Arts **du Canada**

 ONTARIO ARTS COUNCIL
CONSEIL DES ARTS DE L'ONTARIO

We gratefully acknowledge the support of the Canada Council
for the Arts and the Ontario Arts Council for our publishing program

We are also grateful for the support received
from an Anónymous Fund at The Calgary Foundation.

THE CALGARY
FOUNDATION

Cover design: Val Fullard
Cover artwork: J. T. Winik, "Trinity," detail, oil on canvas, 31.5" x 23", 2003
Interior design: Luciana Ricciutelli

Library and Archives Canada Cataloguing in Publication

Tostevin, Lola Lemire
    The other sister / Lola Lemire Tostevin.

(Inanna poetry and fiction series)
ISBN 978-0-9808822-1-6

I. Title. II. Series.

PS8589.O6758O84 2008   C813'.54   C2008-903902-5

Printed and bound in Canada

Inanna Publications and Education Inc.
210 Founders College, York University
4700 Keele Street
Toronto, Ontario, Canada M3J 1P3
Telephone: (416) 736-5356 Fax (416) 736-5765
Email: inanna@yorku.ca
Website: www.yorku.ca/inanna

*For the twins
and their sister*

Epigraph by Hannah Arendt is an excerpt from "Preface" in *Men in Dark Times*, copyright © 1968 by Hannah Arendt and renewed 1996 by Lotte Kohler, reprinted by permission of Houghton Mifflin Harcourt Publishing Company.

Excerpted poem on pg. 21 is by Emily Dickinson, "Poem #26," from *The Collected Poems of Emily Dickinson*, Thomas H. Johnson, editor, Boston and Toronto: Little, Brown and Company, 1960.

Excerpted song on pg. 24 is from Rita Chiarelli, "Eggs Over Easy," *Breakfast at Midnight*, Northernblues Music, 67 Mowat Avenue, Suite 233, Toronto.

The excerpt on pg. 50 is from *Black Dogs* by Ian McEwan. Copyright © Ian McEwan 1992. Reprinted by permission of Knopf Canada.

The excerpt on pg. 132 is from *Martin Heidegger: Basic Writings*, David Farrell Krell, editor, New York: Harper and Row, 1977.

Excerpted poem on pgs. 163-164, "To Awaken an Old Lady" by William Carlos William, is from *William Carlos Williams: Selected Poems*, Charles Tomlinson, editor, New York: New Directions Publishing, 1985.

...even in the darkest of times we have the right to expect some il-lumination, and such illumination may well come less from theories and concepts than from the uncertain, flickering, and often weak light that some men and women, in their lives and in their works, will kindle under almost all circumstances and shed over the time span that was given them on earth...

—Hannah Arendt

ON MORNINGS WHEN MOTHER HEADS FOR THE FRONT DOOR, *pail and coal shuttle in hand, my sister and I rush up to our bedroom and station ourselves at the window overlooking the street. Through a narrow opening in the lace curtains we watch as she follows the horse-drawn wagon, stooping every few feet to pick up the warm manure.*

It is for the garden, she proclaims when father confronts her and the reeking pail, her voice so innocent no one but father would dare question her public display of uncommon self-sufficiency.

It's already a blooming jungle back there, father grumbles, his chin tilting toward the back of the house.

But a toad can die of light, Harlan, mother replies in a feigned whimper.

Father rolls his eyes. Everyone knows that mother is not the whimpering kind and father is often short on patience this early in the morning. Damn the blasted toads! It's like the blighting Plague of Egypt out there, he shouts as mother, head high, makes her way to the side of the house and to a bin at the far end of the yard by the edge of the ravine.

Father is right about the toads. Introduced to keep the garden free of insects deemed injurious to mother's plants, the toads are multiplying so fast that mother can hardly keep up with the planting of trees and plants to protect them from too much sun. Surrounded by the neighbourhood's manicured lawns, clipped bushes, and sparse flowerbeds, our raggle-taggle assortment of trees, shrubs, and vines has earned mother a reputation. She is the neighbourhood eccentric. At least this how she imagines she is perceived. How she wants to be seen. Fastidious gardens are the measures of barren imaginations she often reminds us with pursed lips. To say more would be gossip and gossip is beneath a person of her station although discretion has never been one of mother's strong suits.

The shade garden, she explains as she weeds and transplants with her usual assurance and precision, is a perfect example of nature at its self-sufficient best. The smaller plants rely on larger trees to absorb the contaminants of the city, an essential process if we, clueless city twits who understand nothing of nature's faithful cycles, are to get enough oxygen if only to breathe. A task made considerably more difficult these last few years because of those cursed automobiles and the rampant industrialization since the war. Damned war. Nothing will ever be the same.

"A toad can die of light." One of the many lines she quotes from a small book of poems she carries in her gardening apron along with an assortment of gardening tools, her head keeping time to the cadence of each line, the knot at her nape held in place with one of the hair grips she collects, two-pronged combs with crowns intricately carved into anemones or apple blossom boughs. Except for the one father brought back from when he was stationed in France: two kneeling ivory angels facing each other, their elbows resting on a triangular topaz, the wings of each angel extending downwards forming the two grips.

Oh, Harlan! she exclaimed when she opened the beautifully wrapped box. Two guardian angels for our twin angels.

~2~

MEMORIES WERE PROVING LESS FUGITIVE THAN THE YEARS. It had been several days since Julia had written on the laptop that her daughter and her granddaughter had given her as a move-in present when she first came to Evenholme. For something to do they said, since she was, presumably, incapable of coming up with anything on her own. Each time she remembered something from the past she was to write it down.

It was surprising how much she did remember but she was even more surprised at how little time there was to write. Evenholme was not the lonely purgatory she had expected. People did not simply sit around waiting for the next stage. There were plenty of activities if one wanted to join in and while she did not care much for the organized soirées such as dances or bingo, she had signed up for most of the outings—the theatre, the opera, art galleries, museums, botanical gardens. She even looked forward to afternoons in the lounge where, under the guise of playing bridge or board games, the residents gathered to tell stories, each retelling showcasing particular events of their lives: Love and marriage. Births. Graduations. Careers. Each story a kaleidoscope reorganizing its patterns to emphasize the singleness of an occasion.

For the most part everyone kept their stories light, nostalgia having the uncanny ability of distilling and smoothing over the rougher edges. Strange reversal from when they were young, when days were spent looking to the future where their true lives would be found. Now, most of their afternoons were spent looking back to where those same lives had been lost. The years, no longer progressing in a straight line, circled back and forth, some of them relived over and over again.

The first time she came to Evenholme was to case the place. The move was inevitable considering her age and she tried to face the inevitability with as much stoicism as she could. Not unlike the two straggly evergreens on either side of the main entrance standing guard over wan hyacinths trying to live up to the rumours of spring. *The measures of barren imaginations*, her mother would have said. The light had gathered around a few lagging snowflakes, each one casting its own halo against a flinty April sky. The brass plaque on the left side of the door gleamed: *Evenholme Retirement Living.*

Pretty exclusive living at that, her daughter, Rachel, gushed in a useless effort to cheer her up. Rachel pressed the bell and chimes clanged from inside.

To be fair to her, Rachel had pleaded with her mother to go on living in her own house after her mother told her she could not manage it anymore. Rachel and her husband, Adam, would move in and she could stay put. The thought of her family witnessing her remaining deterioration, however, sent her, to use her granddaughter's vernacular, into one major funk. Plus she had not told either Rachel or Thea that she had fallen three or four times in recent months, once as she was going down the stairs. It was a miracle she hadn't broken anything and she hobbled around for days. A slight touch of rheumatism, she fibbed when they stopped by. Someone was always stopping by. The house was like Grand Central Station what with someone always checking up on her—Thea, Rachel, Adam, the woman from Living Assistance. Even the maintenance man. He'd been doing odd jobs for Julia for more than thirty years, coming around once or twice a week, but now he was showing up every day. Only pecuniary gain would inspire such devotion, so Julia suspected that Rachel was paying him extra. She didn't mind. Faithful old soul. But not as old as she was. No one was ever as old as she was anymore.

She had also started to drop things. Her doctor thought it might be due to a loss of sensation in her fingers. A rather obvious diagnosis, she thought.

Yes, I am fully aware that I am losing sensation in my fingers, but why? she asked.

Likely nerve damage to the extremities, he said as he flipped through her file to remind himself of her medical history. His father never had to do this. His father always remembered from one visit to another. And now his son who was less than half her age had a memory twice as bad. Probably because of those fancy gadgets youngsters were always using nowadays instead of relying on their brains.

Nerve damage to the extremities, she'd never heard of such a thing. She had always assumed that her mental faculties would be the first to go, or her sight and hearing, but these were still functioning relatively well as far as she could tell. Of course, it was always possible that she couldn't tell. There was always that possibility. And this is why I'm falling? she asked.

Yes, it would affect all extremities, the doctor repeated.

What about my head? Is it considered an extremity?

He smiled. Your head is fine, Mrs. Brannon.

His father always called her Julia.

Considering your age, the young doctor continued, Your head is more than fine. But falling down and dropping things isn't. What are we going to do about this?

Oh, spare me the royal *we*, she scolded him. I don't know what you have in mind, but I am going to check myself into one of those fancy places, if any will have me. It should make you happy since you've been urging me to do this for years.

He had not, in fact, been urging her to do any such thing. It had only been five years since he'd replaced his father who had retreated to one of those fancy places himself, but she was not about to quibble with a youngster no older than her grandchildren. Never a model patient, she wasn't about to change because of some juvenile who treated her as if she didn't know anything about her female anatomy or her advanced age.

Have you considered having your daughter and her husband move in with you? he asked and continued riffling her file with an exaggerated show of impartiality.

You've been discussing me with my daughter, have you?

He nodded. She worries about you.

You told her I'd fallen down the stairs?

He blushed like a school boy caught breaking ground rules.

Discussing me with anyone without my permission violates patient-doctor confidentiality. Your father would never have done this.

It's my duty, Mrs. Brannon...

It most certainly is not your duty. My personal affairs are my business and I would expect you to respect my wishes. I am perfectly capable of making my own decisions.

I realize this, Mrs. Brannon, but...

I won't hear of it. It's out of the question. I've been my own boss for too long to give it up now even if it means moving into a room the size of a placard in an old fogeys' home.

He tried to dissimulate a smile. Yes, I understand. I thought your daughter's idea might be a better solution in your case.

What do you mean in *my* case? I am not a case. I don't need you or my daughter to tell me what the best solution is for me. There are only two things I need from you, a proper diagnosis and the name of the best place I can check myself into. Not one of those hospices where they plunk people in wheelchairs, connect them to tubes, and forget about them because it's assumed they don't function anymore.

You mean a retirement home, he said, nodding vigorously, relieved at not having to involve himself beyond providing a vague diagnosis and the name of a retirement home. Some are very nice, he added. He reminded Julia of an overly keen puppy.

Yes, yes, it's what my daughter calls it. Retirement living. Different eras have different euphemisms with which to mitigate the inevitable, I suppose.

*

Her first impression of Evenholme was not as unfavourable as she expected. On the contrary, she was quite relieved until she discovered how much it would cost.

It's going to take every penny I get each month and then some. I'll have to sell the house, she told Rachel.

Rachel wouldn't hear of selling the house. It had been Rachel's home from when she was a slip of a girl until the day she married and she was as attached to it as Julia had been. As Julia was still. For more than ninety years, Julia and the house in Wildwood Park had braced themselves against the outside world. They had stood up to all the metaphorical downpours and windstorms, confident they could always right themselves again.

But now, alien to any promise of a future together, the house was letting Julia know it was time to let it go. Shoving her down the stairs and making her drop things. Even the clock on the mantel had stopped and would not respond to repeated windings, refusing to slice off another minute until she moved on.

Her last will and testament specified that Rachel would inherit the house and most of its contents and Julia saw no reason why Rachel and Adam shouldn't take possession of it now. So, after endless discussions, Rachel and Adam agreed to sell their semi-detached in the Annex and move into the house in Wildwood where they planned to retire eventually anyway. They would take care of its maintenance and taxes and pay Julia a small amount each month to help her bridge the financial gap and meet her obligations to Evenholme. It wasn't an unfair exchange. The Annex semi to which Julia had contributed a sizable down payment had quadrupled in value since Rachel and Adam had purchased it twenty-five years ago. The interest on that amount alone would more than make up for what they would contribute each month, plus they were about to inherit a house worth a fortune. In one or two years at the most, maybe less.

*

In order to give prospective residents a better idea of Evenholme's personalized comforts, the grand tour included the viewing of three occupied suites: studio, one-bedroom, and two-bedroom, the latter for a couple or two people who preferred to share. Certainly not the case for Julia. She had rattled about a large house on her own for decades and she wasn't about to parcel out this piddling space at this stage of the game. She decided on the one-bedroom suite with a kitchenette overlooking a combined living and dining area. It would be ideal for reading and her afternoon tea.

Because they were extensions of former lives, Julia found most of the suites unsuitably appointed. Beds and dressers once meant for two took up much of the bedroom. Less than half-a-dozen steps were required to get from the bed to the bathroom. A favourite reading chair and footstool which might have once fitted nicely in a corner of a large living room, extended half-way across the sitting area. Collections of paintings and photographs, pictorial histories spanning generations, crowded the walls.

I'll bring the single bed and the dresser from the guest room, the bird's-eye maple, she told Rachel. It will need a new mattress. A good one if I'm to spend the rest of my days in bed.

Rachel sighed. You won't be spending the rest of your days in bed, mother.

I'll also need a settee with a footstool, not a full sofa. These rooms are claustrophobic enough as it is.

Why don't you take the love seat we bought for the study? We've hardly used it, but I could have it recovered if you want, Rachel said.

No need to, it's fine as it is. And two of my Persian rugs to cover this nondescript excuse for a carpet. It should be washed. Or replaced. Can this carpet be replaced? she asked the attendant.

It is fairly new, the attendant replied. It would probably have to be replaced at your expense.

Fine. I'll replace it at my expense if I can choose it. I want to make sure it's a flat weave in a neutral colour, not those thick, garish synthetic dust collectors most people are so fond of. My Persians won't lie flat on those.

The attendant nodded and smiled while Rachel wrote everything down without saying much, an indication that Julia was getting to her.

The communal areas—game room, dining room, the two

lounges—bore the indelible stamp of an interior designer's idea of understated elegance on a limited budget. The faux Early American furniture suggested comfort but moderation. Fake flowers bloomed everywhere—on sofas; in paintings; dried or faded silk bouquets on marble-top sideboards. Even the plain chairs and wall-to-wall carpeting were coordinated to the pinks and mauves of the overall floral motifs. Except for a cabinet displaying a collection of Royal Doulton figurines and fancy teapots and cups, the main lounge reminded Julia of a lobby in a high-end hotel that had seen better days.

*

It's all I have to bring today, This, and my heart beside...

Rachel and Adam had intended to do most of the packing and storing and had brought dozens of cartons to the house, but Julia wouldn't let them. This was a chore she needed to do at her own pace. It was important for her to see this through for reasons she didn't examine or question other than it marked the end of her history at Wildwood. The end of her history, period.

It was agreed that Rachel and Adam would assemble and set up the empty cartons in the attic and each day, over a period of a month, Julia carried a few items at a time, wrapped them and stored them until each carton was full. Before sealing the boxes with masking tape, she placed a few sprigs of lavender from the giant lavender plant in the greenhouse. It was the only plant still flowering in there. She would have preferred lilac, but it wasn't the season yet. Whoever opened the boxes in the months or years to come would be greeted by a scent reminiscent of monogrammed linens, sachets between layers of underclothes worn only on special occasions. Perhaps even whiffs of tobacco from when she occasionally retreated to the attic to smoke and recollect, a habit that had persisted from when she and her sister were girls. History would make itself present within this space where souls still dwelled and where her life had taken such a peculiar turn.

Other than the few pieces of furniture she needed, she brought only enough toiletries as if she were going on an extended holiday. Also two long fleecy robes for lounging and six changes of clothes—two each for winter and summer, and two for in-between. The styles didn't vary much—long, narrow skirts, some with jackets to match; white linen blouses, a few sweaters. Two pairs of slippers, two pairs each of summer and winter shoes, and one pair of snow boots although she doubted she would need those, except perhaps on frigid days when the jitney bus took residents to the theatre or the opera.

She packed enough books to fill the available shelves, most of which she had put aside for when there would be more time to read. She had always bought books compulsively and hadn't read half of them. Too many books were read as pretexts for killing time and not wanting her time dead she had put them aside after a few pages. Ironic, wasn't it? So little time left and she now felt she could afford to waste it.

There were also those few items she simply couldn't bring herself to leave behind: her mother's collection of fancy combs; two photographs by Alfred Stieglitz that her mother had purchased on a wedding shopping trip to New York; the strings of pearls she and her sister wore as part of the wedding attire; family photographs including one of the wedding; a dozen or so childish drawings signed either Billy, Tommy, Rachel or Thea. Other than these, she had no need of her art collection and left it behind.

Her first priority was deciding where to hang the drawings, especially the two of the house that Billy and Tommy did when they were barely five years old. One depicted the house and garden in vivid summer colours while in the other the house was buried under a blanket of snow. It was important that they be visible from the love seat. Some of the photographs would go on the dresser in the bedroom and others on the table beside the narrow French doors that also served as the only window for the sitting area. They opened onto a shallow Juliet balcony with an unusually high railing, undoubtedly a cautionary measure to keep the vulnerable from pitching over. Spindly and winter-battered English

Ivy trailed from a narrow planter, looking nothing like the green cascade depicted in the brochure.

On moving day, once everything had been put into place, Julia looked around the two crowded rooms. The mirror on the dresser facing the bedroom door reflected most of the suite giving the illusion of more space. The few things she had brought seemed to have multiplied. Oh dear, she muttered, I didn't manage to rid myself of all my lares and penates.

What are lares and penates? Thea wanted to know.

Possessions. A post-graduate student should know this, Julia told her granddaughter. As she turned around to survey the suite, she caught her dismayed reflection in the mirror and for a fleeting moment she got the disquieting feeling that her twin sister was watching from some other place and some other time. Well, well, she seemed to be saying with a malicious grin. Would you just look at us now.

*

Mother comes upon a young girl going up the attic stairs. It could be either Sissa or me.

Where are you going, Sister? mother asks.

The girl points to the attic door. Up there, she replies.

Why?

Sissa and I are playing hide and seek.

But Sister is hiding downstairs, mother whispers.

The young girl pats herself on the chest and says, I'm looking for me.

~3~

WHILE THE RESIDENTS WERE ENCOURAGED TO EAT AT LEAST ONE meal a day in the main dining room, new arrivals were allowed an adjustment period during which they could eat in their suites until they settled in. Until they decided to get on with it. It took two weeks for Julia to finally venture out for her main meal, which she usually ate at noon. After another week, she followed the residents to the main lounge where many gathered in the afternoon.

As she approached the cabinet with the figurines and the teacups, she stopped and turned to a woman walking by. Aren't those lovely, she said to the woman. She was, in fact, not fond of Royal Doulton figurines, but it was time to make an effort at socializing, a custom in which she had never had much interest until now.

The woman barely glanced back. Oh those, she said in a heavy accent, They were left here by someone who died. I think you got her room, the woman added and shrugged as if to say, I don't care for knickknacks or other people's deaths. Julia noticed her eyes. They were different from one another. One was a bright and clear blue while the other was cloudy. Well, Julia thought, I hope not all residents are as ungracious as this one.

Conscious of a roomful of people appraising the new arrival, she resolutely made her way to one of the sofas while scanning the room for a more likely candidate to whom she could introduce herself. The cushion barely gave as she sat down. Some professional interior designer must have decided it was easier for old bodies to rise from cushions that did not yield.

No sooner had Julia sat down than a fossil of a man she hadn't noticed at the other end of the sofa scuttled toward her fast as a sand crab. She instinctively pushed herself against the padded arm until there was nowhere else to go. As far as her peripheral vision could tell, he kept staring in Julia's direction.

He was hardly the candidate she had hoped for and she debated whether she should get up and leave when a brittle voice cackled: You new here?

His directness and tone sounded more like an accusation than a query. Why, yes, Julia answered, startled. I've been here three weeks. Three of the longest weeks of my life, she thought.

Can't say I've seen you around, the old gentleman said. Can't say I'm surprised either, it's what most people do when they land in here.

There was little for Julia to add. He undoubtedly had more experience with how life unfolded at Evenholme. She waited for him to elaborate, but after a few seconds she gathered he might need prodding. What would that be? she asked.

What would what be? he said.

Her first conversation with a resident was taking off in a peculiar direction. Pronouncing each syllable as if speaking to someone who was not fluent in English, she reminded him: When people first land here, what do they do?

Hide in their room, he stated as if Julia had missed the point.

I was not hiding, she protested. True, she had eaten most of her meals in her suite, but it was none of this man's business. Why should she justify herself to some nosy old coot? Determined, however, to make her transition as pleasant as possible she introduced herself. Julia Brannon. She extended her hand.

Wilkes, he replied, keeping both hands in his pockets, ignoring what she intended to be a gracious gesture. Been here going on ten years, he added.

As it became obvious that he was not about to reciprocate with a handshake of his own, Julia withdrew her hand and placed it on her lap. For a split-second she wondered whose age-spotted and wrinkled hands were resting on her knees. She and her sister had always been so proud of their slender fingers and perfectly manicured nails. Their long legs. *Jane and Julia Crane, legs as long as whooping cranes.*

Really? Ten years! So Evenholme must agree with you then, she said, wondering at the idea of Evenholme agreeing with anyone. She scanned the room for someone who wouldn't present such a challenge. Half a dozen people looking in her direction were noticeably amused.

Yup, going on ten years. Can't complain if you consider the alternative, Mr. Wilkes replied and chortled.

She didn't immediately grasp what alternative he was referring to, but when she did she made a point of not responding.

A few more seconds went by with neither one saying anything until Mr. Wilkes leaned over as if to share a confidence. I have a question for you, he whispered.

You have? she whispered back, more out of courtesy than interest.

He stared ahead and after a few seconds she wondered if he had lost his train of thought again or even lost track of where he was. His eyes, which might have been a nice shade of blue once, were washed out and without expression. The agile luminousness of younger eyes had deserted him, leaving him with an opaque and fixed stare.

You were about to ask me something, Mr. Wilkes.

Pardon?

You were about to ask me a question.

I know, I know, he replied impatiently, implying she had no right to rush him. I ask all newcomers this. Been doing it for years. He wanted her to understand she wasn't the recipient of special consideration.

Yes, you said you'd been here going on ten years.

That's right. Longer than anyone here.

Quite the feat, Julia said, but to herself she thought, Not long enough to have improved the art of your conversation. Her patience was beginning to wear as she noticed the residents with the knowing grins becoming more animated as they discussed amongst themselves. They might have been familiar with Mr. Wilkes's peculiar line of questioning. So, what was it you wanted to know? she asked.

You've lived a long life, he stated emphatically.

She nodded, her lips sealed into a forced smile. She had, over the years, perfected the art of the forced smile although she used it less as she got older. The compulsion to hide one's true feelings decreases with the years. There were a few circumstances, however, when she was still compelled to use it, this gentleman's age being a case in point. She was also aware of being watched by a lounge full of people with whom she would be spending what remained of her life. She could hardly appear callous.

This is true, Mr. Wilkes, I have lived a long time.

Over a century, I would guess, he said decidedly.

A sharp jolt of disbelief ran through Julia. His assumption took her aback and she could feel her forced smile transforming itself into resolve. She was well into her nineties, but she had never looked older than her age. I beg your pardon?

What I want to know is this, he continued without embarrassment or apology. Of everything you've experienced in your life, which event do you think affected you the most? Personally, I mean.

She was, by now, feeling harassed. None of what this stranger was asking was his damn business. It was, in fact, downright impudent. A stranger poking into other people's lives, converting their personal experiences into his hobby. Frittering away the precious months or weeks he had left.

Yet, as he sat there, alert with anticipation, she felt she had little choice but to play along. At least pretend she was playing along. Which event had affected her the most? Obviously, one stood out from all the others, but she had kept it to herself all these years so she wasn't about to divulge it now. Not to a total stranger. Other possibilities jumped to mind—her mother and father; Thomas and William. But she didn't want them to be pawns in this old man's game. She could have mentioned the young woman who threw herself off the top of a building when she and her sister went on the wedding shopping trip in New York. She hadn't known the young woman, yet she haunted Julia for years, as all suicides will. She decided against this too. There was the house in Wildwood

Park where she had lived all her life, but it would hardly qualify as an event and, in any case, it would be too idyllic an oasis for Mr. Wilkes. He was after calamity; she could smell it. She needed something impressive yet impersonal, something to satisfy his morbid curiosity while keeping herself and the members of her family at a safe distance.

Oh, Mr. Wilkes, she said with as much levity as she could muster. So many things have improved the quality of all our lives, so many for which we should be thankful, I wouldn't know where to begin.

He considered this for a moment then frowned. What things? he asked, his voice edged with scepticism.

Why, I could name any number, she said when she was, in fact, scrambling to come up with one. Women's right to vote came to mind. The Pill. But neither the vote nor the pill would be of any interest to a man of Mr. Wilkes's age. Considering his physical condition she wondered if the television remote wouldn't be worthy of a mention. The first man on the moon. Or perhaps the fancy computer Rachel and Thea had given her, but, again, Mr. Wilkes may not have been familiar with what such a small and relatively new gadget could accomplish. So, for reasons she could hardly explain, although she later concluded it may have had to do with an unreasonable and lifelong fear of physical pain, she blurted: Anaesthetics. The development of anaesthetics to deaden pain, now was this not the kindest of inventions, Mr. Wilkes?

Her answer could not have had a more stupefying effect than if Mr. Wilkes had been hit over the head with one of the Royal Doulton figures. He glared, unsmiling. The game they were playing was about to unravel. Anaesthetics. What in the name of heaven had possessed her to say such a thing? She began tittering at the peculiarity of her choice. At the peculiarity of sitting in the main lounge of a retirement home trying to forge a conversation with a stranger to whom she had little to say, with an audience who was growing more amused by the minute.

I see, he finally said. An invention for which a woman with no tolerance for discomfort would be thankful, I'm sure. One that men could have used during the Great War. The right side of his upper lip curled in a contemptuous sneer.

Julia sat up on her unyielding cushion and tried to compose herself. Ah, so your most memorable recollection would be of war then, Mr. Wilkes, she said.

Yes, ma'am, he replied with the pride of an old peacock who is unaware it has lost most of its flamboyant feathers.

And which war would you be referring to as great, Mr. Wilkes? She wished someone, Rachel or Thea, could have been there to see Mr. Wilkes's perfect double-take, like one of those exaggerated reactions from comic movies she used to go to when she was a girl. His hands, still in his pockets, were now shaking uncontrollably. She could not imagine why he would be so agitated or upset.

He took a deep breath. What's your name again?

Brannon. Julia Brannon.

Mrs. Brannon, he began. It was his turn to weigh each word. Unless I have lost the few faculties I have left, the Great War I am referring to is World War I which began in 1914, lasted four years, three months, and twenty-seven days. The war to end all wars. But a woman of privilege such as yourself would not have had to worry about anything as inconsequential as defending her country because she had more important developments to worry about such as anaesthetics. An invention whose influence you seem to be under still, Mrs. Brannon.

Well, well. The old dear was vicious but articulate. Of course, The Great War. How could she have not remembered? As she explained to Rachel on her next visit, she had not immediately grasped which conflict Mr. Wilkes was referring to. As far as she was concerned, all wars were indistinguishable in the suffering they cause and giving them inflated monikers was just another way of granting them a status they didn't deserve. As she also told Rachel, Mr. Wilkes seemed so much older than she was that he might have been alluding to some conflict from before she was born. She'd never had any interest in retaining dates of historical battles and he might have been referring to the Crimean War for all she knew or cared. The Great War. Another event vanished into the void, betrayed for having been forgotten. No, not so much forgotten as deliberately mislaid because of the unpleasant memories it always evoked.

You are right, Mr. Wilkes, she conceded in an attempt to bring an end to their tedious exchange. War remains, for the worst part, men's business, she said. It would be presumptuous of me to guess the misery it must have caused. She had no intention of sharing what the Great War had done to her own family. How her father had returned from it a thoroughly changed man, ulcers eating away at what was left of his leg. The nightmares.

Yes, Julia knew about Mr. Wilkes's Great War. She had even survived the one that followed. But this was hardly the time or occasion to discuss it and for a moment she wondered how a man with so little consideration had gained access to a retirement home as exclusive as Evenholme. Good manners were apparently not a prerequisite for admission to this sorry excuse for exclusivity.

She felt tired. She stood up. If you will excuse me, sir, she said, I have little interest in going over grim incidents. In any case, I have none to relive since mine was a pleasant life and happiness makes for less interesting stories than misfortune, does it not, Mr. Wilkes. So, good afternoon to you, sir.

As she left the lounge she thought she could hear snickering. Not only from Mr. Wilkes, but from some of the men. As the old saying went: Old men are twice children.

*

Sissa and I stand by the front door greeting people as they come in. Forty or more have gathered for the welcoming party. They fuss over the braid sewed to father's shoulders and the medals and the cross pinned to his chest. There are whispers about how gaunt he is, and I am thinking how incongruous it is for a father to return so triumphantly from war as if from some sporting event, but with his left leg missing.

For several months we are awakened in the middle of the night by bloodcurdling screams followed by mother's muffled voice.

Father can't breathe. He can't breathe in the dark. Lights are flicked on throughout the house as mother makes her way to the kitchen to make tea. Sissa and I join father sitting on the stairs, his head between his hands. When he finally speaks, he tells us once again how he personally oversaw the construction of cement bulwarks in the trenches over the corpses of boys not much older than we are. Not much older than you are now, he repeats. He describes how relieved his boys were when ordered out of their rat-infested trenches to face enemy fire, fully aware of the heavy toll it would exact. These accounts are invariably followed by a detailed description of how his gangrened leg had to be amputated without an anaesthetic.

We listen out of duty. It is the least we can do. Until mother emerges from the kitchen with father's chamomile tea. Oh, Harlan, don't go frightening the girls with your gruesome tales, she admonishes and shoos us to bed.

*

Over the next few days, as word of Julia's encounter with Mr. Wilkes began to spread, several women introduced themselves. Two or three even knocked on her door. As one of the women put it, she too had been put through the old fart's inquisition. As far as he was concerned, the twentieth century was the garbage bin of history and he challenged new arrivals to retrieve from it experiences that had most marked or influenced their lives. The incidents couldn't be borrowed, no one was allowed to capitalize on other people's suffering. They couldn't choose the bombing of Hiroshima if they had not been in Hiroshima at the time, nor could they claim the Holocaust if they had not been one of its victims.

As if the entire world wasn't affected by those events, Bella Blanchard said. In spite of her dynamic voice, Bella Blanchard had an unusually inexpressive face.

As the women explained, it didn't matter what answers anyone gave, nothing could trump Mr. Wilkes's Great War. Especially not anything to do with women. A mother's or a wife's grief was but frivolous sentimentality as far as he was concerned. No home front could outdo his battlefront.

Why does he refuse to shake hands? Julia asked the women. Why does he keep them in his pockets?

Probably Parkinson's, Bella Blanchard said. Her silver hair was beautifully thick and curly, but because nothing in her face moved, she reminded Julia of one of those insipid sheep in a painting by Raphael that Julia had seen during a trip to Italy many years before. She wondered if Bella had been injected by that poison Botox, the one that paralyzes muscles of the face and prevents wrinkles. She also wondered what Bella made of Julia's own face, each line a testament to resolve, or so Julia imagined.

Gertrude Mitford guessed that Mr. Wilkes's shaking might have been due to injuries sustained during the war. Someone else mentioned anger because Mr. Wilkes was always angry. No one suggested it could simply be because of old age.

One thing was clear. In spite of his annoying habit of poking into other people's business, in his ten years at Evenholme Mr. Wilkes had managed to earn at least one singular measure of consideration. No one ever addressed him by his first name or by any of those patronizing sobriquets the staff often resorted to: *Gorgeous. Honey. Sweetheart.* For the short time Julia knew him he was always Mr. Wilkes.

~4~

"IT'S ALL I HAVE TO BRING TODAY, THIS, AND MY HEART BESIDE..."
Sissa and I are making our way through the backyard tracking the sound of toads, hoping we can corner one long enough for it to dart out its sticky little tongue. Silver branches weighed down by rows of bleeding hearts reach above our waists. Lady slippers arch their tiny little feet as if testing the air.
It is mother's birthday. Because of this special day, our hair is held back with smooth silk ribbons instead of the usual grosgrain, and we are not wearing our coverall aprons. Black patent leather boots have replaced our usual sturdy brown ones. Guests will soon arrive for ice cream and cake, and Sissa and I will stand in the middle of the garden where the overhead branches don't meet, a perfect, dappled spotlight for us to recite, in unison, a poem we memorized for the occasion:

"It's all I have to bring today,
This, and my heart beside,
This, and my heart, and all the fields
And all the meadows wide.
Be sure you count should I forget,—
Some one the sum could tell,—
This, and my heart, and all the Bees
Which in the Clover dwell."

*

What's that you're reciting? a familiar voice asked from the doorway.

21

Thea! You scared me half to death when I'm already almost there. Except for blond and orange tufts of hair sprouting from behind an armful of lilacs Julia could hardly see her granddaughter.

Let's get rid of the blooms, the smell is killing me, Thea said as she laid the laden branches on the kitchenette counter. Can we open the window? This place needs air. She walked to the French doors and opened them, June air filling the room like a faint sigh. She looked around and reached for a vase on the bookshelf.

Dear Thea, wired package of raw sensibility in her frayed jean jacket, cropped tank top, and a stud diamond in her navel, a residue from her more rebellious days.

When are you going to get rid of the diamond? Julia asked her. It is vulgar. I hope it's not one of your mother's.

I told you before, it's fake. A cubic zirc.

Typical.

Of what?

You can never be sure of anything's true value or authenticity nowadays.

I'm not getting rid of the zirc until someone gives me the real thing.

I thought you were never getting married.

I'm not. But it doesn't prevent someone from giving me diamonds.

How pragmatic of you, dear.

It wasn't that Thea was inauthentic. As genuine a young woman as there ever was in spite of the zirconia and the hacked hair. She had worked against her natural beauty since her early teens when she announced that her life goal was to be different.

Different from what? Julia had asked.

From everybody else, Thea had replied. Barely fourteen and she had already grasped the laws of transgression. In breaking the rules that made young women conventionally beautiful, Thea had assumed an identity delinquent from what was expected of her. Julia liked this about her granddaughter—her obsessive interests in machines such as cars, motorcycles, computers—anything that society didn't consider feminine. It was a vanity Julia preferred to the conventional kind.

To everyone's relief, after high school, Thea had finally stopped piercing various body parts and threatening tattoos like the gaudy serpent winding itself between her elbow and her shoulder. It had practically sent Julia into cardiac arrest.

Don't you like it? Thea had asked with put-on innocence.

Of course not, it's awful. Your parents must be horrified.

Yah, they're pretty pissed. They don't know it washes off. I thought I'd make them sweat a little.

You mean it's not real?

Nah. I'd never get a real tattoo, they're so mainstream now, so many girls are getting them.

Julia had silently given thanks to the poor misguided and mainstream young women disfiguring themselves for some fleeting trend. Why would you put your parents through this? she'd asked. It's so unkind, Thea.

It's like you said, too much kindness kills.

I don't remember saying any such thing.

Are you kidding? I've heard you say it dozens of times.

I wouldn't worry too much about excessive kindness on your part, dear. An unfair comment since Thea was by far the most generous member of the family, at least where Julia was concerned. Thea had never given the impression that she visited Julia out of duty, not even as a little girl. As soon as she was allowed to take the subway on her own she visited Julia's house at least once a week, sometimes bringing friends, putting them to work in the garden, or shovelling snow in spite of the regular handyman who took care of such chores. Julia would hear them whispering, I can't believe she's in her eighties. I can't believe she's in her nineties. A curiosity item to most, but never to Thea.

Tinny sounds were escaping from the earphones dangling around Thea's neck. What's all the racket? Julia asked.

Thea unwound the contraption and placed it over Julia's ears. A gravelly voice with a western twang accompanied by a blast of drums, electric guitar, and other unidentifiable implements belted out: "*Eggs over easy with a vodka or gin.*"

Julia ripped off the earphones. Good Lord, Thea, why would you have this detonating into your brain? You could damage yourself.

Isn't she great?

It's a woman?

Yah, Rita Chiarelli. In concert in Germany. I was there, I saw her.

She's German?

Canadian. She was touring. Isn't she amazing?

I have no gauge with which to evaluate this kind of noise.

Thea emitted an exaggerated groan. You don't need an effing gauge to listen to the blues.

Mind your language and put the blasted thing away. Don't you listen to good music anymore?

Chiarelli is good music.

Classical music is good music. Getting you a season's ticket to the opera was a waste of money and time if you ask me.

Rachel and Julia had been subscribers to the Canadian Opera Company for more than twenty years and had assumed that buying a season's ticket for Thea would automatically make her an admirer and perhaps a devotee. They had felt justified following a performance of *Carmen* when Thea stood at the bathroom door, bath and shower head doubling as a microphone, belting out the familiar aria, "*L'amour est un oiseau rebelle, que nul ne peut apprivoiser….*" Off key but her French surprisingly good.

See? My travels weren't such a waste after all, she'd said to defend the long periods of time she took away from her studies in spite of her parents' objections. Railing it through Europe to find herself, she called it.

Wouldn't you have a better chance of finding yourself in your own back yard? Julia had asked.

Nope, already looked there.

How are you going to support yourself while you're away?

I'll find work.

What kind of work can you do if you don't speak the language?

You don't need to speak the lingo to wash dishes, Nan.

Julia had never been able to understand how washing dishes served as a tool of self-discovery. That production of *Carmen* was good, but you are likely to see better ones especially in Italy, she said.

Oh, I don't have to see it again, Thea answered with a dismissive shake of the head. I can listen to it on CD. The proof is in the music and the voices, not in the tacky costumes and sets. Or those outdated plots, she added, rolling her eyes.

Those stories are timeless, Thea.

Good reason to change them then. Time to make new connections, she'd said, waving her fingers over her head as if she could magically rewire her brain. Nothing is timeless, everything can be rethought, she added.

The last opera they saw that season, *The Marriage of Figaro*, was even less likely to win Thea over. It was so different from *Le Nozze de Figaro* that Julia and Rachel had seen many years before in the Teatro Comunale in Ferrara. The opera house, several centuries old, looked like a rococo beehive with gilded balconies. The super-charged hall and the formally attired audience all combined to give Mozart's opera an atmosphere of fantasy. The very first notes had set off vibrating little mallets inside Julia's ears, tightening a noose around her throat and heart. For the entire length of the performance, eight-year-old Rachel sat transfixed and motionless. Where are the voices coming from, she'd asked after the performance. It was unfeasible to her that such beautiful voices could emanate from human bodies.

This was what Julia had wanted Thea to experience as she and her mother had once experienced it, but the static production of *Figaro* to which they had taken Thea had fallen far short of everyone's expectations. The poor staging had highlighted the naive part of the story and Julia had been struck by how the cast looked embalmed inside a stale praline box. As she went over the array of wigs and fake beards, the musty costumes, the powdered ladies and gentlemen she'd seen and heard over the years, she began to appreciate Thea's point of view. Partly because of the poor production, and perhaps also because of her own age and weariness, the gilded sheen of Ferrara had worn off. As Thea said, nothing was timeless. There was no longer any solace to be found in the puffed-up atmosphere of concert halls. She could just as easily have stayed home and listened to the music and the voices from a comfortable armchair.

Oh well, I tried, Julia sighed. Your mother and I tried. It was thoughtful of you to bring the lilacs, Thea.

Mom sent them. She says they're your fave.

Fave. What did they teach graduate students nowadays? What is your mother up to? Julia asked.

Same old. Writing a paper for a conference she's going to in a few weeks. She said she'd drop by in a couple of days.

Hmm… Probably why she sent the lilacs ahead of time.

What do you mean?

She's always complaining about the smell of this place.

What are you going on about? She sent them because you like lilacs and they were ready to be cut. Don't be such an old cynic.

Thea was right. Julia did behave like an old grump sometimes, a habit she fell into when she discovered that being frankly irritable generated more conversation than fake serenity. In fact, she wouldn't have blamed Rachel if she had sent the lilacs ahead of time. No matter how exclusive Evenholme purported to be, it couldn't mask the strong disinfectants intermingling with the lingering smells of mass-produced food, stale perfume, and perspiration from clothes worn over too many years. Not to mention the rude exhalations from which even women and men of good upbringing were not exempt. As Julia soon discovered, one of the responsibilities of living in close proximity to others was the ability to maintain one's dignity in relation to impolite bowels. Otherwise you were condemned to stay in your suite with little more to do than vent your flatulence while watching flakes of dead skin drifting along narrow shafts of light before settling into carpets and grout lines. It was hard to believe that those flakes of dead skin carried the same genetic material as when they were shed by younger bodies.

Did you know that the Latin name for lilac is *syringa*? Julia asked Thea.

Like a syringe?

Yes. To inject and reawaken numbed bodies after a long winter, I suppose. Except it would take considerably more than a few lilacs to reawaken mine. Lilac doesn't have the same fragrance it used to, you know. Its perfume was exuberant with anticipation when I was a girl.

Anticipation of what? Thea asked.

The end of the school year. Summer holidays. Going to our grandparents' summer house in Hayground Cove, mother's yearly escape. I can still see her with her skirt hem tucked inside her waistband, stalking horseshoe crabs in the surf. Or chasing plover birds, their heads jerking up and down, and their twiggy little legs zigzagging to escape the oncoming waves. When it was too cold to go in the water, we chased dragonflies in the marshes. Oh, Thea, I do wish you'd stop fiddling with those blasted lilacs and visit with me.

You're in a cranky mood today. What's up with that? Thea asked as she stood back to assess her floral arrangement.

You're not listening to a word I'm saying and it's making me nervous. Make us a cup of tea and sit down for goodness sake.

What were you reciting when I came in? Thea asked as she filled the electric kettle. It sounded like a poem, something about heart and bees.

Oh, Dickinson. Emily. There was a woman who wasn't embarrassed to speak to herself.

That's phenomenal, Nan.

Yes, she was pretty phenomenal.

I mean that you remember the poem.

Is it? I suppose it is considering I can't remember what I've had for lunch most days. Probably because of the rhymes. As it gets older, the mind looks for patterns and rhymes make it easier to remember lines.

Your mind's better than anyone I know. You have the memory of an elephant. So was Dickinson one of your faves? she asked as she set two Shelley china cups and saucers on the table. She knew that her grandmother hated drinking tea from coffee mugs.

What's with this "fave" business, Thea? "Favourite" is a perfectly adequate word. And stop using the past tense. I am still here, after all.

Oh, behave yourself. Is she? Thea repeated.

She was one of mother's favourites. My sister and I memorized this poem for her birthday. Mother preferred recitations to presents, which was fine with us; it saved on our stipend.

There are quite a few poetry books in the library at the house, many of them first editions. Were they your mother's?

Most of them were, yes.

She liked poetry?

Yes, she did. I used to think it was an affectation of hers until I read her stack of garden journals after she died and I realized it was much more than that. She sought in poems what she sought in her garden, a place in which she could identify and safeguard feelings. Different people find different places in which to store their sensibilities, I suppose. With some, it's religion, books, money, status. With mother, it was poetry and her garden. They might have given her the illusion of being safe.

Thea filled two cups with tea. Wasn't she safe?

As safe as any of us ever are, I suppose. She was often at odds with the world, especially after the war. Thea, do you remember if I left the gray vase on the mantel? I couldn't find it when I unpacked my things.

What gray vase?

The one with the little mice around its neck.

I don't know what vase you're talking about.

The vase father bought when he was stationed in France.

Oh, for God's sake. You expect me to know about a vase someone bought almost a century ago? I don't remember ever having seen it.

I might have packed it away. It's a Lalique, you know. Not that this would mean anything to you. I hope your mother didn't ship it off to Goodwill or to one of those phoney antique shops.

She doesn't ship anything to Goodwill or to antique shops, but she probably should. The attic is so packed it's impossible to move around up there.

Your mother will get rid of it all soon enough. She really should keep the vase. And the combs. They're Lalique, too. In fact, you should take the combs. They're in my jewellery box in the top drawer of my dresser.

Don't worry about them. It's not important.

It is to me. I want you to take good care of them. What are you going to do with them?

Well, I can't wear them. She pointed to her hair, barely an inch long. I'd frame them for people to see. They shouldn't be hidden in your dresser.

Why Thea, what a good idea! Turning the past into art.

I'll get it done for you if you like, Thea said as she walked into the bedroom and retrieved the box with the combs. They're amazing. They should be in a museum.

I worry about them, Julia said as she watched the combs disappear into a side pocket of Thea's overstuffed knapsack. People have things stolen here all the time.

Are you sure about that? Someone actually told you this? Thea cocked her head and looked at Julia as if apprehending a child telling a fib. Her large hazel eyes twinkled.

I keep wondering when someone will figure out how much those two Stieglitz photographs are worth, Julia continued. You can never be too careful.

No one will take the photographs, Nan. I did find something in the attic, Thea said as she reached down into the main part of her knapsack and retrieved two red boxes, one velvet and one linen with cross-stitch writing on the lid: Treasure what is genuine. Julia recognized the boxes immediately. The velvet one had been kept in the front parlour until her mother's death. It held a stereoscopic viewer and a few dozen sepia cards of places her mother and father had visited over the years, starting with their honeymoon. The linen box with the cross-stitch lid contained photographic cards of the family, relatives, and friends. Each card from both boxes displayed two side-by-side photographs. When viewed through the stereoscope the two photographs merged into a three-dimensional image. Dried bits of lavender stuck to the boxes. It had taken Thea less than two months to start rummaging through the cartons in the attic.

These are so neat, Thea was saying. There's a whole bunch of you and your sister, but it's impossible to tell who's who. She pulled several cards out of the linen box and handed them to Julia. Can you tell?

Julia hadn't looked at the cards in years and it startled her to see them again, especially those of her and her sister in such fixed poses. Immobility was not how she remembered the two of them growing up, not how she replayed the memories in her head. Oh, I'm not sure, she said. This one might be me. This one is definitely my sister.

How can you tell?

I know my own face, Thea.

But how? They're so much alike.

I just do. Julia turned a few cards over. On each one, either Julia or Jane had been crossed out. Now I remember. When mother first wrote our names on the back of each card we convinced her she'd gotten them wrong. She hadn't, she almost never did, but we wanted to tease her. She replaced them all with Sissa out of frustration.

Why Sissa? Where did this name come from?

It was the first word we spoke, the name we gave each other. We were probably parroting mother who always called both of us Sister.

Wasn't it weird, calling each other by the same name? Thea asked.

Not really. We never thought about it growing up, it just was. Until people started to call us by our names, Jane and Julia, and we suddenly became part of a larger world. We spent hours poring over cards like these then. Julia pulled out some of the European sights her mother and father had visited—Notre-Dame, Sacré-Coeur, Chartres, La tour Eiffel, palaces in Florence, Venice.

You and mom did travel to a lot of those places, Thea said. Mom said you almost never left Wildwood except to travel.

Yes, Rachel and I did travel a lot. It was as if I already knew these places because of the cards. Like the time father took us to Niagara Falls in his new sedan. He had bought cards of Niagara Falls beforehand and as soon as we got there Sissa and I went looking for a man walking on a tightrope holding on to a balancing pole, one foot pointed above Whirlpool Rapids. We had seen his three-dimensional image through the stereoscopic viewer and we just assumed he'd be there.

It's still in here, Thea exclaimed riffling through the stack. See? She held up a card with side-by-side images of a man crossing foamy rapids on a tightrope.

This is not even the whole lot, Thea said. There are a few hundred more of you and your sister at home. Who took them all?

An uncle, father's brother. He'd taken up photography as a hobby and it grew into a sideline business. He was fascinated with my sister and me because we looked so much alike and we became one of his pet projects for a while. He recorded different stages of our growing up. Whenever he visited at the house he brought along one of his stereo cameras. They looked like clumsy pairs of mother's opera glasses.

Julia took the stereoscope from Thea and found herself staring at herself as a young girl dressed in what girls typically wore in the early nineteen-hundreds—a pinafore covering most of her dress, which stopped just below the top of her boots buttoned at the ankles. Her dark, waist-length hair was held back with a grosgrain ribbon. She was not looking directly at the camera but to one side, trying to keep a straight face, pursing her lips to stop from laughing.

This is such a neat one, Thea said as she handed Julia another card, a shot of two young women standing face to face, mirroring each other so that their left and right profiles were interchangeable.

Ah, yes. My uncle entered this one in a contest and it won a prize.

31

So, which one is you? Thea wanted to know.

Julia stared into the viewer for several seconds. Which one was she? What difference did it make now? This one's got me stumped, she finally said as she handed the card and the viewer back to Thea.

Thea was inserting and pulling out cards from the viewer like an investigator trying to shed light on a mystery. This one didn't work at all, she said. It's out of focus or something. It looks like a person with a shadow or a weird aura or something.

Julia laughed. Yes, I suppose it does. The question is, who is the person and who is the shadow?

You tell me.

Julia raised her shoulders. I wonder.

How come you never want to talk about your sister?

There's not much to tell.

Did something happen between the two of you?

Things always happen between sisters.

Like what?

We grew apart. I told you, we wanted different things. She died a long time ago and my life went on.

Thea wasn't about to let the matter drop. Was it over a man? Did you fight over a man?

No, no, nothing as mundane as all that.

No big romance? she insisted.

No big romance, Julia answered. Why were entire lives so readily distilled to simple romance stories? she wondered. Each one promising to be unique when each one was but another incarnation of the same? Fleeting moments frantically fanned when they threatened to burn out. Love, she had discovered over the years, blossomed mainly in the absence of such embers. No big romance, she repeated. My life is not a dime-store novel, Thea.

What do you know about dime-store novels? Thea asked, a simpering smile suggesting Julia was either too old or too prissy to know about such things.

Quite a bit, actually. A young woman from Quebec my mother hired to teach us French lived with us for a few years. She used to hide novellas under her mattress. This is how I learned most of my French.

You're kidding! Thea exclaimed in genuine surprise.

Yes, but we didn't learn it very well. We were too busy trying to figure out the silly plots of romance novellas to pay attention to such things as the *passé composé* or the *imparfait*. I don't think even Mademoiselle Jolicoeur knew the difference. I didn't learn until much later that the *imparfait* is used mainly for events that aren't finished and that the *passé composé* relates to an action in the past with a beginning and an end. You could say my life has now become a *passé composé*.

This is what I want to know more about.

What? French verbs?

Everything. The French tutor, the twin boys, grandpa Brannon. Other than you being my grandmother, I don't know much about you or your sister.

Other than being your grandmother and your mother's mother there isn't much to know, Thea.

Mom says she doesn't know anything about her father. She says you never talked about him. Thea was scanning Julia's face as if she might discover buried deep within the wrinkles some relevant clue.

He died when she was barely two years old. She wouldn't have remembered him.

Is it too painful to talk about him? Or about the boys?

Not anymore. But why rehash the past? There are so many other things to talk about. How are your studies doing?

That's just it. I'm putting together a cultural history for a paper and I thought I'd do it through some of the things I'm finding in the attic. It's a regular gold mine up there.

Oh, I wouldn't bother, Thea. Mine wasn't a particularly exciting life.

Something tells me there's more to it than you let on.

No one is interested in an old woman. Old age has not taken its place with love and war among the grand themes of literature. We are irrelevant, just an old species on its way out, Julia said.

Au contraire, grand'mère, I'm very interested. I want to learn more about our family history. There's something weird about it.
There's something weird about all family histories. It's best not to dwell on them too much.
Your past may bear on my future.
A cliché, Thea.
Personal history is important now that so many traditions are disappearing, Thea insisted. It was a surprising comment from someone who never lost an opportunity to break with every tradition that came her way. Someone who once claimed that tradition was for people who couldn't think for themselves so they kept repeating the same old patterns.

Being part of Thea's history did have a nice ring to it though. It gave Julia a place within a context larger than her own inconsequential life. Everyone made history each in their own small way, according to the cards they were dealt. What student had not looked for perspective and direction for their years ahead by looking back? Even if she had become little more than fodder for Thea's project, wasn't it better than nothing?

Thea glanced at the double card she was still holding in her hands, the one of the two Sissas facing each other. These are like mirror neurons, she said.

Mirror neurons? What are those?

They're cells in an area of the brain that can read other people's minds. They respond to seeing another person do something as if they were experiencing the action themselves. Researchers think we understand the behaviour of others, what others do and feel, on the basis of what we do and feel.

How did you learn about the workings of the brain? Is it part of your cultural studies?

No, a friend of mine was telling me about them. He says there's a problem though.

Only one?

Thea ignored Julia's comment. He says that new scanning technologies show that perception activates the same areas of the brain as imagination and the brain can't always distinguish between the two. There's often confusion between what people imagine and what they perceive.

People have been confused about what they perceive and imagine since the beginning of time. This is what good literature used to be about. That's why any rendering of the past is always provisional, Thea. There's a wonderful scene in Oscar Wilde's *The Importance of Being Earnest*, in which Miss Prism says to Cecily that memory is a diary we carry with us. To which Cecily replies, Yes, but it usually chronicles things that haven't happened and possibly couldn't have happened. Another way of saying that one person's truth may be another person's fiction.

Thea would not be deterred. I know, I know, but it's your version of the truth I'm after.

Julia's version of the truth. She hardly knew what it was anymore. There were days now when she could hardly differentiate between her life and her sister's and she wasn't sure she wanted to revisit the brief period when each had been distinctly her own. In any event, the past came back to her mostly in flashbacks nowadays and flashbacks did not serve history well. They leapt about the years with little regard to chronology, cutaways sliced into episodes moving at their own speed, gleaming with their own incandescent truth. Like the stereoscopic cards in the red boxes.

So, Julia ventured out of curiosity but also to change the subject. What new friend would this be who is interested in mirror neurons?

Just a friend, Thea said. Her evasiveness indicated there was more to it than she was willing to admit.

My perception tells me he's somewhat more than a friend. Or would that be my imagination?

Definitely your imagination, Thea said and grinned. Here's a card of our Wildwood house. Jeez, it's hardly changed.

Thea had referred to the house as their house, hers and Rachel's and Adam's. It had now passed into mutual ownership. Peering into the viewer and seeing the two sweeping roofs and the vines creeping up the stucco walls was like looking into a long-range telescope, the house suddenly springing from under the shaded summers of Julia's childhood.

I must say I don't care for all this nostalgia, she said, handing the viewer over to Thea. So where are you working these days?

My usual part-time at the racetrack, Thea said, glancing at her watch.

Julia sighed. Why would anyone want to participate in such an infernal sport? My mother hated cars.

I know. The horseless carriages with the metal heart.

With the metal engine heart, Julia corrected her granddaughter to remind her she didn't know everything about Julia's past or her mother.

Nan, I'm sorry, but I have to run. She checked her watch again.

I know, dear. I am very grateful for your patience. You must be so tired of my rambling.

Are you kidding? I thought I might tape you at some point, if you didn't mind.

I would mind. No taping.

Okay. But you can't stop me from quoting you.

Weariness washed over Julia. She felt exhausted and she still had to get herself ready for lunch. Perhaps she would stay in her suite today, put her feet up, and have a few crackers and cheese. If my rants can be of service, be my guest, she told Thea. I thought you were in a hurry to leave.

So you want to get rid of me now, you wily old woman. Thea kissed Julia on the forehead. Try using the laptop. It doesn't have to be fancy writing, she cautioned as an encouraging directive. God knows I get enough of that at school, she added.

Fanciness is the least of my worries, Thea.

Just the facts, ma'am, she quoted from a detective series that was from another television era for a project on the history of television she was assigned the previous year. Hers was a new language of theories and concepts with which to analyze or—according to Thea's preferred term—to deconstruct the socio-cultural past. In listening to her, Julia often felt abandoned by her own age.

Don't forget, Thea shouted over her shoulder as she rushed out the door. The two Sissas. I want more.

Thea's visit, the scent of lilacs, and the photographs were triggering a flood of Proustian moments. Shouldn't certain events remain unrecorded?

*

Sissa is standing slightly behind and to Uncle's left. She is stroking her thighs and making torrid faces like those we've seen in silent movies.

Try not to laugh, Uncle Warren admonishes as he walks over and positions me in the exact pose in which he has just photographed my sister. Which one are you, again? he asks.

Sissa, I reply.

And what's your sister's name?

Sissa, comes the answer.

He grins and shakes his head. Look sedate like a good girl should, he says and he takes the picture.

It is shortly after this session that we decide to tell mother about Uncle Warren running his hands up our stockings under our skirts during some of the photography sessions.

Oh, I'm sure he doesn't mean anything by it, she says. However, we can't help but notice a deep frown cross her forehead. From then on, she stays in the room with us whenever Uncle comes to the house. Gradually, over a period of several months, our photographer Uncle drops by less often.

~5~

JULIA MADE A MENTAL NOTE TO ASK RACHEL ABOUT THE LALIQUE vase; however, she would have to be careful how she went about it. Rachel would hate having to go through the boxes. If you'd let me do the packing, I would know where things are, she'd say, her reproach different from Thea's who was still directing her rebellion against the entire world. With Rachel it was mostly the usual generational mutiny between mother and daughter, much of her impatience stemming from displaced guilt and fear. Guilt because she didn't want Julia to get old, didn't want her to be at Evenholme, and fear because of what loomed ahead. Julia suspected that Rachel was more afraid of the next few months than she was. Julia had often wondered if, buried deep within Rachel, there didn't linger an element of threat still. Ever since she was little, she had insisted on a life without surprises, which in itself was surprising in a child. Everything having to be planned ahead, everything having to be in its proper order as if the unexpected carried the possibility of ambush.

Whenever she gave Julia her perfunctory hug at the end of her visits, there was the same rigidity in her body as when Julia carried her down from the attic stairs when she was four years old. Or the first time Julia took her to school, leaving her there for a few hours, a betrayal as far as Rachel was concerned. Rachel's refusal to speak to teachers and schoolmates for two years, because to have spoken to anyone but Julia would have broken an unspoken pact between them. Outwardly, Rachel had outgrown her fear, but part of her clung to it still and in an effort to hide it, she often tarnished her visits with impatience. She would have denied all this, of course, but this was how Julia perceived it. Julia

38

had always thought of perception as one of the most basic and important of all the senses, the implement with which the other five were sharpened. It was through perception that another person's thoughts could be detected in a fleeting smile or the intonation of a voice, a creased brow.

Whenever Rachel dropped by, Julia let her do most of the talking. She listened as Rachel told her what was happening at the university and how she was winding down towards retirement; the conferences she still attended and the papers she gave, all of which blended into one long conference and an even longer paper in Julia's mind.

Resigned to Thea's decision not to follow in her mother's footsteps as a literature professor, Rachel complained about Thea's choice of a major, Cultural Studies. What Adam referred to as a smorgasbord with no real focus. All she's done is exchange high school rebellion for university cynicism. I swear, her generation believes in nothing, Rachel had complained.

Julia had thought this to be an unfair assessment. Oh, Rachel, is that really true? Even if it were, isn't it better to believe in nothing than in anything? From what I read in the papers and what I see on television these days, people don't think for themselves anymore. So many resorting to simplistic self-help books, gurus, and New Age whimsies.

Julia knew nothing about Cultural Studies and had her own reservations, but she also remembered everyone's reaction when she first announced that she wanted to study philosophy. Not surprisingly, her father's had been pragmatic. Philosophy is not going to put food on anyone's table, especially not a woman's, he'd said. You better make sure you get married.

Her mother had been sceptical although she wasn't entirely adverse to having a daughter enter such an unusual field. There had been so many contradictory sides to her mother. Feisty, but also aspiring to refinement while seeing through its pretensions. Mindful of how limited opportunities were for women, yet she played her roles of wife and mother well, aware they often meant compromise. She admired women who didn't fit the mould, like her favourite poet, but she was also wary and cautious when it came to her daughters.

During her visits, Rachel also filled in Julia on her sons' families, Andrew's and Alan's, but it was like hearing about strangers. Julia hardly knew them and, truth be told, she found herself losing interest in life outside Evenholme. Life in the real world. As if Evenholme didn't have its fair share of reality. Rachel asked about the people Julia was meeting there and Julia believed Rachel was genuinely interested, but she wasn't inclined to tell her much. As if these new friendships were in need of protection. From gossip or misinterpretation. They couldn't be assessed according to the same standards as if they had been forged on the outside.

It was during one of the bridge sessions with Gertrude Mitford, Bella Blanchard, and Sonny Walsh that Julia noticed once again the woman with the mismatched eyes. She was seated on a sofa near the card table, having a heated discussion with a middle-aged couple. From what Julia gathered, she was complaining about the man's cologne. He had doused himself too liberally and it was making her dizzy. Her head was resting on her hand propped on the arm of the sofa.

Maybe it's you she can smell, Sonny, Bella whispered and everyone at the table snickered except Sonny. Sonny Walsh with the oversized moustache still considered himself a ladies' man despite being in his late eighties and he always wore too much aftershave.

After a few seconds of silence from the sofa, the younger woman leaned over: Why are you always so critical? That aftershave was a present I gave Zach.

Oh, oh, here it comes, Gertrude said as she peered over her cards and her bifocals.

The woman with the mismatched eyes sat up. I am sorry, but I cannot help this. Some colognes make me dizzy. They make me sick to my stomach.

It's okay mama, the Zach fellow said and took his mother's hand in his.

I may be critical sometimes, as she says, but… The woman's voice trailed into insecurity. Then, as if encouraged by her son's attention, she found her voice again: If I am mean it is because I am too polite to be rude to her, so I be rude to you instead.

Everyone sitting at the table, eyebrows raised, waited for the next development.

Always bad-mouth, bad-mouth, the woman with the mismatched eyes continued. The two of you bad-mouth me to feel closer. Better to find something else to glue the two of you together.

Mama, please. This is very stressful.

Stress! Ah! What you know of stress I could put in a… She was searching for a word, pointing to the tip of one of her fingers.

Yes, I know, a thimble, Zach said, nodding, indicating he'd heard it all before. I know, mama. Please. He raised his two hands as if to stop oncoming traffic. I will not wear the aftershave again. I should have been more considerate. I forgot.

Julia almost felt sorry for the poor sap. He was trying to play all sides, assuming the role of an impartial arbitrator when, in reality, he was caught between the proverbial rock and hard place and there were no harder places than being caught between a wife and a mother. Julia wondered if he had any idea that his wife was using criticism as an emotional magnet between herself and her husband as his mother had said. After a few seconds of awkward silence, the older woman got up and walked towards the door.

Oh, for fuck's sake, Zach hissed as he got up and ran after his mother.

The next day, as Julia was leaving the dining room, she saw the woman sitting by herself staring at a mass of congealed lasagne on her plate. Cereal flakes clung to the front of her dress and Julia instinctively looked down at her own blouse to make sure she had no remains of breakfast or lunch still lingering there. Was it an incontrovertible law of nature that the more birthdays people had, the more food stuck to their clothes? Julia wondered.

Julia guessed the woman to be younger than most of the residents, certainly younger than she was. She was slight, almost fragile. Except for Julia, most women at Evenholme wore slacks, but the woman with the mismatched eyes wore dresses that reminded Julia of another era, what European women wore in movies about the forties or the fifties.

Julia decided the woman needed company. May I join you? she asked although she had already eaten.

The woman looked up, startled, nervous, her upper teeth tugging at the corner of her lower lip, a habit Julia had observed on several residents.

Of course, she answered, distracted.

Julia introduced herself.

Lena Kohn, the woman replied.

Julia had barely sat down when Lena leaned over and placed a hand on Julia's arm. Have you had your test yet?

My test? What test?

You know. The one they give everyone.

No, I don't know. There's a test they give everyone?

Yes, yes. The geriatric assessment, she said, carefully articulating each syllable, her ts and rs rolling against her palate, her vowels coming from deep inside her throat, what Julia imagined to be typical of an Eastern European language.

Why, no. No one mentioned any such test to me. What in the name of heaven is a geriatric assessment? What do they assess?

Our physical and mental abilities. She nodded several times as if to confirm both the factuality and the absurdity of such a practice.

To evaluate mental and physical abilities? No one mentioned any such thing to me.

Oh, they give them to everyone. I had mine this morning. Lena paused, looked around to see if anyone was eavesdropping or watching, then whispered, I think I failed it.

The idea of women of a certain age worrying about passing or failing tests to assess their physical and mental abilities struck Julia as being so preposterous that she began to laugh. One of the few advantages of getting old was not having to adapt to the expectations of younger generations, least of all coddled professionals who made their living trying to fit the elderly within the parameters of their research. This is the most ridiculous thing I've ever heard, Julia said.

Ridiculous maybe, but it's no bloody joke, Lena Kohn protested, her North American vernacular incompatible with her accent.

But it's not so serious either, is it? Institutions may have to rely on rules to function more efficiently, but you can't take them personally.

Of course you can, Lena replied, puzzled. It is humiliating.

Her glumness, the untouched meal on her plate, the din of voices and clicking of spoons in tea cups and coffee mugs in the background, all contrived to contribute to the humiliation Lena must have felt. The poor dear was in need of commiseration and not Julia's flippant callousness. Are you going to finish your lunch? Julia asked.

No, this is not for eating, Lena said as she pointed in the general direction of her untouched food.

Why don't we have tea in the lounge then?

Yes, this is a good idea. Lena rose from her chair.

Lena Kohn said nothing as she resolutely made her way to the lounge, obviously still upset at what had transpired earlier that morning. Failing her test was taking on a disproportionate significance.

Julia tried to lighten the mood. Here we are. There should be rewards for people as old as I am reaching their destination.

Lena Kohn laughed. The sudden flash of a young person crossed her face and again Julia noticed her eyes. How very different they were from each other. The clouded one speckled with brown.

Mr. Wilkes was sitting by himself and Julia whispered to Lena Kohn, Speaking of tests, did Mr. Wilkes ask you about your most meaningful life experience yet?

Oh yes, Lena said. What chutzpah this man has. I sent him packing. So you haven't had yours yet? she asked again as they sat down.

My test? No, I haven't.

How long have you been here?

Going on two months.

Maybe they think you don't need it. Maybe I'm the only one.

I doubt you need assessing any more than I do or anyone else. What are those tests? What were you expected to do?

Lena became very animated, but didn't address Julia's question. I did very well at first, she said. I answered everything. Everything I could remember about my medical history, but I cannot remember everything. And my personal one, too. I had no trouble with the movements. She flailed her skinny arms about. The sharpness of her features, her dried, permed hair dyed a peculiar shade of burgundy reminded Julia of an exotic bird. Many people at Evenholme reminded Julia of different species of birds.

Movements? What do you mean? You were expected to move your arms in a particular manner?

Yes, that was the motor assessment test. That's what the nurse called it. Again she accentuated each syllable, pleased to have met another challenge.

Julia had agreed to routine tests when she first signed the admitting papers, but no one had mentioned them since. She requested two pots of tea from one of the young volunteers who came to Evenholme for a few hours every afternoon, then turned to Lena: So tell me more about these exercises you had to do.

They are easy, Lena said. This part is easy. To tap my foot, to reach my arms, and to turn my neck, like this. She rotated her head effortlessly. But there was this other one and I failed it.

What other one?

A mental one.

Well, Mrs. Kohn, Julia reassured her, I'm sure this test has nothing to do with your mental abilities.

Please, to call me Lena.

And call me Julia. Julia smiled while seething inside. How dare they presume to give them mental and motor tests? Lena, Julia said, I would like you to describe every detail of those tests. What do they involve, exactly?

There are several.

Yes, I understand. But tell me about the one you think you might not have passed. She couldn't bring herself to repeat the word "failed."

I had to name twenty animals.

That's it? Julia thought. What could be so difficult about naming twenty animals. Not wanting to appear insensitive or unsympathetic, she simply asked, And you couldn't?

There was only one minute, Lena cried out in indignation. One minute to name twenty animals. No problem, this is no problem, I told the nurse. Cat, dog, bird, turtle. I had to stop a few seconds to think of more: wolf, bear, mouse, rat, lion. Oh, and elephant. How many is that? I was sure I had done very well. Ten, the nurse said as she kept her eyes on her watch. Only ten? I did not believe to be only ten. You have twenty-five seconds left, the nurse said and my mind went, how to say, like a blank? So I repeated: Cat, dog, mouse, rat, lion, and all the others, and giraffe. Yes, giraffe, Lena exclaimed, reliving the episode over again. Yes, good, Mrs. Kohn, the nurse said. That's eleven. Can you think of any other?

Lena grew more agitated as she mimicked the nurse. Can you think of any other? Can you think of any other? she repeated, her eyes on the lookout, searching the room.

Fear had such an erratic way of resetting a person's features, Julia thought. The mouth struggled to keep from distorting, the voice quivered, eyes darted about. Julia followed the movements of Lena's eyes around the room. One was a dark, clear blue, while the other was mottled as if it had been robbed of much of its brown pigment. The different colours accentuated the physiological working of each eye, the mottled one conveying almost nothing while the blue eye assumed the task of expressing for both. Julia wondered if each one perceived differently. Did the cloudy brown eye greet each day differently from the other? Did it cast an opaque film on whatever it captured, a cloudiness extending beyond the narrow radius of the here and now?

How long have you been here? Julia asked.

Julia could see Lena counting in her head. Three months and two weeks, she replied.

A little longer than me. So I'll probably get mine soon then.

To search and to search my head, Lena continued, knocking a closed fist on her head. Then the nurse pressed a button on the watch and said, Time's up. She wrote something on a form on her clipboard. Always those clipboards. I have known minutes to last a life, but this minute was gone in a few seconds. Lena snapped her fingers to communicate how elusive those precious seconds had been. Time's up, she repeated, mocking the assessor with the time watch.

Julia couldn't understand how anyone could get into such a state because of some irrelevant, institutional test. She found Lena's lack of assertiveness irritating yet her outrage at Lena's humiliation made her want to help her.

I'm glad you warned me, Julia said. I won't take these tests. I'll refuse.

You cannot refuse. If you do, God knows what they'll write on their clipboards.

Oh, Lena, what do we care what they write on those silly clip-boards. These are not records of our lives, we're not in heaven yet. I may be at the gates, but I'm not about to go in just yet. Let them write whatever they want. They need something to do; it's their job.

Lena clasped her hand to her mouth and a girlish giggle escaped from behind her hand. It triggered a familiar and mischievous impulse. It goaded Julia into going a step further much as Sissa's giggles always did when they were girls. She seized the bait.

Unless I took the test but prepared for it first, she said.

What do you mean?

I assume it's a standard test, one they give everyone. I'm sure they'll get to me eventually. If they don't, I'll ask about it. If you can describe it very carefully, I can prepare. I can memorize the names of twenty animals beforehand. Learn them thoroughly until I can easily name all twenty in a minute.

Lena's body language changed. She sat up, the lines of her face rearranging themselves, making her look unconventionally attractive, both eyes gleaming, even the clouded one.

Encouraged by her reaction, Julia added, There are books on animals in the library. I could look up the names of rare animals, ones she wouldn't expect, ones she's never heard of. Now, wouldn't this impress our little gal with the clipboard?

You would do this? Lena muttered. You would not be afraid?

Oh for goodness sake, Lena, what is there to be afraid of? In any case, memorizing is good for an old brain. You can help me. It will be fun. My mother always said two heads were better than one. Let's do it.

Okay, Lena said, nodding. Let us do it.

By the end of the first afternoon, Lena and Julia had collected an impressive list of names, some familiar, others the most alien creatures Julia had ever come across. They listed them in alphabetical order to make it easier to memorize. From what Julia had once read when she first began misplacing her keys or forgetting familiar telephone numbers, short-term memory was not very robust. Unlike long-term memory that can retrieve facts and events after years, even decades, short-term memory required practise and tricks to keep it functioning relatively efficiently.

The next two weeks burgeoned into a tempest of memorizing, Lena drilling Julia until she could recite forward and backward twenty animals to which they added an extra five in case Julia forgot a few at test time.

This reminds me of when my sister and I played tricks on our friends and teachers, Julia told Lena.

You and your sister liked playing tricks? What kind?

Oh, we used to think up all sorts of tricks. The manure one was our favourite.

Manure? Like horse shit? Lena asked.

Yes, like horse shit, Julia said, laughing at Lena's casual use of coarse language. We would retrieve trowels full from the bin my mother kept at the edge of the ravine at the back of our house and pack it into jars and take them to school. If a boy was mean to us we'd put some in his boots, or in the desk of girls who put on too many airs. Once, Sissa and I hid some in the wastepaper basket by the teacher's desk. You should have seen the look on her face as she kept inspecting her boots and the hem of her skirt.

Lena placed a hand over her mouth as she usually did when she laughed. Oh, Julia, you have too much nerve.

Yes, that's what I've been told. I had more than Sissa, that's for sure.

Who is this Sissa? Your sister? Lena wanted to know.

Yes, my sister.

I have never heard this name, Sissa.

It was a nickname we both had.

Both?

Yes, it was a name we gave each other when we first began to speak. Maybe it's like this with twins. The inability, initially, to differentiate between each other's name. Perhaps even between each other sometimes.

As Julia talked, Lena's expressions varied from puzzlement to incredulity. She may have even paled a little, although it was hard to tell since she was already so wan and wore too much rouge. Julia had assumed Lena to be a little younger than herself, but it had been a shock to discover that she was almost twenty years her junior.

You are a twin? Lena asked. She attempted a smile that quickly disappeared. She could so easily disappear behind those eyes. I was also a twin, she said.

Really? You are a twin too? Coincidences had always fascinated Julia, but she had never believed in their preordination. However, she couldn't help but wonder what had incited her to speak to Lena Kohn in the first place.

I was, yes.

Were? Which means she is gone now?

Dead, Lena said tersely as if to admonish Julia for using a euphemism. Your twin, she is dead too?

Her directness always astounded Julia. Yes, a long time ago.

Lena said nothing and looked away. She had a peculiar and

restless way of playing with her hands, of repeating the same movements over and over again.

After a few moments of silence, Julia asked, Did the two of you have a special name for each other?

Yes, we did, was all Lena said for a while, debating perhaps whether she should divulge to a stranger a detail as intimate as a special name that sisters once shared. Julia knew the feeling, the resentment at having the world intrude on a bond between twins. It had been the beginning of their undoing, hers and Sissa's.

Julia tried to appear only casually interested while gaining Lena's confidence. There were few opportunities to compare the experience of growing up with someone identical to yourself. Of course, I wouldn't want to butt in, Julia said after a few seconds of silence.

Nali. We called each other Nali, Lena said. My sister's name was Lili, and from Lili and Lena we must have made up Nali. Or maybe my mother did, I can't remember. I don't think it was father. He always called us by our proper names. This was before Uncle Pepi. She pulled on the sleeves of her sweater until they reached her knuckles.

Nali. It's a nice name. Original.

So is Sissa, Lena said smiling.

Julia wanted to know more, where Lena came from, her background and her accent, what had happened to Lili, but she sensed she couldn't push for too much too soon. There would be more opportunities. They wouldn't be going anywhere, not for a while. Their list of rare animals would fill in for whatever could not be discussed for the time being. Julia also instinctively understood that she could not call Lena Nali, just as she would not have wanted Lena or anyone else to call her Sissa.

So, Lena Kohn, she said, Aren't we lucky to have found each other to practise our homework? Let's hope I don't panic in the middle of my test and forget it all.

Oh, you will remember, Lena said. She then added a peculiar comment: They don't put bromide in your food here to make you forget.

Sissa and I are looking through one of mother's books on mythology for a school assignment. We have to find a myth we can apply to real life. At least this is what we're supposed to be doing. Every half-hour or so, mother opens the door of the library to check on how we are progressing. When we hear her approaching, we insert what we call our life plans inside our books and pretend we are working on our school project.

Because we can't agree on a mutual strategy for each of our futures, we make separate lists:

SISSA'S LIFE PLAN	SISSA'S LIFE PLAN
At 12: To put my hair in an up do.	*At 12: To have my hair cut short.*
At 14: First kiss from a boy.	*At 13: First kiss from a boy.*
At 16: To become an actress.	*At 16: To become an actress.*
At 17: To be the belle of Toronto.	*At 17: To be the belle of the world.*
At 20: To be engaged.	*At 20: To have many suitors.*
At 21: To be married.	*At 21: To travel the world.*
At 22: To become mother of a baby girl.	*At 22: To become engaged.*
At 24: To become mother of a boy.	*At 24: To marry a millionaire.*
At 25: To live happily ever after.	*At 25: To be as famous as Mary Pickford.*

We both love the cinema, a recreation mother doesn't entirely object to because of the recent release of the movie Hulda from Holland *starring Mary Pickford, which was filmed in Hayground Cove. Although it was converted into a mock Dutch village with a windmill as backdrop, the Cove was easily recognized in the film and mother cannot bring herself to deny her daughters what she now calls this delightful art form.*

The next time mother looks in on us she adds, Remember, two heads are better than one. One of her favourite sayings. Two heads are better than one.

We're hardly surprised then when we come across a picture of a woman with two faces in the mythology book. In one hand she holds a book and in the other a quill.

We could write about her, I tell Sissa.

I guess. But what does it mean?

The caption beside the image reads: Memory: One face turned toward the past, the other to the present.

We could write that two heads are better than one, like mother says, I tell her.

~6~

IF MEMORY WAS A TWO-HEADED WOMAN RECORDING THE PAST with a quill, Julia was now determined to extract hers from her laptop. Laptop, as misleading a designation as she'd ever heard. She had, over the years used a lap-robe to keep the chills at bay; she'd owned a few lap-dogs; she'd read about lap-dancing, a sorry substitute for a lap-robe or lap-dogs, but she'd never heard of a computer meant to be used on a lap, especially one as unsteady as hers. Nevertheless, she now made an effort each morning to jot down a few thoughts. Nothing elaborate. She wasn't about to ruminate or pass judgment on what could not be undone. A glass full of milk falling off a table and shattering could not suddenly gather itself up and jump back to form a whole glass of milk like in the movies. There was a big difference between the forward and backward directions of real time in an ordinary life. Plus she still carried a built-in command preventing her from revealing too much.

The small room in which she pecked away each morning was comfortingly quiet. Except for the occasional muffled sound from the hall it was almost impossible to detect anything from the other side of the door. She felt calm inside her solitary confine-ment as it filled with familiar images, events she hadn't thought of in years.

The laptop wasn't as easy to use as the old typewriter she'd left behind. A pen would have been as efficient and as fast, but she was determined to make use of Rachel and Thea's gift if only to prove that she could. The instruction book was easy enough to follow, certainly easy enough to read in its oversized type. Rachel and Thea must have thought she was going blind. The problem wasn't her eyes but her fingers, as the young doctor had already told her. Not only were her fingers restricted by the small keyboard, they felt like little stumps cut off from their command centre, but, because she was losing her sense of touch, she was never sure if she had struck a key unless she kept her eyes on the monitor hoping the right letter would appear. The slightest hesitation kept a letter repeating itself as if tumbling into an abyss. It sometimes made her want to throw the silly gadget out the faux-French window. She had been much quicker touch-typing on her old Underwood.

Rachel and Thea had also *hooked her up* to the Internet. Hooked her up was their terminology not hers, as was *surfing*, which had nothing to do with water. Another perfectly good word modified to accommodate yet another newfangled contraption. Although surfing the net was often more interesting than writing about her commonplace life.

Her first venture on the net was to find out all she could on the physiological process that hands go through as they age, how nerves connect or, in her case, no longer connect. In the *search* slot she wrote, *sense of touch*. After a short interval of staccato Morse code tapping, the number 11,900,257 appeared. Almost twelve million! Considerably more information than anyone needs to know on any given subject. But, as she was about to discover, few had anything much to do with the physiological workings of the hand.

Some promoted simplistic concepts of touch healing, the so-called art of placing hands over ailing areas of the body, while others offered resourceful massages, whatever resourceful was supposed to mean. Lingering Touch sold lingerie while Italian Touch sold pasta recipe books. There was Scandinavian Touch, Finland Touch, Australian Touch, English Touch, all of them selling products supposedly representative of each country.

Some of the sites could have been the clever fantasies of science fiction minds: Touch Control, Touch Screen, Touch Panel Monitors, all had the uncanny ability to respond to the touch of a finger or a hand. Intuitive Touch Interface suggested interaction based on a person's feeling and insight. One ultimate goal was to have them on military command posts to make war more efficient and Julia wondered at the idea of making long-distance killing more productive.

After visiting a few dozen sites and not finding anything vaguely resembling the old definition of touch, that subtle physical contact of a caress or a gesture of endearment, Julia was about to give up when she stumbled upon a site called French Touch. As it turned out, French Touch was a porno site.

Curiosity got the best of her and she pressed the porno site bar ever so quickly, as if testing the temperature of an old iron. She could hardly believe her eyes. Naked bodies and body parts, enlarged penises and inflated breasts flashed and pulsated like gaudy neon signs. She couldn't, for the life of her, remember anyone's skin, least of all her own, as pink or as unwrinkled. Faces and bodies unblemished by age and uninjured by passion or misjudgement, those painful but necessary states that waylay people when they least expect it. Where had diffidence gone since she and Sissa first learned about sex?

*

My monthly, as mother calls it, has made its appearance before Sissa's has.

It's not fair, she whines to mother. Why does she get hers first?

Yours will be here soon enough, mother tells her. No point rushing it if you don't have to.

It is time for our two daughters to learn about the birds and the bees, she says to father who is standing with his back to the fire, a glass in one hand and steadying himself with the other on the mantel. Father proceeds to expound on mother's exceptional knowledge of subjects such as poetry, art, gardening, and her remarkable flair for furnishing a house, the essential aptitudes of the New Woman, he tells us, the new freedoms of the day. Because mother is an American, father has always believed he married a free spirit and an import.

Sissa turns to me. I know what she's thinking and she knows what I'm thinking—mother, promoter of the new freedoms of the day? If mother is imported china, as father claims, are his twin daughters supposed to be pieces of a matching set? Sunlight streams through the leaded windows on either side of the fireplace and catches a gray vase beside the clock. Perfect little glass mice run against a background of glass foliage around the vase's neck.

Father excuses himself and it is obvious that mother is no more comfortable than father as she begins: as an essential part of their education, girls and boys should receive proper instruction in pro-creation. Girls and boys should know how and why relationships develop between them. We should read her books on the reproduction of plants, she adds, since the concept is not dissimilar.

At the end of one hour, Sissa and I are as confused as when mother began and we realize that this is likely to be the extent of our education on sexuality and procreation. Should we want to learn more we'll have to fend for ourselves or, better still, ask Mademoiselle Jolicoeur.

For two years we've had a young woman from Quebec living with us during the school year. She is supposed to be teaching us French and in order to prolong her undemanding job, she teaches us only enough to impress mother. Our slow progress is blamed on our indifference to learning a second language and our singular lack of linguistic ability instead of Mademoiselle's questionable teaching methods. Sissa and I don't mind. Barely seven years older than we are, Mademoiselle treats us more as companions than students. She lets us rummage her room and never complains when we try on her clothes and her high-heeled shoes, her perfume or makeup. She even helps us create outlandish get-ups from the clothes she brings back from Montreal. Toilettes, she calls them. She dabs our cheeks with rouge and winks at us when mother marvels at our healthy complexions.

The books that Mademoiselle likes to read are slim novellas with covers of men and women kissing, their titles simple enough for us to understand: La vendeuse d'amour; Minoune; O ma Nadia! *and, one of the most intriguing,* L'homme vierge. *The words "virgin" and "man" in the same phrase spur such interest that Mademoiselle finally agrees to read it to us, translating the story as she goes along. It is then followed by another, then another; fanciful stories of beautiful young women whose true loves are briefly thwarted but always resolved into happy endings, each novella exactly thirty pages long.*

How much to you know about sex? she bluntly asks one afternoon.

We try to paraphrase mother's books on plants and organisms and Mademoiselle laughs so hard we assume mother must have gotten it all wrong. Ah, ben non, c'est pas possible, Mademoiselle keeps repeating. Qu'ils sont niaiseux, ces maudits anglais. She then puts forward a strategy, the kind of threat we are getting used to. She will not tell our parents, she whispers.

Tell them what? Sissa whispers back, frowning.

She looks directly into our eyes. She will not tell mother what she is about to tell us about women and men.

A DISCREET KNOCK. TIME FOR THE DAILY ROUNDS.

Good morning, Mrs. Brannon, one of the two women said in too loud a voice.

How many times have I told you not to shout, Julia asked her? I am old, not deaf.

The same routine every morning. The one with the vacuum making a big show of cleaning while the one with the medical tray and the stethoscope made an even bigger show of taking Julia's blood pressure and asking impertinent questions. Julia assumed she was a nurse, but considering what nurses wore nowadays it was impossible to tell. They were both efficient enough, at least at changing linens, registering Julia's pulse and blood pressure, and taking her for her walks, although she hardly needed them for this since Daniel Browne had moved in. She hadn't taken to him right away. She had, in fact, found him a little forward in the beginning, but she was rather pleased now that he had been so insistent and that they were going out three or four times a week, weather permitting.

Ah, this is where the smell of roses comes from, the one with the stethoscope said.

It's time we threw them out, they're starting to smell, Julia said.

Did your daughter bring them?

Yes. And my granddaughter. They're always bringing me flowers.

You're a very lucky girl, the nurse said.

Don't call me a girl, Julia replied.

The nurse disregarded Julia's request. Your granddaughter is a very attractive girl, she said as she rolled up Julia's sleeve. I like her hair, she added.

Well, you must be the only one then. I suppose you also approve of the tank top two sizes too small and the thing in her navel.

Why not? She has the figure for it. Might as well enjoy it while she can.

Julia cast an appraising eye up and down the nurse's baggy pants and sweater. Not even a sweater, one of those shapeless sweatshirts young people wore nowadays. Imagine, a professional wearing a garment with such a name. There was a time when working women were fired for wearing trousers, Julia told her.

Is that a fact? the nurse said absentmindedly without interest.

Yes. Nurses, in fact. Two of them. It was in all the papers.

They were fired for wearing slacks at work? the nurse asked.

No, at work they wore their regular uniforms, but they wore flannel trousers after their shifts. They fancied themselves as Marlene Dietrich look-a-likes or something. At least Marlene Dietrich had the figure for it and her trousers were always wide and roomy. If you don't have the figure, you shouldn't wear trousers. Especially those tight, skinny ones. Makes a woman's backside look like the rear of a horse.

The cleaning woman and the nurse glanced at each other. Julia could tell they were trying to keep a straight face. How overbearingly conceited they were. Which only spurred Julia on.

Some of the nurses didn't think the hospital could dictate what they wore on their off hours and they continued wearing the trousers regardless of the ban, so they were sacked. Of course, this was way back when, before nurses were allowed to wear any old thing. Things have sure changed since then.

The nurse smiled. Julia knew she had gone on too long and the nurse was indulging her, waiting for the appropriate moment to ask what Julia knew she would: Have you had a bowel movement today, Mrs. Brannon?

The nurse should have known better by now. She should have known that Julia would let a few seconds go by before answering, Dear Child, you, or someone exactly like you has asked me this question every morning since I got here, and every morning I have given you, or someone exactly like you, the same answer: My body's elimination habits are none of your business. If I do develop problems in this area, I will inform you, or someone like you, as soon as I deem it necessary.

The nurse shook her head and recorded something on her chart. Those damned charts, as Lena Kohn called them.

Don't you get tired of always writing down the same thing? Julia asked.

How do you know I'm writing down the same thing?

What else would you write? Nothing ever changes around here. I have dipped into the future and seen the wonder that will be. Who wrote that?

The two women looked at each other again. I don't know, Mrs. Brannon, the nurse said.

It's getting harder for me to retrieve names these days.

You're one of our brightest, the nurse offered as she summoned another one of her artless smiles.

What condescending temerity, Julia thought. Which reminds me, she said. Some of the residents were given a test. An assessment test. Do you know anything about it?

The standard test given to new residents?

I guess so. I haven't had mine yet and I was wondering why. A few people who came here around the same time I did already had theirs.

There might be a priority list. The psychologist who administers them comes in only a couple days a week. Maybe you're not as urgent as some.

Yes, anyone who remembers as much as her name around here is considered a genius. I think I should have the test soon. I don't know how much longer I'll be around and I'm curious.

I'll look into it. Is everything alright? You're not unhappy here, are you? It was the nurse's awkward way of asking if Julia intended on kicking the bucket soon.

I'm not complaining, considering the alternative. Julia was using Mr. Wilkes's line. It had come to this. Making people feel uneasy was one of the few pleasures she had left.

You have one of the nicest suites in the building, said the one who did the cleaning.

It's the same as all the one-bedroom suites, isn't it? It's disgraceful how we're crammed in like sardines. Especially the studios.

I meant you have such lovely things, the cleaner said as she draped Julia's cashmere throw over the footstool and placed her needlepoint cushions against the back of the settee. She then began dusting the table by the window, rearranging the photographs, which annoyed Julia to no end. It was important to keep the photographs in their proper order if she were to remember who everyone was. She could hardly keep Andrew's and Adam's families straight. No, not Adam, Alan. Adam was Rachel's husband and Alan was one of their sons. She had to keep them in their proper order.

What a wonderful wedding picture, the cleaner said pointing to the wedding photograph in which Julia and Sissa were wearing identical dresses.

A handsome groom, the nurse added.

Yes, unfortunately, Wilson was a very handsome and charming man, Julia said.

~8~

FATHER HAS INVITED A YOUNG LAWYER WHO RECENTLY JOINED *his law firm to a social gathering at the house. In addition to practising law, Wilson Brannon also lectures at the University of Toronto and since Sissa and I are planning to attend university in the fall, father suggests we might want to meet him. A bright, personable, young man, he tells mother.*

How young? Sissa wants to know.

I'd say in his mid-thirties, answers father.

Sissa and I look at each other. But that's not young, I say.

Why should we meet him? We're not going into Law, Sissa says to remind father she has been accepted to Normal School while I intend to pursue philosophy in spite of his objections.

Yes, yes, but it's a good idea to meet someone who knows his way around the campus. And mid-thirties is hardly ancient. I want you to be on your best behaviour, he warns. The two of you are getting too cheeky for your own good. Getting too big for your blooming bloomers, if you ask me, he adds.

What strange sayings father has. Our cheekiness, as he calls it, stems from the prospect of attending university in the fall, but it is also because Sissa's and my interests have diverged. Our futures are disengaging like Siamese twins who are being separated after eighteen years, our confidence nurtured by an unfamiliar yet exhilarated independence.

On the night of the party, Wilson Brannon is clearly taken by the fact there are, as he says, two of us. This is not unusual since Sissa and I seem to be an ongoing source of fascination whenever we are first introduced to people, especially men. Their eyes jump back and forth trying to confirm they are not seeing double. Wil-

son Brannon is one of the few who manages to keep his reaction in check, but just. He also has the presence of mind to direct his charm towards mother.

I can see how one child could inherit such elegance and beauty, Mrs. Crane, but two? How is it possible to duplicate such perfection?

His instincts are impeccable, but then so are mother's. She giggles. Mother often tries to arouse in men the very reactions against which she warns her daughters. She makes sure we understand that it is merely part of a social game for which she has established a catalogue of rules: a man will make a great show of talking to you when he is, in fact, talking mostly to himself; give the impression you are attentive and he will conclude that you are a brilliant conversationalist even if you've hardly uttered a word: dream of courtship, wake in wedlock.

You make courting sound like the plot of a nineteenth-century novel, I complain.

Oh, I doubt it has changed much since or ever will, she acknowledges and laughs. She is not blind to her contrary advice, encouraging independence as long as it does not exceed by too much what she refers to as a coarse but necessary duty.

Oh, Mr. Brannon, how very kind of you, she gushes, But I assume it is my husband's elegance to which you are referring. The girls have, indeed, inherited his best features.

Beauty and modesty, how charming. Wilson Brannon nods as he looks at me squarely. He has noticed how tedious I find mother's remarks. I hold his gaze as it lingers over every feature of my face until it finally shifts to Sissa. As she often does in social situations, she turns beet red.

Ah, this one blushes, Wilson Brannon exclaims, pleased to have had such an effect.

Yes, this one always blushes, mother says as she shakes her head. As far as mother is concerned, blushing is a sign of ill breeding.

Mr. Brannon turns to me, his eyes prancing with amusement. And you? Do you ever blush?

Never, I reply.

And why not? he asks.

I have never encountered anything worth blushing about.

And she's the bold one, mother whispers in Mr. Brannon's ear as a sign of friendly confidentiality.

The bold one. Interesting. And what does this make you? he asks Sissa.

Her colour burns deeper. *I'm as bold as my sister,* she replies with defiance. *Only I can't hide it as well as she does. She's better at deceiving.*

Sissa stares me down, challenging me to contradict her. We are rivals for the first time in our lives.

Two bold beauties including a deceptive one. Well, well. How challenging. I was wondering, Mrs. Brannon, if your daughters could accompany me to a box social this coming Saturday?

You would have to ask my husband, Mr. Brannon. He's the one who decides the company the girls keep. Another of mother's misleading ploys. She's the one who decides everything where Sissa and I are concerned. *What is the occasion?* she asks.

The university is raising money for the girls' basketball and hockey teams. Both teams play intercollegiate games with McGill and Queen's. They are very good and need our support.

Girls playing basketball and hockey? mother chides, mildly disapproving. But only mildly.

Why not? Sissa asks.

Wilson Brannon turns to Sissa. *My sentiment exactly, why not indeed? The basketball team is very good, it wins most of its tournaments,* he repeats.

Then Jane and Julia would undoubtedly approve. They are modern young women. But I do hope they don't start imitating men once they get to university.

Oh, please, I mutter. Given the chance, Mother would be the first one to pick up a basketball or a hockey stick.

Mr. Brannon turns to me. *Your father did tell me the two of you were planning to attend university in the fall. What will you be studying?*

The two of us answer at the same time: *Philosophy. Teaching.*

Wilson Brannon raises his eyebrows. *Philosophy? How unusual.*

He looks to both of us, unsure which one has made such an uncommon choice. He's about to ask when father joins us, pleased the evening is progressing so well. The noise has increased considerably throughout the house due to the crystal punch bowl having been filled several times.

Harlan, mother cries out, Mr. Brannon has invited Jane and Julia to a box social on Saturday to which I will gladly donate two lunch boxes should you agree to let them go. But if you do, we should warn the poor dear that he may end up having to buy both boxes himself.

Mother has already sensed how much Wilson Brannon longs to display her daughters as double trophies and she is letting father know she has no intention of preventing him from doing so. In fact, she plans to contribute. A handsome bachelor in his thirties who is already establishing himself as a university lecturer and a law partner presents infinitely more promise than the young scallywags Sissa and I have been bringing home recently, most of them barely out of high school.

Mr. Brannon beams. I would be the envy of every gentleman there, he says.

I decide it's time to throw a wrench in mother's and Mr. Brannon's plans. But no one has bothered to ask us if we want to go, I protest.

Mother, father, and Mr. Brannon laugh as if Sissa and I had anything to do with the decision.

As I was telling Mr. Brannon, Harlan, this is our bold one, mother says bowing her head in my direction.

And deceptive, as I'm given to understand. Wilson Brannon keeps scanning my face for a riddle he can't quite grasp or solve.

For the rest of that spring and summer, the first time mother agrees to forego a month in Hayground Grove, Wilson Brannon is turned into the Crane twins' project. He drops in so often that father complains we are keeping him from his work.

The young man may be grateful for the distraction, a delighted mother tells father.

I'm sure he is, mother, but the business isn't exactly benefiting from so many of them, father replies.

The girls are our first business, Harlan.

Father knows exactly what mother means and acquiesces.

He is right about the diversions. If Wilson fails to show up at the house for a few days, Sissa and I make excuses to visit father at his office. We bring picnic baskets and talk father into letting Wilson escort us to Hanlan's Point or to the Kew Beach Bathing Pavilions. Sometimes we skip dinner and take in a movie at the Oakwood or the Madison or a vaudeville act at the newly opened Pantages. On weekends we cruise Lake Ontario aboard the Corona or take trolleys around the Belt Line. Since the three of us are always together, mother has no need to worry about Wilson Brannon's intentions. Her work is done and it is now up to her two daughters to settle the outcome.

A few weeks before classes are due to begin, Wilson takes us on what he calls an insider's tour of the campus. He knows everything there is to know about the buildings, when they were built, and to what purpose. He commands such authority it's as if he were personally responsible for the university's progress. But then, the confidence with which he approaches everything is precisely what makes Wilson Brannon so interesting and impressive.

The Normal School on St. James Square where Sissa plans to attend teachers' college conveys a placid but practical refinement. Much like Sissa. Unlike the scholarly architecture of Osgoode Hall with its vaulted ceilings where Wilson has his office.

It must be wonderful to work here, Sissa tells him. She approves of everything Wilson does. It is obvious to me, and probably to Wilson, that she is falling head over heels in love with him.

As if he had intentionally saved the best for the last, we proceed to University College on King's College Circle, the building in which I will be taking my classes. With its massive triumphal arches, turrets, and corbel head gargoyles, it looks exactly as I imagine a Benedictine abbey or an English castle might look. I have seen buildings like these on the stereoscopic cards. The silence of the marbled halls and carved staircase with a dragon resting on its newel post conveys the solemn and portentous aura of a sequestered shelter where knowledge waits to be discovered. This is where I want to spend the rest of my life.

Wilson Brannon is a very handsome and seductive man and I have, in the last few months, longed to have him kiss me. I love the way his hair grows over the edge of his shirt collar at the back. I yearn to rest my cheek on his dark gray woollen coat. I want Wilson Brannon. But I also want to go to school. I want an academic career and to spend the rest of my life in buildings such as these. I couldn't possibly do this and be married. This is when it suddenly strikes me. It would be simpler and better for everyone if Wilson were to fall in love with Sissa instead of me.

~9~

ON THE APPOINTED DAY OF THE ASSESSMENT TESTS AN EFFICIENT and pleasant young woman showed Julia into her office. Lena had referred to her as a nurse, but the framed certificates from various gerontology programs and a graduate degree in Clinical Psychology indicated she was a psychologist and not a nurse. It seemed a considerable amount of training to be administering tests on aging minds suspected of malfunction. Any more specialization might have had her in a laboratory doing research on some obscure project such as The Molecular Pathways of the Right and Left Brain of the Embryonic Zebrafish, a creature Julia had come across in one of the library books on animals.

As a relatively new resident, Julia would be undergoing certain evaluations, the psychologist explained. She should have had them sooner, but there were more urgent cases, plus she had been away on holidays. She related this with the professional detachment of those people who believe that individuals can be defined by what is measured and recorded on charts.

What kind of evaluations? Julia asked innocently. She wished Lena could have been there to witness the playing out of their conspiracy.

They are only routine assessments to evaluate different skills, Mrs. Brannon. You'll have no trouble with them at all, you'll see. Her smile suggested that Julia was about to be the recipient of a prize, a child's trinket.

And which skills would those be? Julia asked.

The assessor pretended to flip through her files. Oh, motor skills and a few other tests, she said, trying to make her flat voice more animated. Anyone would have seen through her affected enthusiasm.

No problem, Julia said. What are the other tests? she asked hoping she hadn't memorized the names of all those damn creatures for nothing.

Memory tests, the psychologist added as she sorted out pages, tapped them on her desk, clipped them to a board. She reached for her stopwatch and placed it beside stacks of what looked like children's books. Toys sat on a table beside the desk.

You must think I'm into my second childhood, Julia said, pointing to the books.

Oh no. People of all ages take these tests. It's just routine. We just want to make sure everything is in order. She gave Julia another one of her smiles which convey nothing except the ability to pull facial muscles up or down at will. We'll start with the motor assessment tests, if it's okay with you, Mrs... She looked at her chart to verify Julia's name. Brannon. Are we up for it?

Was it part of medical or psychological training to use the royal we, Julia wondered? Sure, she said, I'm up for it. Go ahead, assess.

The motor assessment tests were exactly as Lena had described— foot tapping, arms reaching upwards, sideways, behind the back, sending fingertips toward the vicinity of the toes. They presented no problem whatsoever.

Very good, Mrs. Brannon. Very good. You are in very good shape. She glanced at her file again to verify Julia's age. My, my. Very impressive. Very unusual.

Ever since she could remember, Julia had walked several miles a week and had, until moving into Evenholme, tended to the lighter tasks in the garden. She had even taken Tai Chi classes. Yes, she said, I'm in good shape for the shape I'm in. Had I known I would live this long I wouldn't have bothered taking such good care of myself, she said.

She expected the assessor to acknowledge Julia's remarks as amusing or at least give another one of perfunctory smiles, but she continued entering results on a form, a thoroughly efficient way of invalidating what Julia thought were two pretty good jokes. Undeterred and in a louder voice, Julia added, I would have lived it up a little.

The assessor finally looked up. Fine, I'll ask you a few easy questions, which will give us time to rest, she said.

During the weeks of preparation, Julia had decided she would not answer certain questions about her personal history. No one had the right to the particulars of her existence. She had, since giving up teaching, retreated into a sort of exile, a shielded solitude she did not want invaded, even now. As she had gotten older and people became more patronizing and took her less seriously, she had become even more protective of who she was. Who she had once been. So, she decided that if some of the assessor's questions were too personal, she would either say she didn't remember or that it was information she was not prepared to share.

The psychologist was sympathetic enough when it came to Julia's memory lapses—she expected as much—but she was clearly annoyed by what she perceived as Julia's lack of cooperation. She was used to residents eager to please, grateful for a few hours of her attention, and she must have assumed that Julia would also accept her tests as co-operative teamwork. She paused after each unsatisfactory answer, pencil hovering above her clipboard before recording Julia's non-compliance. It wasn't long before her disinterested cheerfulness gave way to outright exasperation.

When it came time for the mental status test Julia could hardly contain herself. As Lena had explained, it required that she name as many animals as she could, twenty within a minute. It occurred to Julia just then how unnecessary it was to specify a time limit. Without it, and without the grand spectacle of a stopwatch, the number of animals retrieved could be recorded without making a person feel like a failure.

Any animal, Julia asked innocently? They don't have to be particular ones, domestic, wild, or indigenous to North America?

The woman looked up. Of course not, she said.

Or in alphabetical order?

Any animal will do, Mrs... It doesn't matter if you don't get twenty, do the best you can.

She was doing it again, establishing an expectation and setting Julia up for failure. Yes, I can only do the best I can, Julia said with a defeated shrug. Let's see. She pretended to reach deeply and began: aardvark, anteater, cheetah, capybara, echidna, ferret, kangaroo, lama, lemming, loris, mongoose, manatee, ocelot, otter, possum, red panda, tapir, Tasmanian tiger, weasel, wallaby, zebrafish. Twenty-two. She was keeping count on her fingers and since her minute wasn't up she added another for good measure: the hairy-nosed wombat.

The assessor kept her eyes on her clipboard and said nothing for several seconds. You have been doing your homework, Mrs... She glanced at her clipboard again. Brannon.

One must always do one's homework when facing a test, Julia said.

I see.

Julia almost felt sorry for the poor dear who didn't know where to look or how to react. Surely, Julia said, There isn't some kind of geriatric law forbidding the elderly to prepare for a test?

No, there is no such law, of course. But this will have to be recorded on your chart. It is not a proper representation of the word cognitive test.

Would it have been a better representation if I had failed? Julia asked. Would that have corresponded better to my cognitive decline?

Of course not. Many people do quite well without having studied first.

But I would guess that most don't, which doesn't mean anything about their cognitive whatever you call it, if you ask me. Are we almost finished with this nonsense? Julia asked as she got up and without waiting for an answer, left the office.

She hadn't felt this euphoric in decades and couldn't wait to tell Lena how successful their little venture had turned out. Lena wasn't in the lounge or in the dining room, so Julia went to her suite and knocked several times.

Julia burst into the room as soon as Lena opened the door. Oh, Lena, you should have been there, she was so ticked off. This will have to be recorded, Mrs... Mrs... She couldn't remember my name, for God's sake, her memory is worse than yours or mine.

Lena kept smiling, as happy with Julia's achievement as Julia was. It didn't matter if she had failed and Julia had passed. Lena Kohn did not have one envious bone in her body.

Did she measure your head? Lena asked.

Measure my head? Why, no. Why would she measure my head? She noted the span of some of my movements, but not my head. Why? Did she measure yours?

Julia noticed that the light that usually made Lena's blue eye so radiant had vanished. Uncle Pepi ordered Lili's head shaved, Lena said. Then he measured it. Hers and mine.

Lena, Julia said, Lili has been dead for a long time. Remember? This is a different time and a different place. No one measures or shaves our heads here. Then, to lighten the situation, she added, My hair just fell out as I got older.

Lena didn't react. The Lena Julia knew had gone somewhere else. Julia reached for Lena's face and held it between her hands. No one shaved our heads, Lena, she repeated.

Lena suddenly looked bewildered, as if she were waking up from a deep sleep. No, of course not, she said. She composed herself, trying to take stock of what had just happened. Julia directed her to the sofa in the sitting area and they sat down. Did you tell the assessor about your sister, Lena finally asked?

No. She did ask if I had siblings and I told her I had a sister who died. When she asked her birth date, I made Sissa two years older than me. Sissa would be furious.

Why didn't you tell her?

I don't know. I didn't want to share any information I didn't have to. I have so few memories I can call my own any more. Did you tell her about Lili?

No. Only about my younger brother and sister.

What happened to them?

Relatives hid them in a Catholic convent in Budapest. They didn't go to the camps.

Why do you think we're lying about having twin sisters, Lena?

I don't know. To protect them, maybe. They are safer if they don't exist.

Safe from what?

Lena hesitated. From intruders. Intruders can change destinies.

Did intruders change your destiny?

Oh yes.

How? It was a crass and unnecessary question. Yet something about Lena urged Julia to cross a boundary she normally wouldn't have. There existed beneath Lena's fragility an impenetrable distance, a truth Julia could not fathom yet she wanted to move closer to it. How did intruders change your destiny? Julia asked again.

Lena paused, searching for the right words, ones that would not betray her or her sister. Lili and I always assumed we would have the same lives as our mother's. We didn't know any other.

And you didn't.

No, no. We had no idea what was coming.

No, no one ever does, Julia said.

November. *When abandoned nests balance vicariously in the skeletons of trees and the only sound in the garden is of two pairs of boots and a red sled tracing their way toward the ravine.* Usually not her favourite time of year, Julia now found herself looking forward to the first snowfall, to the velocity of each snowflake tumbling toward her window. Each tiny and brilliant existence encompassing the entire world. Julia had been at Evenholme for seven months and there was a reasonable expectation that she would make it through another winter.

The daily rounds were becoming intrusive, the nurses entering her suite as figures of authority. Because they often saw the residents at their most immodest and vulnerable, they assumed they could allow themselves anything, most of them on automatic pilot. Their simulated patience reminded Julia of parents trying to cajole their children. Their presence and their incessant questions about bowels and their inane comments on the weather disrupted Julia's thoughts, contested her space.

There were a few exceptions. Like one of the male nurses, a charming Québecois with a ready smile, who never stooped to condescension. Unfortunately, Julia seldom saw him. He tended to the more delicate requirements of the male residents and had little to do with the women. He was spending a fair amount of time with Mr. Wilkes who apparently was not doing at all well.

A burly man who spoke English with a French accent, René had been nicknamed Descartes by the residents, partly because he was French-speaking, partly because in an environment where people were starting to lose the ability to think clearly about who they were, René left no ambiguity as to who he was. He had already discovered in his thirties a commonality between himself and his elderly patients, a rare occurrence in someone so young. He reminded Julia of Thea.

The day nurse who was now on her daily rounds checked her watch and asked if Julia was going to Tai Chi. There's a class before lunch, she said.

We'll see, we'll see, Julia said. Julia had no illusion as to the limited version she now did which could barely be recognized as Tai Chi. She used to be able to do all 105 movements and she could still manage a few, but not all at once and mostly sitting down.

You should go, the nurse said. It's good for you. Do you want me to help you get dressed?

I can get dressed by myself. If I need help, I'll ring. Julia wanted her and the cleaning woman to leave. Their youth, the facility with which they worked and talked exhausted her. They had not yet earned the right to think and move at Julia's pace. She waved them in the direction of the door.

The nurse gathered her instruments and cast a last glance around the room. Okay, then, she said. Just ring if you need anything.

Julia didn't care much for the couple who taught Tai Chi twice a week. The woman wore crudely made sandals with thick socks, her long, gray hair tied back in one of those sixties no-styles. The residents were supposed to call her Sifu, teacher, but Julia refused, so she never addressed her by any particular name. Truth be told, the woman got on Julia's nerves. She had the kind of smile that managed to convey both humility and condescension at the same time. And she was always pointing to a place above her belly referring to it as her chi, the inner strength at her core, as if Julia didn't know anything about inner strength.

She had, a few days before, reprimanded Julia for leaving before the end of the class. It might disturb the others she'd said.

But I'm too tired to go on, Julia had told her.

Yes, I understand, the woman replied, closing her eyes ever so slightly, and only for a split second, to emphasize the magnitude of her understanding. If you get too tired you could sit and meditate.

Have you ever meditated? she asked. It's never too late to start, to open one's mind.

How had a person less than half Julia's age arrived at such certainty? Julia wondered. She must have been one of those people who, having seized on a simple solution to define her entire life, was now hell-bent on converting everyone to her way of thinking. Open my mind? Julia asked.

Yes. Through introspection, the woman said. This time her smile could only be described as beatific. The beatific smirk of saintliness. She had the hard, lean body of someone who has deprived herself of life's excesses and pleasures, a body that invites other people's vulnerabilities to call upon its resources. You could not respond to her without risking exposing yourself to her judgement. Through meditation, she continued, Your sense of self vanishes while consciousness remains vividly aware of the continuum of experience.

It was more than Julia could bear. Oh, Ms Sifu, she said. Do you honestly believe that I, having lived almost a century, would be oblivious to the continuum of experience? If I cared enough, which I don't, or were I presumptuous enough, which I am not, I could probably teach you a thing or two about self-vanishing. Believe me, I'm a pro at it. But it is your class and if you would rather I didn't attend, I won't.

No, of course not. I thought it might be a good opportunity for you to meditate, that's all.

I think I'm in a very good position to decide what is best for me, Julia replied.

The man, also a strong but more silent type, usually let the woman speak for him, giving the impression that he functioned on a higher plane. Sifu requested the class address him as Master. Julia had always been suspicious of adults who needed to shore up their identities with labels, plus her days of addressing anyone as master were well behind her, if there ever were such days. So she didn't address him either.

Julia requested they keep a chair at the back of the room so she could sit if she had to. She greeted the sun as wide as her arms would allow, not as generous a greeting as it had been a few decades ago. She spread her wings like a white crane and waved her hands like clouds. She combed the wild mare's mane and worked shuttles like a fair young maiden. When she'd had enough, she got up and left even if the class was still in progress.

11

A FAIR YOUNG MAIDEN.
*I am nearing the end of my first term as a philosophy student.
It is dusky by the time my last class ends and if Wilson is on campus he walks me home. I suspect he is on campus more than he needs to be.*

Sissa assumes Wilson plans these walks as pretexts to come to the house to see her. In spite of the early nightfall, the first snow has dusted the campus with unusual brilliance.

Have you thought of what we talked about last week? Wilson asks.

I can't marry you, Wilson.

Why do you keep saying that? I know you care for me. You wouldn't kiss me the way you do if you didn't. You certainly wouldn't be coming to my rooms...

Before he can go any further, I cut him off. I like kissing you, Wilson. In fact, I like it very much, I tell him with a half-giggle.

You don't kiss men the way you do and expect them to walk away, he says and catches me by the waist.

Wilson, there are people.

Marry me.

I can't.

Why?

School is very important to me right now.

There's no future in philosophy for a woman, if you'll pardon my saying so.

No, I won't pardon you or father for saying so. There isn't much future in it for men either, but it's more acceptable for men to pursue impractical professions than women who are expected to enter fields better suited to their instincts.

Better suited than philosophy.

I have no interest in occupational therapy or nursing, Wilson. Even less so in household science. I could never look after a man the way mother looks after father.

Be reasonable, Julia, the man is missing a leg, for heaven's sake. He needs looking after. But I can look after myself.

I'm sure you can, although I would probably end up looking after you in spite of your two legs.

What about teaching?

What about it?

You could go into teaching. Like your sister.

Maybe eventually. But not the lower grades.

I have no objections to you attending classes after we're married.

No objections until the children came. Biology has a way of determining the agenda.

I would have thought you wanted children.

I do. But not now.

You shouldn't wait too long.

I'm barely nineteen, Wilson. I have all the time in the world.

We walk in silence along Philosopher's Walk. Students, their faces red from the cold or exuberant because of the first snow, rush by. I can sense Wilson's frustration.

You don't care for me then.

I do care for you. I can't tell you what these last six months have meant to me. I wasn't sure about studying philosophy before. Now, mainly because of you, I know I can. You make me believe I can do anything.

You can. This is why I love you.

I want more, Wilson.

All the while I thought I was courting you.

I thought you were courting Sissa. She cares about you deeply.

She's sweet, but she's not you. She's what most men want in a wife. As much as the two of you look alike, you are different.

And I'm not what most men want?

You're more of a challenge.

You would soon tire of the challenge. I would not make you a good wife, Wilson. Surely you know why.

Why?

Sissa. She would do anything for you. I wouldn't. As far as she's concerned, there's nothing or no one in the world but you right now, which means she's in love with you more than I am. I can't give up school to marry you and have children. Not yet, I'm not ready. It's only been a few months since I've realized who I could be without Sissa. I can't attach myself to another person right away; I have to give myself time.

How much time?

I don't know, Wilson. Until I get my degree.

But that's another three years, he says with is a sharp intake of breath, a gasp.

I hadn't had the courage to talk to him like this until now. Am I in love with him? Did we confuse our kisses with love? Sissa has no doubts. She's absolutely sure she wants to spend the rest of her life with him. How can I jeopardize Sissa's happiness with my uncertainty?

Sissa loves you very much, Wilson, I repeat. His chestnut hair is covered in snow, a proliferation of glistening ribbons lifting gently as he walks. Any woman would jump at the chance to marry this man. But I can't. My sister loves him. The love I have for Wilson is new and tentative while the love I have for Sissa has been with us since we were born. It overrides doubts or any pain I would cause her. Knowing this generates immeasurable joy and tempers the sadness I should feel for not agreeing to spend the rest of my life with Wilson Brannon.

His astonishment lasts but a few seconds and quickly shifts to retaliation: The only thing left for me to do then is to marry your sister. If she loves me so much and you don't.

She does love you Wilson.

I don't love her, he says.

How could you not?

We continue to walk in silence. There is no reason to worry. We confused our kisses and flirtation with love and this will soon burn itself out. He will learn to love Sissa, I am sure of it.

12

JULIA PHONED RACHEL AND THEA TO WARN THEM SHE WOULD BE busy in the afternoon and evening, in case they were planning to drop by. Relieved to learn that her mother was keeping busy, Rachel didn't bother asking questions. Julia hadn't been able to reach Thea and left a message on her machine. So, what's up, what are you up to? Thea wanted to know when she returned the call.

Julia didn't say anything about meeting Daniel for an early dinner, only that several people were gathering in the lounge to be introduced to a woman from Hungary. A few days earlier, the residents had received a letter asking for volunteers. A schedule had been organized for people to help with a temporary resident, Gizi Magris, who would be staying at Evenholme for a few weeks.

A concert pianist, she had, two years before, awakened one night to find her apartment in flames and had passed out in a hallway trying to escape. In addition to extensive burns to her body, both hands had been destroyed.

A Canadian doctor visiting the hospital where she was a patient had arranged to bring her to Canada where a team of doctors and surgeons donated their time and skills for several bouts of reconstructive surgery to prepare her hands for prostheses.

Younger than the usual residents, Evenholme had nevertheless agreed to let her have one of the studios while she recuperated, and volunteers were needed to help with ordinary tasks such as helping Gizi wash herself, get dressed, comb her hair, cut her food and feed her, functions the residents still took for granted. It was obvious from the tone of the letter that this was meant as a double blessing. In allowing the residents to help her, they were supposed to feel wanted and useful. As transparent a plan as it was, Julia looked forward to having a younger person in need of her help for a change.

This is great, Nan, Thea said at the other end of the line. I don't want to hear you bellyaching about being useless ever again.

Don't patronize me, Thea.

You are impossible. Anyway, I'll see you in a few days and you can tell me all about it.

Gizi Magris sat in one of the large, stuffed armchairs in the lounge. She wore a silk blouse with a high lace collar camouflaging much of her scarred neck. Long lace cuffs were sewn to the end of her sleeves covering her bandages. She imparted calm and self-assured elegance. The woman with lace hands, Julia thought.

Everyone gathered around her and after the necessary introductions she spoke about the accident, the surgeries, her love of music. As she talked, her features rearranged themselves into smiles, which threatened to become grimaces because of the extensive disfigurement. The residents greeted her comments with polite and sympathetic nods of understanding and admiration. When the meeting was over she stood up to thank everyone for volunteering. Exceptionally tall and slender, she towered over almost everyone and carried herself with the dignity of someone who has walked away from calamity and turned tragedy into strength. As the residents left the lounge, someone near Julia whispered that they might have been in the presence of an extraordinary human being.

Julia's duties would consist in helping Gizi with dinner three times a week starting the next evening. She could hardly wait. Because Gizi couldn't manoeuvre doorknobs each volunteer was given a key to her suite.

When Julia opened the door it was stone quiet and dark inside. The curtains were drawn and it took a few seconds for Julia's eyes to adjust. Gizi was curled up in the corner of a love seat, eyes closed. Hello? Julia said tentatively.

Oh, come in, please come in, Gizi said.

Did I wake you? Julia asked.

No, I was resting my eyes. They are sensitive and the overhead light is too bright, so I keep it off as much as possible.

Should we keep the lamp off then? Julia asked and wondered how she was going to navigate in such a dim room. Perhaps we could use the side-table lamp, she suggested

Yes, please, do turn on the lamp. I can manage switches on walls, but knobs on lamps are a problem, she said, raising the two bandaged stumps where her hands should have been.

As Julia flicked on the lamp she hit the shade and wobbly shadows appeared against one of the walls. They reminded her of a lamp with a carousel shade that she and Sissa had when they were girls. When the lamp was turned on the shade rotated, projecting patterns of a merry-go-round on the walls of their bedroom.

There, that's better, Julia said and introduced herself again in case Gizi didn't remember her from the night before. I'm to help you with your dinner tonight, she added.

Gizi nodded, a token gesture to replace the shaking of hands.

Is it here, yet? The dinner? Julia asked.

No, not yet. It's just as well, it will give us time.

Time? For what?

To get ready. Wash my hands, Gizi said and laughed.

Julia made a pretence of laughing too if only to acknowledge Gizi's attempt at humour. Because Gizi was not wearing the lace blouse with the high collar and the add-ons at the wrists, the mangled skin on her neck and her arms above the bandages was clearly visible. Poor child. Julia's legs faltered a little and she questioned whether volunteering had been such a good idea.

It occurred to Julia that perhaps Gizi was hinting that she should wash her hands too. Of course, Julia said, I wouldn't dream of handling your food without washing my hands.

No, I mean I have to go to the bathroom.

Oh, is there anything I can do? What was Gizi expecting, Julia wondered?

I can manage, Gizi said. I only need you to put the paper between my hands. She held up her bandaged stumps again. They looked liked two large paws. Her body had gone through too much to claim modesty or vanity now.

Oh, of course. Of course, Julia repeated. To her own ears, she sounded like a babbling idiot. Her nervousness was interfering with her ability to communicate. Of course, I understand, she added. I've been doing it myself for over ninety years.

Gizi gasped. You are that old?

Yes, I am. Julia didn't add that she was, in fact, on the downhill side of ninety. She could picture Rachel saying, Why, it's so nice of you to be doing this, mother, while Thea would be outraged. She didn't expect you to wipe her ass, did she? For all her compassion, there were boundaries Thea wouldn't cross unless absolutely necessary.

Gizi kept staring at Julia. Over ninety, extraordinary, she said. She struggled from the love seat with a weariness Julia hadn't noticed the night before. Julia had, upon meeting Gizi, imagined a bond, an equivalence between their frailty, their vulnerability, the kind that came from exposure and loss. More so in Gizi's case since her hellfire had so recently descended upon her. Now, Julia was struck by the sheer vanity and presumption of such an idea. How could she put herself in this woman's place?

As soon as the dinner arrived Julia proceeded to cut up the meat and made a joke about the difficulty of feeding someone peas on a fork and Gizi suggested she use a spoon. They made polite conversation, mostly about Gizi's accident and her thwarted ambitions. There was little else to talk about. The fire had drawn every detail of her past and her future into a giant vacuum.

Would you like me to help you get ready for bed? Julia asked after she had tidied up.

No need to, someone else is coming at nine. But you could read to me a while, Gizi suggested. I can't hold a book very well and turning the pages is awkward. She pointed to a pile of books sitting on a chair.

Any particular one? Julia asked as she picked up the books one by one. They were all in Hungarian. I'm afraid I can't read these, she told Gizi.

There are two or three in English in there, Gizi replied. One of them was nominated for the Booker Prize. Yes, that one. She pointed to a slim volume that Julia was holding. *Black Dogs* by Ian McEwan.

Julia turned the book over and scanned the blurbs. *The New York Times* believed it to be a novel with "vision ... *vivid in its moral complexities.*" *The Washington Post* called it "*a study of the fragile nobility of the human spirit....*" Appropriate, considering the situation, Julia thought. Sounds interesting, she told Gizi. Here? She pointed to a bookmark.

Gizi nodded and Julia began to read: *Turning-points are the inventions of storytellers and dramatists, a necessary mechanism when a life is reduced to, traduced by, a plot, when a morality must be distilled from a sequence of actions...*

What an extraordinary statement, Julia reflected as she read on. And real lives? What about real lives? Were they also in need of plots to identify their turning-points? Such as this woman's accident? And Lena Kohn? Lena hardly needed storytellers to identify her turning-points.

As Julia was about to leave, the next volunteer having arrived, Gizi asked if she, or someone she knew, had a tape deck she could borrow. And tapes. She liked to listen to music, she said.

What kind of music? Julia asked.

Mostly classical, Gizi said. Piano, she added.

Ah, a woman after my own heart. I don't own a portable tape deck myself, but I'll ask around. If I find one I'll bring it next time I come. In two days, I believe. Julia realized she should have told her she would bring it as soon as she found one, but she wasn't as keen to return as she had been volunteering, not as excited about the prospect of feeding Gizi again. Beneath Gizi's graceful bearing and cultured veneer Julia detected entitlement. It was not a quality she admired in people especially since she had only recently discovered it in herself and she was still searching for an effective antidote. There would not be the same opportunity for friendship with this woman as there had been with Lena Kohn or Daniel Browne.

She made a mental note of placing a reserve for the book by Ian McEwan at the library the next day.

~13~

IT WASN'T LONG AFTER DANIEL BROWNE MOVED IN THAT THE proverbial grapevine had him and Julia spending an inordinate amount of time in each other's suites. There are people who, as they get older, assume the right to pass judgement on everything and everyone around them. Ironically, as far as Julia could tell, they were the very people most lacking in good judgement.

The time Julia spent with Daniel Browne was far from inordinate. Two afternoons a week at the most. And it certainly wasn't what anyone thought. Julia no longer had the energy or the interest to do what anyone thought. In spite of her promiscuous reputation as a young woman, she had long given up on the kind of love that feeds and dies on genitals, the kind that names itself romance or being in love, but has more to do with brief spasms of pleasure. What she and Sissa once shared, now that was true love. Sissa had been the template from which Julia extracted love's definition. Sissa, then Rachel and Thea.

It had never occurred to Julia, nor did Daniel Browne ever indicate, that anything physical could happen between them, even when they started to hold hands. There was such cruelty in nakedness now, this assailable, almost laughable body once thought of as an object of desire. Each ache and wrinkle, each failing organ inscribing itself as its own evidence.

Julia had never been a prude. She had never thought of her body as a yardstick of someone else's morality. Having a twin sister whose body reflected hers might have provided her with a mirror in which all bodies resemble each other, their differences the minor details of a general biological reality. Nor had she ever thought of the female body as a source of mystical knowledge as some women would have the world believe. She remembered reading an article during the so-called sexual revolution of the sixties in which the vagina was compared to a sacred, translucent chamber and she had thought, Well, there's a perception emanating from too many hallucinogenic drugs. No, she had never been a prude. On the contrary, her sister had often accused her of being a little too loose with her affections.

There was a fair amount of flirtation at Evenholme, but Julia doubted there was much sex in spite of a few residents who still conducted themselves as if sex should always be on one's mind. Half-a-dozen women behaving like schoolgirls. The extraordinary lengths they went to. Bella Blanchard's poisonous injections. Gertrude Mitford, whom everyone referred to as Mrs. GM, not so much because of her initials but because her face had been lifted so many times someone said she looked as if she had been Genetically Modified. Mrs. Gilbert in 209 with her astonishing collection of wigs. She smeared her face with so many layers of makeup, no one would have recognized her without the makeup or the wigs. Why was it still so important to attract attention, Julia often wondered. Did it make women who felt invisible feel more visible, a plight as true at eighty as it had been at eighteen?

The men weren't much better. In fact, they may have been worse, broadcasting their imagined conquests to anyone who cared to notice. Sonny Walsh placed flowers on the dining tables of the women he imagined he was wooing, while Graham Porter left notes under plates and doors. Youth's swagger replaced by the bravado of old age. Memories of the flesh carrying their own deceptive rhetoric in order to deal with the palpable dread of being alone. In a setting where people lived together from breakfast to bedtime, there was still the dread of not being loved enough. In this, even the aged were insatiable.

Julia noticed him immediately. He ate alone, preferring his own company, which meant he was either a widower or a bachelor. In either case, he looked after himself rather well, unlike some of the other men whose clothes looked as if they had been thrown on with a pitchfork.

He owed much of his pleasant appearance to his ramrod posture and his white mane. He was one of those rare and fortunate gentlemen whose dorsal alignment hadn't shifted with time. His barrel chest and the extra pounds around his waist served him rather well. They conveyed strength, as did his legs straight as timbers inside his dark gray trousers, or so Julia imagined.

Daniel Browne had also managed to keep most of his hair, which was never too long or too short unlike some of the men who got shorn to the scalp to defer a visit to the barber for several months. Nor did he need to pull long strands across his pate to camouflage the hairline's retreat. Silver curls barely cleared his shirt collar at the back. Julia had always found this attractive in a man.

Because he was a retired Professor of Mathematics, the women assumed that Daniel Browne thought himself above everyone else. Julia had undergone the same scrutiny and bias when she first arrived, so she should have known better than to join their gossip. But it was the old story. You found fault with others as a basis for the admiration you bore for yourself. Julia knew this yet it didn't prevent her from telling the women an ongoing joke when she was at university about the antisocial tendencies of mathematicians. Mathematics, the joke went, was invented for those who lack a flair for conversation because they spent so much time playing with themselves. Not in the best of taste, but appreciated by the other women nevertheless.

Daniel Browne usually kept his nose in a book while he ate, either an indication he was well read or a tactic to avoid people so Julia was surprised when he turned to her at the dining room door one day and asked if he could join her for lunch. She had looked in on Lena who wasn't feeling well and by the time she got to the dining room the meal was almost over. Nothing was more depressing than two individuals sitting at opposite ends of a dining room as it slowly emptied, so Julia accepted the invitation.

In spite of Julia's crude remarks regarding mathematicians, no one could have accused Mr. Browne of lacking in conversation.

She didn't always agree with what he said, but he had plenty to talk about. He spent several minutes complaining about the tardiness of doctors and how his appointment had been delayed for over an hour. He could not understand, except in cases of emergencies, why doctors could not adhere to schedules. It made one suspicious of their accuracy in other areas, he said. He then went on for several more minutes on the importance of punctuality. As he rattled on Julia wondered if Daniel Browne was undergoing a slight case of the nerves.

Human needs are not always mindful of the clock, Mr. Browne, Julia finally offered as a reminder that illness didn't necessarily adhere to schedules and perhaps he needed to spend less time on the subject.

He grinned, partly to acknowledge her remark, but also to dismiss it. Please, call me Daniel, he said. He then asked why Julia almost never went to the dining room for her evening meals. Surprised and flattered he had noticed, Julia explained she preferred a light supper of fruit, tea, and biscuits in her suite. Except on the occasional Sunday when she felt compelled to honour tradition.

What tradition would that be? he asked.

Sunday lamb or beef, she replied.

Tradition is important to you then?

Not so important as to do it on a regular basis, she said. But I still enjoy a dinner of lamb or roast beef on those rare occasions when I am unable to keep myself company.

Yes, yes, so do I. Lamb and roast beef are also favourites of mine, he said, pleased to have identified at least one common point of interest. Considering his mathematical background and his views on punctuality, Julia wondered if a traditional dinner wasn't one of many items on a list of equivalence formulas, Sunday dinners of lamb or roast beef equalling close family ties, equalling order and certainty. Julia decided to goad him a little.

Except our family dinners usually deteriorated into family squabbles, not a tradition I care to uphold, she added.

It was impossible to tell if her comment had any effect, so she pressed further, aware she was paraphrasing Thea: In fact, I have often wondered if tradition is important to people who can't think up new ways of living and thinking.

If provoked he did a good job of hiding it. And how did you arrive at this untraditional conclusion, he asked as any unflappable deductivist would, soup spoon poised in mid-air.

Tradition dictates how people should behave. I find this lazy.

He smiled. I see. I hear you taught at the University of Toronto, he said, then added, As I did.

Julia nodded. I did teach introductory courses in Ethics and Literature, yes.

I taught Mathematics.

So I've heard. But I doubt I taught there as you did. My courses were broad, liberal, college courses. Mathematics would have been university courses of a higher learning.

Do I detect a note of sarcasm, Julia?

You might, for which I apologize. As someone once wrote: Sarcasm is a blow turned stupid, Julia said.

He let out a loud and surprisingly unrestrained guffaw. He then asked if Julia would care to have tea in his suite the next afternoon. Instead of dinner, he added with a knowing grin.

As generous as it was of Daniel Browne to suggest that Julia had once taught at the University of Toronto as he did, it was an inaccurate assumption. In spite of holding a graduate degree in philosophy, Julia had never been allowed the same privileges as a male professor. The prayer carved in stone at the entrance to the Great Hall at Hart House may have purported to draw into a "common fellowship" all members of the Colleges and Faculties, but at the time of its installation it was not meant to include women. When Julia lectured at University College, women were allowed, on special occasions, to attend functions at Hart House on the condition they entered by a lower side door, a rule extending, at least metaphorically, to most areas of the university. It was not until 1972, long after she had left, that women were admitted to Hart House on equal terms with men.

The first course taught by a woman at the University of Toronto consisted of demonstrating food chemistry: Clara Benson, the first woman to earn a doctorate in chemistry, taught courses in household science designed to help young women organize the home. Although no one admitted as much, many felt it was also designed to keep them there. Making domestic work the result of a woman's education would not only maintain the status quo, it would safeguard the illusion that women were in charge of the home while men were in charge of everything else.

After Sissa's wedding, Julia had buried herself in various school activities, made several friends with women and men, and realized the extent to which she and Sissa had kept to themselves growing up. She enrolled in several language courses including classical Greek and French. Mademoiselle Jolicoeur's French lessons had not been as hopeless as they had once seemed. She joined the Women's Literary Society of University College and participated in the few debates in which women were allowed. Because the men usually outnumbered the women in such debates, she spent hours preparing for each one. Especially when University College debated St. Michael's. University College defined itself as a non-sectarian institution, but it leaned heavily towards Anglicanism. On the other hand, St. Michael's offered a philosophy curriculum based on Catholic theology influenced by the metaphysics of Thomas Aquinas. A spirited competition developed between the two. It was a pity, chided the students from University College, that Saint Thomas Aquinas's saintliness had not made him or the students of St. Michael's more rational.

As much as Julia loved school, it wasn't long before she realized that she was not entirely suited for philosophy. She should have been since she was, by nature, a sceptic. Her brand of scepticism, however, was based on mistrust of what often passed as wisdom. She grew impatient with much of philosophy's theoretical bent. It seemed reasonable to her that ideas should, at some point, profit real lives, just as it seemed reasonable that logic should be relative. On this, she agreed with her mother—life belonged to those who lived it, not only those who thought about it.

When she decided to pursue a graduate degree, she was more

or less coerced into combining philosophy with literature. As her advisor pointed out, the combination would open more doors for a woman who wished to be employed. Since she already held several credits in English Literature and she was an active member of the Women's Literary Society of University College, she was already half-way there, he said.

Partially out of interest and partially out of spite, Julia proposed a thesis on the philosophy and poetry of Lord Byron. The climate at the university was conservatively English and as far as she could tell Byron did not represent the typical English soul.

Why Byron, her advisor wanted to know. Why not Wordsworth? Coleridge?

They were not philosophers, Julia reminded him.

But Byron was of the Ishmaelite race, he whispered. Even he understood the racial implication and his eyes went darting past Julia's shoulder.

He died fighting Moslems, she reminded him.

True. But he had a reputation.

Julia presumed he was referring to Byron's many love affairs including an incestuous relationship with his half-sister. Or perhaps it was because Byron drank Burgundy from a human skull or because he had written and published satirical rhyming couplets called English Bard considered a slight to English poets.

Plus he was such a melancholic, her advisor added and sighed, his eyes, once again, darting past her shoulders. Anything written under the influence of melancholia, a state associated mainly with women and the weak-minded, was clearly not a proper area of study.

Julia also had mixed feelings about Romantic and melancholic writers and their self-absorbed rhetoric about passion and suffering, but she felt she needed to stand her ground. She decided to shore up her argument by quoting Byron: *Sorrow is knowledge.* A few days later she was given permission to begin her research for her proposed thesis: *A Philosophy of Rebellion in Lord Byron's Poetry.*

Upon completing her thesis eighteen months later, she was hired to teach two introductory courses, one in English Literature and another in Fundamental Ethics. She did, eventually, teach more advanced courses, but she was never considered for a full senior post. She might have been had she gone on to obtain a post-graduate degree and had she not lost her enthusiasm for philosophy, or if circumstances had not intervened.

If Daniel Browne's claim was not entirely accurate, Julia hoped it would nevertheless help them establish a kinship in something other than old age.

~14~

DANIEL'S STUDIO SUITE STOOD IN SHARP CONTRAST TO JULIA'S. To describe it as sparse would have been an understatement. A single-sized bed doubled as a divan; two chairs as straight-backed as Daniel stood dutifully at each end of a small square table. In fact, except for a few dozen shelves overstocked with books, the room gave no impression of being inhabited. No family photographs, no paintings, no used plates or cups abandoned in the sink. The only hint of a human presence was a silver salver bearing a tea set, two cups and saucers on the counter by an electric kettle.

The first time Julia visited him in his suite she wasn't sure how to fill the awkward moment when one is supposed to comment on a host's lodgings. So she said nothing and walked directly to the shelves to peruse his books where she hoped she would find something on which she could comment. Instead, all had to do with some branch of mathematics or science. There was no fiction, poetry or philosophy, nothing much to do with human beings other than a few biographies of mathematicians or scientists and one other volume titled *An Introduction to the History of Human Stupidity*. It reminded her of something her father might have said.

You don't read fiction? she asked.

No, none of that romantic, sentimental stuff for me.

She bristled. Fiction is not necessarily sentimental or romantic. Serious literature gives us insights into the human mind and human nature.

Not much point in digging too deeply into those, Daniel answered. Your discoveries will either appal or disappoint.

How depressingly cynical, Julia fired back. Perhaps you haven't read enough good literature.

Perhaps. But I'm not so sure anything new about human beings can be learned from fiction. Or history. Most of it is just the recording of man's nastiness toward his fellow man.

And mathematics, what do they explain? Certainly not cruelty or war.

Neither do novels.

Good ones do. If they're perceptive enough.

I tend to be a more pragmatic sort of person.

Even pragmatism is rooted in perception, Daniel, Julia shot back.

True. You have me there. His eyes twinkled. Julia could tell he liked to exchange opposing views. Oh, I'll admit to having read fiction a few times, he conceded. Not often, but sometimes I like to see what the fuss about a book is all about.

Is it so disappointing then?

Not always. I've been surprised a few times, but not often.

I suspect there are only as many great authors as there are great mathematicians, Julia said. But it shouldn't stop people from reading or studying mathematics.

Well, new mathematical solutions are new. In fiction, the dates, the names of people and places change but the events stay pretty much the same. It's basically the same story. Variations on a few themes.

You must be one of those people who believe in eternal recurrence then.

Which is?

The theory that everything repeats itself in cycles.

People don't seem to learn much from one cycle to another, do they? You believe this cycle stuff?

I try not to. I cling to the hope that history is progressive.

I'm afraid I'm more cynical.

Julia took a book down from the bookshelf without looking at the title and walked to the table, which wasn't much sturdier than a card table, and sat down. Well, I may be also, actually. I do believe that imagination helps to bridge the gap between facts and solutions though. Wasn't it Einstein who said that imagination was more important than knowledge? She glanced at the cover of the book she held. *The History of* DNA.

Yes, he might have said something like that. That's a fascinating book, he said, pointing to the book in Julia's hands. You can borrow it if you like.

I don't think so. Learning the basics of the human body doesn't strike me as crucial these days.

Daniel laughed. I know what you mean.

She put the book down and scanned over scribblers and textbooks stacked on the table that also served as his desk. You still do math? she inquired.

I spend a few hours each morning solving problems from my grandson's exercise books, Daniel explained. It gives me the illusion that I still have a schedule. And a brain.

Like most residents, he had gotten into the habit of laying out his hours and days with specified tasks and appointments, if only with himself. The need to stabilize time prevented surprises and alleviated the anxiety of not having the strength to handle them.

I do the same, Julia said.

How so?

I spend a few hours each morning writing on my laptop. Julia rather liked the sound of this. It gives me the illusion that I am a writer, she added.

What do you write?

Oh, nothing much. A daily journal, except it's about the past. It's for my granddaughter although she doesn't know I'm doing it yet. May I? Julia asked pointing to the scribblers and textbooks.

Sure, go ahead. He walked to the cupboards in the kitchenette.

Julia flipped through a few pages. Strings of letters, numbers, and other mute signs glared back.

Do you have any interest in algebra or geometry? he asked.

Not in the least, Julia said and laughed.

You'd be surprised how much those equations hold some of life's most important mysteries, he said as he poured water into a measuring cup, gauging the precise amount he needed. He poured the water into the electric kettle, and glanced at a clock with large, black numerals sitting on the counter. A split second before the water was due to boil, he poured some into the teapot, sloshed it around, pushed the boiling button on the kettle to start it boiling again, emptied the teapot, dropped the tea ball infuser into it, then poured in the boiling water. He checked the clock once more, warmed the cups while the tea brewed. It was an extraordinary display. His concentrated preciseness transformed the routine of making tea into a fluid, choreographed ceremony. He reminded Julia of the proverbial creature by which people set their clocks. Like Descartes's sparrows returning at precisely the same time each spring. Or Linnaeus's flowerbeds whose flowers opened at different hours of the day—the passionflower spreading its petals at noon, the primrose at six in the early evening. The eternal recurrence of the plant world when left to its own device.

Julia picked up a textbook. It dealt with geometric forms, spoke of areas and volumes, empty realms to her eyes. She wondered why anyone would continue to devote so much time to such a demanding and abstract subject in retirement. She understood mathematics' utilitarian importance. Without it lives would be primitive and naive. Yet, she felt lost when confronted with mathematical abstraction. It reminded her too much of the Greek idea of perfect truths or ideal worlds which never reached the real world. Hadn't the geometrical simplicity sought by Plato proved illusory in the end? The same illusiveness that Daniel felt when he read literature, perhaps.

Do you have many grandchildren? Julia asked. Because Daniel rarely broke into reminiscence, it was best to be as direct as possible. He had mentioned visits to daughters and sons, but this was the first time he had referred to a grandson.

Yes, yes. Several grandsons. And a great-granddaughter. Little epsilon, he added and chuckled.

Julia remembered two definitions of the word epsilon: an unusually brilliant star of a constellation, or a person of low intelligence.

She chose the former. Yes, grandchildren are such bright stars in our otherwise dimmed lives, she said.

A quizzical expression crossed Daniel Browne's face. Had he not expected her to know the meaning of his quaint simile? Had he expected her brain to have shut down because she was a few years older than he was? At least she assumed him to be younger.

He removed the books from the table and replaced them with a meticulously ironed linen tablecloth and matching napkins. The fine white china cups and plates were plain. The worn silver utensils, substantial in weight, bore an engraved G on each handle, not the B of his own initial. Whoever had owned the china and the cutlery before him had preferred unadorned, classical styles. Perhaps an inheritance from a relative with a different name.

I haven't seen your friend around these last few days, he said as he arranged fruits and biscuits on a plate.

Which one? Julia knew he meant Lena but she didn't want to give the impression that her social life had been reduced to one friend.

I think her name is Lena. Has she been ill?

Yes. Well, no, not exactly. She likes to spend time in her room sometimes. Julia had been about to say bed, but thought better of it.

Nothing serious, I hope?

Not really. Julia was reluctant to say more lest he or anyone else found out about Lena's erratic episodes. Just a phase she's going through, like everyone else around here, she said.

What kind of phase? Daniel asked.

Julia began rearranging the cups and saucers on the table and the biscuits on the plate. Oh, sometimes she thinks she's somewhere else, she said as nonchalantly as she could. It's not so unusual, I don't know where I am most mornings when I first wake up.

She hated the forced levity in her voice. *Those little levities so commonly incident to young ladies.* Where did she remember this from? She was neither young nor was there anything commonly frivolous about what was happening to Lena.

Where does she think she is during those phases? Daniel asked, avoiding Julia's eyes as people do when their questions are cautious and meant to sound casual when they are, in fact, calculated. Not unlike Julia's answers.

Julia shrugged. Who knows? Another time. Another place. Julia suspected he already knew, but she wasn't about to confirm his suspicions.

What time? What place? he insisted.

The past. Don't get me wrong; it only happens sometimes, not very often.

Going through her second childhood is she?

Good Lord, no! Julia exclaimed. The thought of Lena's dreadful memories being interpreted as innocent as childhood struck Julia as outrageous, until she realized this was precisely what they were: memories of a childhood turned nightmare relived over and over again.

You can trust me, Daniel said, searching Julia's eyes for a link to which he could connect and she could trust. I won't repeat it, he added softly.

Oh, you mustn't. People here spend so much time chatting up other people's business.

I'm not the type to chat up other people's business, Julia.

I didn't mean to suggest you were. It's just that, well, sometimes Lena thinks she's back in one of those camps that she and her twin sister were sent to during the war. Sometimes she seems to think she's back there, especially when something happens to upset her. It's very peculiar. Kind of a chain reaction, I guess. She gets upset, then the first thing I know she's somewhere else or she's retreated to her bed.

Has something happened to upset her lately?

Her son and his family are away on holidays. She assumed she was going with them and when she realized they'd already left she took to her bed. I've hurried to her suite before the housekeeper or the nurse these last few days to spruce her up although I doubt we're fooling anyone. This morning I couldn't find her hairbrush in the usual place in the bathroom and I opened the drawer of her night table and the drawer was filled with pieces of bread, most of them dry and mouldy.

She's saving bread?

I guess so. When I asked her about it she raised herself on one elbow and stared into the drawer. It was so strange. She just kept staring. You don't have to save food here, Lena, I told her. We have plenty to eat.

Did she say anything? Daniel asked. He seemed genuinely interested.

No, she just continued staring at the bread. I knew it didn't have anything to do with not having enough to eat, I knew it was something else. So I asked her again: Are you confused this morning, Lena? There's no danger here, this is a nice home. I wanted to engage her into telling me what was going on, the reason she was storing food. I had to repeat two or three times, Do you know why you are saving bread, Lena? Can you tell me, so I can understand? I was hoping my questions would jolt her back.

Did they? Daniel asked.

Well, not really, not then. She motioned me to come closer. For Lili, she whispered. Lili gives me her bread, but now that I have too much I give her mine. Lili was Lena's twin sister, Julia explained to Daniel. Lena once told me that she saw a little boy beaten to death because he gave his bread to his sister, so Lena must have felt she had to whisper in case someone overheard. Hearing Lena refer to Lili as if she were still alive, lowering her voice as if it she had to keep someone from hearing, sent me into a panic.

Has this happened before?

Yes, but nothing like this. A passing remark now and then, but she usually snaps out of it pretty quickly.

She'll probably snap out of this one too.

I hope so. Having to go back to that period in her life must be terrible. Surely, once is more than enough.

Her sister died in the camps, did she? Daniel's voice sounded flat and for a moment Julia wondered if he was bored. So many people didn't want to hear about the camps anymore, about the Holocaust. Perhaps he felt the same way.

No. They both survived the camps. Lena told me if one of them had died in there, they both would have died. They kept each other alive. But after the liberation, Lili lost her will to live. Her sight had suffered terribly because of experiments done on her eyes, more so than Lena. Food was scarce and she gave Lena most of her rations. It sounds like Lili might have starved herself to death. A kind of suicide, I guess.

They were two of Mengele's children, were they? he asked without surprise.

Why, yes. You know about Mengele?

He gave a wry little laugh. Doesn't everybody?

I didn't. The name was familiar, of course, I knew he was part of the machinery, but I didn't know what he had done, precisely. I didn't know about his experiments on twins. I was a twin too, you see, and it upset me to hear what he did.

More so than if you hadn't been a twin?

Julia couldn't tell if the contempt in Daniel's voice was directed at her or at Mengele. Oh no, she replied, somewhat rattled. Well, perhaps. Not being Jewish had always exempted me from these events. It was something that had happened to them. But as a twin, I was no longer exempted; I could envision the possibility.

As a Gentile you would have been exempted, even as a twin.

I suppose. Even so, I was drawn to Lena the moment I met her. Especially after learning she was a twin and what she'd gone through because of it. Ironically, being a twin saved her.

But not her sister. What was your sister's maiden name? Not Brannon, I suppose, he said.

His sudden shift surprised her. Pardon?

Your sister's or your maiden name, I was wondering what it was.

Our maiden name was Crane. My sister was Jane Crane.

Jane Crane. Did she study philosophy too?

Not really, no.

He stared at Julia for a while. He pointed to the book on the history of DNA. You should take that book; it's interesting. Sounds scientific but you won't have any problem with it. It claims that human DNA is almost identical in everybody, that only a tiny proportion of it accounts for differences between people, and those are mainly superficial—eyes, hair, the physical stuff. Except for identical twins, of course.

He picked up the book off the table and flipped through several pages trying to find written confirmation for the case he was making. Here it is, he said and began to read: Only one thousandth of our genetic make-up accounts for differences between any two human beings who are not identical twins. He looked up. Imagine that. If our DNA was a thousand-page book, nine hundred and ninety-nine pages would be identical. Only one page would be different. Only one thousandth of a difference between any two people. He hesitated, then added, Between any two men, say Jesus and Hitler.

Oh, I wouldn't be shouting this from the rooftops, Daniel.

I know. What a source of indignation science can be. To think of all the misery that's been caused because of one thousandth of a difference.

Well, I don't know, Daniel. It doesn't add up.

What do you mean?

It's too small a difference. What if the findings were interpreted the other way around? What if we mess up because of the other nine hundred and ninety-nine pages. Everybody is practically the same, yet we all have this insatiable need to be different. Not only different, but better. We keep saying we should respect each other's differences when what we really want is to be better. This may well be our blind spot, that's why we can't see it.

Julia thought of Lena. Mengele injecting her brown eye in an attempt to make it blue. To make it better in his own eyes. The swastika a symbol for a blue eye, the Star of David a symbol for a brown one.

You know, Julia continued, I remember the exact moment when I decided I no longer wanted to be like my twin sister. We'd always thought of ourselves as essentially the same until suddenly I no longer wanted to be like her. I wanted my own life and I wanted it to be better than hers. It was about the time we started to make lists, life plans we called them, and I made sure my lists were different from hers because I thought hers were so ordinary. I couldn't understand why she wanted such an ordinary life. I thought I could discover who I truly was by not being ordinary, the reason I studied philosophy, I guess. I assumed it would tell me who I was, separate from my sister. Perhaps this is why identical twins are such a curiosity. They undermine people's sense of individuality. No matter what that book says, Daniel, as long as there are two people on earth, one will always try to outdo the other.

Daniel didn't say anything for a while. Julia could hear the minute hand of his old-fashioned clock with the large, black numerals slicing through the seconds. She could see he was mulling over what they'd discussed. Until, finally, he said. Jesus Christ, Julia, you're just as cynical as I am.

Julia sighed. Maybe more so. Philosophy may have raised these questions well before science did. Of course, while Heidegger was working on his grand concept of Being and commonality between human beings, he was turning Jewish colleagues over to the Nazis. After the war, he wrote: *He who thinks greatly errs greatly.* Maybe he should have written, He who thinks greatly betrays greatly. If one of the greatest philosophical minds of the century got it so wrong, what chance is there for the rest of us?

Oh, I suspect he was adapting to the situation like most people did at the time. Perhaps this is something else we all share, the need to adapt.

Not everyone adapted. Some people refused to go along.

Not enough, obviously. I've often questioned this notion of individual responsibility in time of war. It seems to me that it makes little sense to hold individual soldiers accountable when they've been trained not to think for themselves.

My father used to say that much of the bravery those eighteen-year-olds exhibited was nothing more than bravado.

Sorry little scapegoats.

But Heidegger wasn't a soldier, he was a thinker. He was supposed to think for himself.

To change behaviour, the environment has to change, even for a thinker.

And Mengele? asked Julia.

What about Mengele?

He was a doctor, a scientist.

No, no. He was a soldier. Bent on fulfilling his duties. If he had been a scientist, he would have seen how engineering his own genetic mutations was scientifically absurd. Not to mention the sadism of his experiments and the wanton murder of the twins he worked on. He was an ambitious officer in a war machine. He adapted to a monstrous situation. As entire nations did and are doing still. Daniel shrugged as if stating the obvious.

This is too depressing to bear. Why do our conversations end up like this?

Like what?

So serious. Two old has-beens with nothing better to do but sip tea and grow more cynically weary with each cup.

Daniel sent Julia an encouraging smile. This is what people do when they've reached the age of reason. But we adapt to good situations too. Take this place, I never thought I'd get used to it, but I'm having a rather nice time. It's awfully good to be able to talk like this, Julia. You're a wise old broad.

Normally, Julia would have objected to anyone calling her an old broad but, curiously, coming from Daniel, it didn't bother her somehow. She was either getting tired of always being on the defensive, or she could read what Daniel meant even if he didn't always use the right words.

How about another cup of tea to go with our next round of cynicism? Daniel asked.

I don't think so. There isn't any more. Daniel had poured precisely four cups from the pot, no more, no less.

Let's throw caution to the wind and brew another pot, he said. His eyes twinkled, his silver hair an incandescent aura as the room grew dimmer with the setting of the sun. Julia was so grateful for this man's friendship, their easy conversations, their common source of sociability and also, strangely enough, the incompleteness they both felt now that they were no longer part of the world out there.

I would like another cup, but I better not. I'll be up all night,

Julia said, discreetly referring to her overactive bladder, but Daniel misunderstood.

It's decaf.

No, I shouldn't, really.

As she got up to leave, he suggested a walk as if he were reluctant to let her go. It's a beautiful evening. He nodded to the opened window from which birds could be heard chirping in a small tree.

Are those sparrows or starlings making all that noise? Julia asked.

I don't know anything about birds, except I'd venture they're probably not ducks. He chuckled. Daniel was very fond of his own jokes. I'm feeling too energized to sit or go to bed just yet, come on, Julia, let's go out.

A walk would be good, Julia conceded, But I should check on Lena first. And I'll need a jacket. Why don't I meet you downstairs in twenty minutes?

~15~

LENA WAS ALREADY ASLEEP WHEN JULIA LOOKED IN ON HER. HER dinner had been delivered to her suite but hadn't been touched. The next morning, Julia made up a tray of coffee and muffins, determined to get Lena up and going. To Julia's surprise, Lena was wearing fresh clothes and sitting in her favourite chair, a little rouge on her cheeks, hair brushed, reading a letter. Her mind had returned from where it had wandered the day before.

A letter from your son? Julia asked.

My granddaughter and grandson, Lena replied and pressed the letter to her chest. They are in Hungary. They will be home soon.

That's wonderful, Lena. In the meantime, we mustn't let ourselves get too lonely. Have to keep those spirits up, don't we? Julia was aware that she was sounding like some of the nurses, but she wasn't sure how else to handle the situation.

Lena looked down and said nothing.

You were in quite a state yesterday. Had you been thinking about Lili? Julia did her best to sound casual as she sat on the edge of the bed facing the chair where Lena was sitting.

I guess so. Lena sounded tentative, then she brightened up as if she had just thought of something. Thank you for throwing out the bread, she said.

It pierced Julia's heart whenever she saw the elderly do this, appealing to the compassion of people who are assumed to be stronger and more understanding.

We don't want the housekeeper or nurse finding your night table full of mouldy food, Julia said. You know how they are; they would blow it all out of proportion. But you are feeling much better now.

No more confusion that I can tell.

Lena started to say something, hesitated, then began again. Do you believe... She stopped again.

What is it, Lena?

Do you believe the older we get the more we become who we truly are? Lena asked. Someone said this to me once. Do you think it is true?

I might have heard something to that effect, but I'm not sure it's true. It probably means we become more set in our ways. Probably a rumour started by Mrs. Genetically Modified, except she's going backward.

Lena laughed. So you don't think we become more who we are as we get older? she asked again.

I doubt it's as simple as that. I'd say we're an accumulation of everything we've experienced. As soon as Julia uttered the words she realized that this was not the best answer, considering Lena's past.

I keep going back, Lena said. I don't know why. For several years after the war, I never thought about what happened. You couldn't think about it and go on with your life. But now I can't get away from it, it's always there. Burned inside my head. She pounded at her head with her fists.

I can only imagine, Julia said.

Sometimes I think remembering is worse than living it.

How could it possibly be worse?

We were so numb then. In shock. And we kept hoping it would end. But now, over and over in my head. It won't go away until I am dead.

Julia thought of something Daniel had mentioned, something he'd read. Or was it Thea? It had something to do with surgery that can erase memory. If there was a way of making you forget, would you do it? she asked Lena.

What do you mean? What way?

Someone was telling me about an operation that makes people forget. Surgeons can locate specific events stored in the brain and erase them.

Nothing can erase. Nothing can make me forget.

Well, apparently this is possible.

No, no. Lena shook her head vigorously. You mean to take the memories away?

Yes.

This is a stupid idea, Julia, she said with uncharacteristic confidence.

You said that remembering was as bad or worse than living what you went through. So, since your memories are so painful, I was curious…

Yes, but they are my memories. Of my life. They are my life, who I am.

In that case, shouldn't you have the right to no longer remember?

So the memories will turn into ashes too? No, no. They tried to do this, you know. After the war they tried to burn everything so no one would find out. Soon, those people who lived this will be dead too. Our children want to forget but we cannot let them. And the children of the people who did this, they want to forget, but they shouldn't. No one should forget.

Isn't this a heavy burden for the children to carry? Is it their duty to have to remember? Always be reminded?

Lena shrugged. It is history. You cannot change history. My children and grandchildren have to know who their mother and grandmother is. The girl from Auschwitz. One of Uncle Pepi's children, Lena said casually as if stating an ordinary fact.

But that's not all you are. You are so much more.

Yes, but I am also one of Uncle Pepi's children. This is all I can think of these last few months. He moved in and won't get out.

Again, Lena knocked on her head with her fists, a gesture she repeated whenever she wanted to convey how hermetically sealed the past was, as insulated from the outside world and from the present as if trapped behind barbed wire. No, no, she repeated. You can't undo the past, not just like that, she said as she snapped two fingers. You cannot undo history.

It struck Julia just then how Lena's mind and body had become an archive, revisiting events she had managed to keep at bay for so many years. Now, as the layers of memory peeled away, the process of remembering had been set into motion. The impact of this repetition established a permanent significance in the annals of her history, her clouded eye a magnifying glass through which the possible could always be envisioned.

There was a moment's silence as the two women thought about what had been said and what it meant to each of them. There was something else that Julia had seen in Lena's night table that she was curious about, a clear plastic box with broken pieces of crayons in it. Pieces so small that children usually don't save them. Julia decided to ask Lena about them.

I couldn't help but notice the box with crayon pieces in it. Do you keep them for your grandchildren?

Lena lifted herself from her chair and walked nervously to her night table, opened the drawer as if to make sure the box was still there. Then, abruptly, almost as a reproach, she said, No, they are mine. I have kept them since the camps. I don't want anyone to take them.

I wouldn't dream of taking them, Lena, Julia replied somewhat offended. She felt like adding that she wasn't in the habit of taking what didn't belong to her, especially a few useless pieces of crayons. However, she could see how upset Lena was and thought it best not to pursue the matter. Well, she said as she got up, I guess I'll go and get ready for lunch. Do you think you can make it to the dining room today?

No. I don't feel up to sitting in the dining room with all those people. Maybe tomorrow. You know, Julia, instead of people trying to erase my past, they should try to imagine it. You should try to imagine your feet, yours and your sister's in my shoes, and my sister's. If people could imagine this, truly imagine what we went through they would not be so quick to erase it.

As Julia walked to her suite, she thought of how Lena's eye reminded her of an eye without an eyelid, exhausted with seeing and with being seen.

~16~

FOR SOME RESIDENTS THE PAST NEVER CAME TO PASS. LIKE A divining rod in search of a source, it worked its way to a well-spring, a place frozen in time where events replayed themselves as if they were happening in the here and now.

It didn't happen right away. Only people deemed relatively healthy in body and mind were admitted to Evenholme. As Daniel put it, considering how many people their age were impaired, they could thank their lucky stars that most of them had been spared. But it did happen, sometimes as with Lena, or to residents who had been at Evenholme for a long time, as Mr. Wilkes.

As much as Julia disapproved of Mr. Wilkes's peculiar habit of asking people about the most influential circumstances of their lives, it hadn't been important enough to pay it further attention. Like most of the women, Julia avoided him. A dividing line was drawn between herself and a handful of men who spent a good portion of their days rehashing war stories.

One morning, six or seven months after their first encounter, Mr. Wilkes entered the lounge dressed in the most bizarre attire. He wore a khaki jacket too loose at the neck and shoulders, yet it hardly contained him at the waist. Medals dangled from a ribbon pinned to his chest similar to those in a box of odds and ends that Julia's mother kept, one of those boxes in which the past is stored away for future generations. Julia's mother never displayed any war memorabilia around the house, her husband's nightmares and artificial leg having served the purpose all too effectively.

Perhaps because her father and Mr. Wilkes had been of different ranks, Mr. Wilkes's woollen jacket looked similar to yet different from the one that Julia's father wore the day he came home from the Spadina Military Hospital.

Mr. Wilkes marched directly to the sofa where Julia was reading, and stood at attention. Below his military coat, his pyjama bottoms had been tucked inside khaki woollen socks bulging out of leather slippers. She half-expected a rifle to be resting on his shoulder. She was about to ask Mr. Wilkes why he was dressed in such a peculiar manner when he suddenly saluted and informed her that he was about to undergo a physical examination.

I see, Julia said. And you dressed up for your physical? She knew her question didn't make sense, but then neither did the circumstances.

Yup. Make sure I'm fit for the Overseas Expeditionary Force. He tried to snap the heels of his slippers.

Ah, the Overseas Expeditionary Force, Julia repeated, deciphering what this meant. So you must be going overseas then.

That's right, sir. On the RMS Saxonia, sir.

Warships was not a subject Julia cared for. Large, ungainly vessels meant to stay afloat had proven too unreliable and treacherous to be granted any kind of consideration. They promised so much and delivered nothing but grief.

I'm Julia, Mr. Wilkes. Remember? Julia Brannon?

Sir?

He had no idea where he was let alone who she might be. The old dear stood so proudly and confident that for a split second Julia saw the eager eighteen-year old he might have been when he had joined his precious Expeditionary Force. What else could she do but go along? You must be excited then. I hear the Saxonia is a fine ship, she said.

It will have to be damn sound to carry all those horses.

Horses on a ship? What a preposterous idea, she thought. But no more so than the war Mr. Wilkes was still fighting. She looked around the lounge for an attendant.

The Saxonia is so overcrowded that some of the men and horses will have to transfer to the Manitou, he continued. Imagine, men separated from their horses, he said shaking his head. He looked around and frowned, realizing perhaps that his time lines had crossed. He seemed confused as to what had already taken place and what, in his mind, was about to happen. A beautiful sight, he went on, staring into the distance. It was in all the newspapers, you know. Thirty-five ships lined up in three columns in the St. Lawrence, sparkling in the sun. A beautiful sight.

And you will be on one of those ships then? Julia asked.

Damn right. Got to get to Salisbury, you see. They need Canadians in Salisbury.

Salisbury? In England?

Damn right. Pleasant enough for the men but damn hard on the horses. It took so long before we sailed that many of them deteriorated before we even set out. Then, what with all the rolling and pitching, most of the horses were crazed by the time we landed and had to be destroyed. Damn waste, if you ask me.

Those poor beasts. Why do we involve them in such stupidity, Julia muttered.

Her compassion and criticism must have struck Mr. Wilkes as incongruous given the more urgent affairs going on in his head.

How do you expect the men to get around over there? he asked, indignant at Julia's misunderstanding.

I don't know, Mr. Wilkes. It seems such a long way to transport horses only to have them destroyed.

Julia was getting caught up in this man's delusions and she didn't like it. But she also understood then why it had been so important for Mr. Wilkes to ask the residents about their most memorable experiences. The Great War was all he had left.

As if he'd read her mind, he proclaimed in a loud voice, This is The Great War. We have no fancy jeeps as in World War II. He stopped short as soon as he uttered the words. Events were not proceeding in their proper order. He looked as confused and alarmed as a horse on a rolling and pitching ship.

Julia needed to divert him somehow. What happens once you get to Salisbury, she asked?

He hesitated for a few seconds. Training, he replied, his voice doubtful. Then on to France where the real fighting begins. Where boys become men.

It was too much for Julia to take in. Or where boys are killed to prove themselves men, she said.

Pff! Woman talk, Mr. Wilkes spat out and shook his head. Do you know where the doctor's office is?

Julia gestured to another resident to find an attendant. The doctor will be around soon, she told Mr. Wilkes. All this preparation and excitement must be exhausting for you. Why don't you sit down and wait for him here? She patted the cushion beside her on the sofa.

He furrowed his brow and looked around the lounge to confirm his bearings. Are you a nurse?

No, but here comes René now. Mr. Wilkes, she explained to René, has an appointment for a physical examination to make sure he is fit for overseas duty.

An understanding but barely perceptible smile slid across René's face. Yes, he said casually, he is to see Dr. Davidson today. Dr. Davidson, one of two doctors who came regularly to Evenholme, had the final say on whether it was time for a resident to be transferred.

Come, Mr. Wilkes, René said, we're running late for your appointment. You mustn't keep the good doctor waiting.

Mr. Wilkes glared at René for several seconds and abruptly pulled his arm away. I need to lie down, he said, his body rigid with the stubbornness of old age. The nurse here says I'm tired and I need to lie down. Never any room on these damn trains.

Don't worry, we'll find you a nice place to rest, René said. Have a little nap, maybe.

Be sure to ask one of the French farmers for a straw mat, Mr. Wilkes said. The French know how to make good mats.

We can do better than that; we have a nice clean bed for you today.

What about my horse? Mustn't leave him standing in the mud. It'll sink so deep, we'll never get him out.

We'll look after your horse, don't worry, René said as he gently led Mr. Wilkes out of the lounge.

For the following two or three days and nights, whenever the door of his suite opened, Mr. Wilkes could be heard shouting commands to invisible troops. Over the top, over the top, he would yell.

One morning, when his door had been left ajar, Julia entered his room. He looked so fragile and small curled on his side, as if the space he occupied was closing in around him. He stared at her, his vacant eyes glistening. She wanted to ask him why he was alone at such a time, where was his family, but she didn't dare. He probably wouldn't have understood anyway. If he had, it might have only exposed him to more pain. Julia considered taking his bony hands in hers to let him know he wasn't alone, but she couldn't bring herself to do so.

She had seen death before, several times. It was not an event one ever got used to. In spite of grief that so weighed the heart it could hardly keep beating, she had been the one to take charge, because she'd had to. There had been so many details to attend to that there had been no room for fear.

Now, it was as if this stranger was her own death sentence. His rigid, curled fingers reminded her of hooks that might reel her in. She steadied herself by gripping the foot of the bed, not wanting to stay but not daring to leave, bewildered at her powerlessness to help this dying man and her inability to simply walk away. As the first time she encountered death on a street in New York. Then again in the house in Wildwood. She could feel the ground swaying beneath her feet and she held on to the bed to prevent from being pulled into its gravitational field.

There was no sound other than Mr. Wilkes's laboured breaths escaping from his gaping mouth, each breath reminding her of a ship struggling for equilibrium on a rough sea. Until, suddenly, he shouted so loudly she nearly jumped out of her skin. Over the top, he repeated several times. Over the top. There were no other words left to his vocabulary.

What is Mr. Wilkes shouting? What does he mean? she asked René in the afternoon as he was wrapping a blanket around the legs of a man in a wheelchair, preparing to take him out for fresh air.

Over the top? It's the cry of infantrymen as they climbed out of the trenches during the war. Is he disturbing you? He will be transferred in a day or two. We're waiting for a bed.

No, no, not at all. I only wondered what he was shouting and what it meant. She didn't want René to think she was complaining about a dying man.

The man sitting in the wheelchair looked up and smiled. Hello, I'm Jack Ross.

Hello, I'm Julia Brannon. How are you this morning?

Can't complain, considering the alternative, he said. He beamed at the cleverness of a joke she'd heard too many times now.

Mr. Wilkes believes he's reliving a period of his life, René explained.

So I gathered. It must be horrible.

Oh, I don't know. He's been a war hero ever since I've known him. Going out a hero isn't so bad.

I can see why everyone calls you Descartes.

He laughed. Really? Can't say I've read him.

I majored in philosophy. I never use any of it now, it was so long ago. A lifetime, really. Julia was about to tell René that Descartes was one of the philosophers she had most enjoyed studying although many people thought he had become obsolete. She had liked him because his method, albeit unrealistic, consisted mainly in granting thinking people the power to conceive themselves as they wanted to be.

I guess philosophies come and go, René said. He took a tissue out of his pocket and wiped the nose of the man in the wheelchair. I think Mr. Ross might be getting a cold, he said.

You're very patient, Julia told René.

Not always. More so some days than others. Believe me, I'm no saint.

Oh, yes he is, said Mr. Ross. He's a saint alright.

A place like this needs understanding more than it needs sainthood, Julia said to the two men. The important thing is to make people think you care.

People think I care, therefore, I care? René said. Isn't it how it goes? He smiled a Mona Lisa kind of smile suggesting he knew more than people generally gave him credit for.

Ah, so you do know your Descartes.

He does too care, Mr. Ross insisted in a loud voice, making sure Julia heard and understood.

Julia nodded. I'm sure he does. I don't know how he does it, looking after old wrecks like us day in and day out.

Old wrecks, alright. I sprained my ankle, the man said pointing to his swaddled legs.

I'm sorry. Does it hurt? she asked.

Naw. Not anymore. Don't care for the physio, though.

Julia turned to René. I went into Mr. Wilkes's room yesterday. I wanted to comfort him, hold his hand, but I couldn't bring myself to do it.

I wouldn't worry too much about it, René replied. It takes getting used to.

I thought I was getting used to it. You did.

Working here will either make you callous or more understanding. I decided on understanding.

A very existential choice for someone as young as yourself.

He gave a resigned shrug. We're all heading in the same direction, he said.

Faster than you think, said Mr. Ross.

I didn't think I'd last at first, René went on. I even gave my resignation once.

I gather you changed your mind.

Another nurse changed it for me, actually. She was the most uncaring, abusive person I'd ever met. One day I saw her shoving underwear in a resident's face because the woman had soiled herself. I realized then this job depends on the dignity you bring to it. I remind myself of this one resident and one day at a time. So, Mr. Ross, are you ready for our walk?

You bet. Mr. Ross gave René and Julia an outsized smile.

As Julia watched René wheeling Mr. Ross away, she wondered if the residents didn't call him Descartes because in sensing their own powers declining they needed someone to help them bear the weight of their increasing vulnerability. After all, wasn't this what was expected of philosophy?

No one ever asked about residents once they had left Evenholme. For several weeks after Mr. Wilkes was transferred Julia wondered how long it had taken Mr. Wilkes to climb over the top of his former life and escape the war still raging in his head.

✻

I'll be darned, a policeman is saying. A Colt automatic. Anyone living here in the first war?

Yes, I reply. My father.

Yep, quite a few of 'em still around. The government smuggled thousands from the States. This here's an officer's model. He turns the pistol around. A Slimline, beautiful, he whispers with admiration. He then points to the rifle lying beside the trunk.

And this here's a Mark III Ross, he says. Damn things jammed so badly, they killed as many soldiers behind it as they did in front. He begins to smile until he remembers why he has been called to the house.

~17~

JULIA AND DANIEL WERE TAKING TURNS HOSTING THEIR AFTERNOON teas although she suspected that Daniel preferred her suite to his. It was brighter, more cheerful, he said as he scanned Julia's books, the pictures on the walls, and the photographs on the tables. Tea with biscuits had gradually been supplemented with different kinds of cheese, bread, and fruit. Sometimes they added a small glass of port or wine.

Daniel peered at the wedding photograph on the table by the French window.

This your wedding picture?

Yes.

You and your sister looked exactly alike, didn't you?

Yes, we did. Few people could tell us apart.

The two of you sure look sassy in those get-ups. Very bold of you, I mean for a wedding.

The wine always made Daniel effusive, using words like sassy and get-ups.

Sassy was my middle name, Julia replied.

I can see why.

Those dresses caused quite a ruckus in their day, she said.

Whose idea was it to wear identical ones? You can't tell the bride from the bridesmaid.

Both our idea, I guess. Wilson loved it.

Your husband?

Yes. He often joked that he had married two sides of a bad penny.

Had he?

Julia shrugged. He liked to think so, she said. I was writing about that dress only this morning.

You're still writing? Daniel asked.

Yes. My granddaughter keeps nagging me about it. I'm not sure I want to give her any of it, but you never know.

Can I read what you've written? Daniel asked.

His request startled her. You certainly may not, she replied with a laugh. You're not interested in human stories, remember?

This is not any human story, Julia, it's yours. I'm interested in what you've got to say.

And I'm flattered. But you should interest yourself in all good stories, Daniel. My story could be anyone's story. One thing I will tell you, I've always associated that wedding dress with death.

Whatever for? It looks anything but.

The week we spent in New York shopping for our dresses was the first time I saw death up close. It stayed with me for a long time, forever I suppose. The circumstances were so peculiar.

How so?

A woman threw herself from the Flatiron Building and landed a few feet from us.

Jesus, lucky she didn't land on you. She could have killed you.

That's what my father said. It didn't occur to me right there and then. All I could think of at the time was her state of mind, what it must have been just before she jumped. Had she planned it for a long time? Or, perhaps, in an impetuous move, she lost her balance and there was nowhere to go but down. I kept playing it over in my mind. Trying to imagine the weightless feeling, the wind filling her lungs. I kept wondering if she had considered the impact on those left behind. It haunted me for years.

Did you ever find answers?

Yes, I think I might have.

How? Daniel waited for Julia to go on. When she didn't, he asked, Are you going to tell me?

No, not now, Daniel. I'm feeling very tired now. I may have had a bit too much wine.

Another day, maybe?

Maybe.

Okay. So why don't I let you rest. I'm feeling a little spent myself, he said as he got up and stretched. It's going to be an early night for me.

Yes, for me also. One of the few luxuries of being old is not needing to justify going to bed whenever you feel like it.

Goodnight then, Julia. I would still like to read some of those things you're writing, he said, as he bent down to kiss her on the lips. A bird's peck.

Maybe you will, eventually, Julia said.

~18~

A FEW WEEKS AFTER THE ENGAGEMENT, FATHER ANNOUNCES HE *will soon have to go to New York on business and mother decides we should go with him. New York is more auspicious than Toronto for the innumerable unmentionables a bride-to-be is expected to acquire. Not to mention those outrageous dresses Sissa and I are bent on wearing. Mother is hoping that once in New York, once we see traditional wedding dresses at the various department stores on the Ladies' Mile District, we will change our minds.*

We establish a routine as soon as we get there: mornings and early afternoons are spent purchasing more matrimonial linens than one couple can possibly use in a lifetime, and shopping around for the dresses: a mother-of-the-bride ensemble, a wedding dress, and a maid-of-honour's, although we insist the latter be identical to the bride's, much to mother's dismay.

From the moment we started planning the wedding, Mother disagreed with us on almost everything. Or perhaps it was Sissa and I who disagreed with mother. She had envisioned a formal affair, the bride in traditional veil and gown, skirt flaring into a train, but we decided otherwise. We wanted a small reception in mother's overgrown garden, the two of us wearing cloche hats, short skirts with dropped waists and long strands of pearls.

This is a wedding, not a dancing soirée, mother complains.

Why can't it be both? Sissa wants to know.

Of course it can be both, I state as emphatically as I can, hoping this won't leave mother any room to negotiate. Her resolve usually disintegrates against her two daughters, perhaps more so against mine. Sissa tends to yield more readily, a pattern that only strengthens my own determination.

It's the curse of having two of them, we often hear mother complain after losing an argument or a battle of wills, a grievance Sissa and I don't take seriously because we also often overhear her boasting to relatives and friends what blessings we are. No bond is as powerful as between two children who have shared a womb, she tells everyone, a strategy meant to reinforce this special bond between Sissa and me. Since we were small, every time we fought or disagreed, we imagined a space between us growing wider and more vacant. A devil's playground, mother called it.

On our third afternoon in New York, after another morning of disagreements, mother suggests we take a break from shopping and visit an exhibition, a forty-year retrospective of photographer Alfred Stieglitz. Your Uncle Warren has told me about him. Mother and father have decided it is time to set aside any grievances they may have against Uncle Warren and they have invited him to take the wedding pictures.

Usually, when mother enters a gallery, in a voice low enough to be a whisper yet loud enough for everyone to hear, she announces that much of what is presently displayed is of dubious merit and taste. But on this particular occasion, she falls silent as soon as she enters the first room.

The exhibition is being held in two large, sky-lit spaces filled with more than one hundred prints in tones of white, silver, bronze, black, pearl, perfectly centred on white mats, and hanging on red-plush-covered walls. The effect is dramatically spectacular. Mother is so captivated by the first photograph, "The Terminal," she doesn't move for a good five minutes. It is a photo of draft horses, the kind used for pulling omnibuses that are now being replaced by trolleys. The owner, his back to the camera, dressed in a rubber coat and hat, gently and lovingly tends his horses as frozen clouds of steam rise from their bodies.

She is equally entranced by the next photograph, "The Flatiron," a thin gray building reaches into space, its steely silhouette softened by blowing snow. It conveys a vulnerable quality in spite of its steel construction. A tree trunk in the foreground, the branches bare except for a half-moon of snow in the crook of the trunk and a limb, defies the building's stature and strength.

This building isn't far from our hotel, mother says. We should see it before we leave New York.

She is less enthusiastic about the last half of the show depicting nudes and she keeps hurrying us along. A crowd has gathered around one photograph in particular, a headless, nude torso showing a good amount of pubic hair. In fact, it would appear that Mr. Stieglitz is quite taken with female body parts. They have been grouped into sections: Hands, Feet, Breasts, Torsos, and Interpretations. The catalogue claims there are many more which could not be exhibited as the general public may not be ready for them.

One can only imagine what those are like, mother scoffs. Mr. Stieglitz's talents would be better spent on horses than on those kind of women, she tells the man at the desk from whom she orders copies of "The Terminal" and "The Flatiron." These she simply had to have. Sissa and I can't think of anything more titillating than what we have just witnessed.

The next afternoon, having finally found the dresses we want, to which mother reluctantly agrees, the three of us decide to walk by the Flatiron Building. It is easy enough to locate, its twenty stories tower above everything around it, a dark surface gridded with darker windows. We are standing too close to it at first to get the photograph's perspective, so mother suggests we cross to the other side of the street toward the park. As we step off the sidewalk and begin crossing the road, we hear a noise behind us, a muffled yet decisive thump as when an object hits an unyielding surface. I turn. On the sidewalk, a few feet away, a woman is sprawled in the most awkward position, partly on her back, partly on her side, one leg bent under her.

The position of the woman's body in relation to her head seems odd. How has she managed to trip and fall so clumsily? Her coat and skirt are bunched above her thighs, elastic garters rolled around lisle stockings, the kind women wear when the occasion doesn't require silk ones. The blank stare of one eye peers through her hair.

We should help her, Sissa whispers, but instinct tells us otherwise and no one moves. Blood trickles from behind the woman's head. Mother holds on to my arm. The driver of a car, annoyed because we are blocking the road, shouts as he drives around us.

Two people on the north side of the street, heads arched back, point to the sky. For a brief moment I wonder if the woman hasn't fallen from heaven. But no, they are pointing to an upper floor or the roof of the Flatiron Building. The woman jumped.

As I realize this, my entire body goes limp, threatening to send me to my knees, but mother and Sissa pull me to the other side of the street. We stand on the sidewalk with two other people, necks craned, looking to the top floors, the windows glinting blindly. There is nothing to see yet we keep this position because there is no other place to look other than at the woman, her inert body prompting questions we want to avoid. Within a few minutes, several more people join us.

She seems so young, one woman says.

How can she tell? Except for the one eye peering through her hair, her face is covered. Even so, something about her does seem young. Maybe the shape of her legs. The white expanse of flawless skin between the elastic garters and her underwear. Her coat. It is a young woman's coat with a fur collar tied securely under the chin although it is a bright and relatively warm day for February. Was she afraid of getting cold at such a height? How did she manage to clear the canopy over the entrance? someone asks.

Two men rush out of the building. We've called the police and an ambulance, one of them shouts while the other man directs gawkers around the body, pleading with them to walk on. One woman screams and joins the crowd gathering where we are standing.

What are we supposed to do? Sissa asks mother.

I'm not sure, mother answers. I guess we'll wait until the ambulance comes, it's the least we can do.

As soon as the ambulance arrives and the attendants bring out a stretcher, mother tells us we now owe it to the woman to leave. Propelled by the five o'clock traffic, the three of us walk back to our hotel without saying a word.

Father is incensed. She could have killed you for Christ's sake, he shouts when he learns what happened. She could have landed on one of you and killed you. The stupid ... He stops upon seeing the horrified look on mother's face.

The woman is dead, Harlan.

Still, she could have killed you, he repeats. I suspect it isn't so much the woman with whom he is angry, but the circumstances. Father can't bear to think he can't protect us. Since the war, any event unable to account for itself in father's scheme of how life should unfold frustrates and angers him. He will not have his family subjected to the laws or the whims of the real world.

People should think of the consequences, he adds. Just because she was depressed doesn't mean she should put other people at risk.

I don't think other people's welfare was foremost on her mind just then, Harlan. The restraint of mother's voice belies her shaking hands as she accepts the drink father has poured from a bottle in a silver ice bucket sitting on a tray on the desk.

Do you girls need anything, he asks? He then turns to mother. Do you want me to call room service? Salts? A doctor?

Of course not, we're fine, Harlan, mother tells him. We'll rest a while and go out for dinner later. You should make reservations at Child's.

I'm not sure I even want to eat, but Sissa wants to go to Child's for some of their butter cakes.

Father picks up the bottle from the desk and pours some of its content into a leather-covered flask he always carries with him. Yes, yes, we'll make a special evening of it, he mutters as he surveys the slow progress of the liquid being transferred from one bottle to the other. There will be no more drinks tonight, mother tells him sternly. Then, having held his gaze for several seconds she adds, At least not before we get back to the hotel.

Of course not, darling. No more drinks until my nightcap.

The next morning, we scour the papers for mention of what we now refer to as the accident, looking for information on the woman who jumped. A more intimate knowledge of who she was, even a few details, would make us feel less like mere spectators.

But we find nothing.
They probably no longer report suicides from skyscrapers, father says.
Why not? I ask.
Too many of them. They are no longer an event.
The death of strangers has become irrelevant to father.

The next months are a blur of preparations, each step met with resistance from mother, although Sissa and I manage to hold our own. The religious ceremony will take place in an Anglican church we never attend, but mother makes the arrangements through the wife of the officiating minister.

He thinks he may have a few possible conversions on hand, mother says. Of course we should attend church more often, she adds partly to lessen any misunderstanding she may have conveyed to the minister.

The reception will take place in the garden and that sends mother into a whirlwind of pruning and uprooting until she finally hires a gardener. A canvas tent will have to be found or one will have to be made in case of rain, and everyone agrees that mother's guest list will have to be reduced.

Why, oh why couldn't you have had a normal wedding, mother grumbles. And why couldn't you have worn decent dresses. Your legs are too long and gawky for those silly flapper get-ups.

It is not a particularly effective admonition since Sissa and I are very proud of our long legs. Jane and Julia Crane, legs as long as whooping cranes.

Freed from encumbering skirts, we dance the shimmy and the black bottom, two of several dances we practised for weeks before the wedding. White clematis clings to the length of the garden fence like unwieldy wallflowers in frayed wedding lace. Wilson, handsome and radiant in a cutaway coat, takes turns to dance with the bride and the maid-of-honour.

Sissa and I are nineteen years old and there is no need to question where our lives will lead. Father's war is behind us and we move toward a future that holds countless possibilities. It never occurs to either one of us what a fickle escort possibility can be.

~19~

THE SECOND NIGHT JULIA RETURNED TO GIZI MAGRIS'S SUITE TO
help with her dinner she brought a tape deck and tapes. She had
gathered a nice assortment from several residents plus a few of her
own, one in particular she thought Gizi might enjoy: Hungarian
Gypsy Dances, lively piano pieces that she and Lena often listened
to when they played cards.

In case Gizi asked for help with her bathroom duties again, Julia
rehearsed a ready reply suggesting that an attendant would be more
appropriate for such a task. She made a mental note to remember
to tell Rachel and Thea of a pun she'd just invented—how spontaneous courage failed her when it came to piddling matters.

Gizi seemed pleased enough to get the new tapes. She nodded
her approval at Haydn's String Quartets, Bach's Violin Concertos,
especially Liszt's Sonata in B minor. Her attitude changed, however,
when she came across the Hungarian Gypsy Dances. She made a
face and tossed it aside. You can take this one back, I won't play
it, she said.

Since these were piano pieces, as were Liszt's, Julia blamed Gizi's
response on her destroyed hands. She should have been more sensitive. I'm so sorry, she said. It was very tactless of me.

No, no, it doesn't have anything to do with that, Gizi replied.
I never played Gypsy music on the piano and I won't listen to it
now.

Oh. Why not?

I won't listen to anything associated with those people, she said
with an air of grim satisfaction. Not even classical.

It's a strange way to assess music, Julia thought. But why? she
asked.

127

I detest Gypsies and anything associated with them.

So I gather. But why? Julia repeated because she was so taken aback that nothing else sprung to mind.

I just do. I dislike them.

In that case, we won't play it, Julia said and put the tape in her bag. Without saying a word, she proceeded to cut the meat and mash the potatoes on Gizi's plate with considerably more vigour than required.

Gizi could see how angry Julia was and in an attempt to smooth things over she presented what she must have thought was a proper justification. Gypsies were a serious problem in her country.

Julia considered letting the matter drop, but her curiosity wanted to learn more about this serious problem, the magnitude of it. She didn't know anything about Hungary and perhaps there was a legitimate grievance for Gizi's attitude. After all, no one was above discrimination, Julia reasoned.

So why are Gypsies such a problem in your country? she asked as she impaled an oversized piece of roast beef and stuffed it into Gizi's mouth.

They won't work, Gizi tried to enunciate while chewing.

It was hardly the calamity Julia expected. Many people don't work, she said.

But they won't work. They would rather steal. She finally swallowed her meat and opened her mouth for a fork full of potatoes. She reminded Julia of a fully grown bird still dependent on an aging mother for worms. She stabbed a dozen or so peas and placed them in Gizi's beak.

Have they stolen from you? Julia asked.

No, but they've stolen from my grandparents. They steal food from farmers and money and jewellery from people in the city. And they beg. They have no pride or scruples, they beg from everyone.

It was an ironic comment from a woman who had been dependent on the generosity of Canadian doctors and hospitals for two years, and who was presently dependent on the elderly for her most basic necessities. For some inexplicable reason Julia felt compelled to come to the defence of Hungarian Gypsies.

Perhaps your grandparents had food to spare, she offered. Is it so bad for farmers to give a few surplus vegetables to hungry people?

They wouldn't be hungry if they worked and bought food. And they steal more than surplus vegetables; they can strip an entire field in one night. Not a potato left. And chickens too, they steal chickens.

This happened to your grandparents? An entire field of vegetables?

No, with my grandparents it was chickens.

How could they be sure the Gypsies took them?

In an accent and intonation similar to Lena's, Gizi patiently explained: The next day, when grandfather went to the place where the Gypsies often set up camp, they were boiling chickens and two of the men had chicken feathers in their hair and on their clothes.

Her evidence, as irrefutable as it must have seemed to her, lent her such an air of authority that, for a moment, Julia considered it valid. Until the image of chicken feathers sticking to men's hair and clothes struck her as so preposterous that she began to chuckle. I don't know, Gizi, she said. It hardly seems fair to brand an entire group of people as habitual thieves because of a few errant feathers. She expected Gizi to at least acknowledge the humour of her remark. On the contrary, Gizi seemed offended.

You do not know, she said as she forcefully pushed away Julia's hand, annoyed at Julia for not understanding a problem of such calamitous proportion.

I'm sure I don't. I will have to take your word for it, Julia said. Then, in an attempt to change the subject she told Gizi that she had a friend at Evenholme who was also from Hungary. Julia suggested that Gizi might like to meet Lena.

Gizi agreed. It would be nice to meet someone from home. What is her name? she asked.

Lena Kohn, Julia said.

The scorn remoulding Gizi's face was even more pronounced

than the sneer when she had talked about Gypsies. It accentuated her scars. The disdain of the previous diatribe transformed itself into downright revulsion. This is not Hungarian, she spat out. This name, it is not Hungarian.

Yes, she is definitely from Hungary, Julia insisted.

This family name is not Hungarian, it is Jewish. Kohn is a Jewish name. The entire sentence hissed out of her mouth.

Yes, but she is originally from Hungary.

Perhaps so, but she is not a Magyar.

She was from Hungary, Julia repeated.

A Jew. From one of those camps, no doubt. Gizi snickered.

If you are referring to the concentration camps, yes, her entire family was sent there.

Yes, another one. All of them from concentration camps. They were not very efficient, those camps, were they.

What do you mean?

They missed so many.

Julia had often heard people describing how their blood ran cold in certain situations. It had happened to her at least twice before, once when her sister received the telegram about William and Thomas and once at the attic door, unable to move or cry out, shivers running down her arms and back, their edges as incisive as razor blades. It was happening again. Little blades running up and down her spine. She placed the fork and knife on the plate. There was no doubt who and what Gizi was referring to, yet Julia wanted her to say it. She wanted her to confirm that an educated person, in this day and age, was still capable of this kind of thinking.

Who are you referring to, Gizi? Who was it that they missed?

The Jews, Gizi said without hesitation. There is a saying in my country: First the Jews, then the Gypsies. Her scarred chin tilted forward in confrontation.

Julia's first reaction was to bolt from her chair and leave, but she felt too shaky. The blood had drained from her limbs and she could hardly gather enough strength to move. So, you hate Gypsies because they steal chickens. And Jews? Why do you hate them?

You wouldn't ask if you had to live with them.

But I do live with them. There are Jewish residents here. And French Catholics, English Protestants. There may be a few people of Arab descent, but I'm not sure because I don't go around asking where people come from or what church they attend. There's a black couple and an interracial one.

Yes, I noticed. It is not my business.

But the Jews are? Why would they be your business?

Gizi shrugged, her face still locked in a contemptuous scowl.

Tell me, Julia said, I'm curious, how many Jews have you lived with?

Gizi still said nothing.

How many?

There were several at music school, she spat out.

Yes, I'm sure there were. And maybe a few Jewish doctors operated on your hands and your other burns.

I don't know who operated on me, I didn't ask.

Maybe you should have. Maybe you could have stopped them.

Why would I stop them, some are very capable. In any event, I was in a coma.

How convenient. I dare say we have all been in a coma at one time or another, but some of us eventually wake up.

Gizi kept staring ahead, her face flushed with anger. Julia should have stopped, she should have gotten up and left, but the thought of Lena, the one missed, the one who was now reliving her days in the camps, prevented her.

You wanted to be a concert pianist. How many of the composers you played were Jewish?

I'm sure there were many. She dismissed Julia's question.

And it didn't bother you to play them? Does it bother you to listen to them now that you can no longer play?

Of course not, she countered. She appeared genuinely surprised by Julia's question.

But you won't listen to Gypsy dances that were not, in all probability, composed by Gypsies but by classical composers.

Gypsy dances, this music is not sublime.

Sublime, I see. So Gypsies don't have passion, like everyone else?

It is not an elevated passion.

But Strauss waltzes or Tosca are sublime?

I would say so, yes. More so Tosca.

Julia was reminded of a line from Heidegger, a line that had often replayed itself over the years: *Authenticity is often allied with sublime and heroic values that are beyond ethical evaluation.* What I don't understand, Gizi, is how, in reaching for the sublime, so many of us end up with our faces in the muck. You know, I thought I was doing a good thing in volunteering to come here, but I feel soiled. So, she said as she finally recovered enough energy to stand, I will leave you to your warped thinking however sublime it may be.

Julia gathered her tapes and those she had borrowed. From now on please get your music from someone else, she said and walked out.

She couldn't wait to tell Daniel.

~20~

CLARA WEBSTER HAD SUBSCRIBED TO A CHANNEL OFFERING pornographic films and half-a-dozen men and women often congregated in Clara's suite to view one. They even had a name for their little clique: *The Old Degenerate Club*. They tried to talk Julia into joining, but she declined. After a scant few minutes viewing French Touch on a website, she had concluded that the most remarkable outcome of looking at sex on a screen was how unremarkable it truly was.

She was being unfashionably uptight, they told her, an old bluenose, and it occurred to Julia that the great taboo of today may no longer be sex as it had been in her days, but on the archaic concept of love.

*

Sissa is pregnant. Until now our bodies were essentially the same, but now we no longer mirror each other. The larger her belly grows, the more distended her breasts, the wider the distance between us.

An old wives' tale claims that the birth of twins skips a generation, but Sissa has proven it wrong. Half way through her pregnancy, the doctor detected two heartbeats. She is carrying twins.

Mother is delighted. Isn't it wonderful how they keep coming and coming. Oh, Sister, I can't wait to see if you too will have twins some day, she tells me.

Sissa's stomach is as big as a giant's glove. What two-hearted animal is brewing inside her? The bigger she gets the more complacent she becomes. An immovable sphinx absorbed by her own enigma,

133

her body the irrefutable proof of some unwavering instinct. There are so many other things to do with one's life than give birth to twins, I keep trying to convince myself to no avail.

We are astounded when we first set eyes on the boys. They couldn't look less alike, one blond, the other dark, like two sides of the sun. Sissa and Wilson name them after each grandfather: Thomas Wilson, after Wilson's father, and William Harlan, after ours. Each day, Sissa's love for them grows more binding than the two of us ever shared. William and Thomas have become Sissa's sole reason for living. Some nights I dream they are mine.

Whenever Wilson is called away on business, I either go to their house in Balmy Beach or Sissa brings the children to Wildwood and they stay for however long Wilson is gone.

These are the occasions when Sissa and I find each other again. We stay up 'til the wee hours, carrying on as when we were girls. She asks about my life as a single, career woman, but only perfunctorily. She doesn't attach much importance to whatever accomplishments I claim for myself. Undoubtedly the reason I go out of my way to shock her with my tales of casual affairs, the most recent with one of my philosophy professors.

But you are not sleeping with him, are you? This would be the third one, she exclaims. She is genuinely scandalized.

The fourth, but who's counting, I tell her as we fall back on the bed.

How did you know what to do? she asks.

What do you mean?

You know, how did you know? I had to rely on Wilson to teach me everything.

Little wonder, considering what mother taught us, I tell her. More hysterical laughter.

What's so great about going from one man to another? she wants to know. Sex can get so tedious when you're not in the mood.

That's not what you thought when you first got married, I remind her.

I know. But I get so tired now. The children are so demanding and having to pretend with Wilson when I'm tired is such a bore.

Maybe this is why I jump from one man to another, to stave off the tedium. Do you think Wilson feels neglected? I ask as a tactic to find out if she's aware of Wilson's roving eye. So much of your attention is going to the boys, I add.

It was great at the beginning, we use to do it all the time, but it's different when you have children. They take so much energy, there isn't much left for anything else. He might feel neglected, but I'm looking after twin boys. You have no idea how exhausting it is. Sometimes I think he's more interested in his sex life than in his children. I don't know why love always has to be about sex.

It doesn't. But men may want us to believe it does so they can keep getting more.

More giggles.

Don't get me wrong, Sissa says. I love Wilson and the boys. I wouldn't trade my life for anything or with anyone else.

It's her trump card, the one she always plays.

Yes, I know, Sissa, I reassure her.

No, you can't know unless you've gone through it. I love Wilson and the children more than anything else, she repeats with a note of triumph and, perhaps, a little provocation.

It's a card well played. As overbearing as Wilson is, she holds him and her children up as trophies, something she's won over me. She takes every opportunity to remind me because she thinks this is what I yearn for. Not Wilson or the children per se, but the kind of love that justifies her entire life, the kind we used to share. When we are together like this, I am reminded how much we are growing apart. It's as if part of me was disappearing.

And it's exactly how it should be, I tell her, careful not to display envy or regret. You should love your husband and your children above anyone else.

My response has disappointed her. Wilson should understand, she continues as if to drive home a point. The boys are my first priority. I can't always be at his beck and call.

I'm sure he does. Wilson is a big boy, he can take care of himself, I tell her. Is everything alright between the two of you? I ask.

She doesn't look directly at me, but I can see the hint of a sardonic smile. Of course, everything's fine. Why wouldn't it be?

*

I would never betray Sissa, I tell Wilson, the two of us standing at my office door.
We've betrayed each other, he replies.
Nonsense. How?
By not being together.
We can't talk about this here, Wilson. People will hear us.
Then let's go into your office because I'm not leaving.
It takes all the self-restraint I can muster to keep from screaming or pounding him with my fists. It's all such nonsense, I tell him. Utter nonsense.
I can't control how I feel, he says.
Of course you can. Except you would rather control how I feel. This obsessive and ridiculous notion that you married the wrong sister is a ploy to control the two of us. First Sissa and now me. I didn't marry you because I didn't love you and nothing has changed.
You did love me. You wouldn't have kissed me the way you did if you hadn't.
Oh, Wilson, why do you keep bringing this up? Yes, I loved kissing you. I liked being with you. It doesn't change the fact that I didn't want to marry you.
Love isn't some rational option.
It doesn't have to be irrational. Why does everyone buy into this romantic and fallacious idea that love makes people behave irrationally. It's not my fault if you married my sister when you didn't love her. All I know is that she loved you more than I did, there's nothing illogical or irrational about this. Frankly, I don't see why you would love me over her.
You're different.
We're the same. Difference is in the eye of the beholder.
She doesn't have any spark. No fireworks. She's so damn needy.

Her neediness stifles me.

But that's what you wanted. You needed her to need you. I think men go for needy women so they'll feel needed, then they resent them because the needy women stifle them. You stifle yourself, Wilson.

When I make love to her, I pretend it's you. I always have.

Oh, for goodness sake, lower your voice, the entire department will hear you. This is just another phoney excuse to go after a woman who might give you sex. Sex is what you want from me.

No, I want you to love me. I want to marry you. Even now I would marry you. I would leave her and marry you.

You're insane. Do you really believe I would do this to Sissa? To your boys?

He clenches his jaw as his temper takes over, his voice escalating from pleading to reprisal as on our walk that November when I refused to marry him. I've heard rumours about you, he spits out. About you and Bruce Evans.

I'm seeing Bruce Evans, so what?

You're sleeping with him, aren't you.

It's none of your business.

I could get the two of you fired. I've also heard you've done this before, you've slept with others.

His words have barely reached me when I realize who told him. Sissa. As virtuous wife and mother, she deemed it her duty to tell her husband the truth about the woman to whom he pays too much attention. This is the lever with which she keeps her husband and maintains the life she wants. It will be impossible to confide in Sissa ever again. What little confidentiality and intimacy was left between us has slipped from under my feet.

Really? You would have Bruce and me fired? I would give anything to see how you would explain yourself to the family. You would never be able to set foot in the house again. Never. Now go, Wilson, I'm meeting someone in a few minutes. Bruce Evans, in fact.

Everyone thinks Bruce and I are well matched, that we have much in common. He is such a good catch. As it turns out we share few interests other than philosophy, plus he bores me to tears. I refuse his proposals and mother is mystified. Boredom is hardly a valid excuse to turn down a marriage proposal.

Shortly after breaking up with Bruce Evans, I start dating Andersen Biggs, a professor in the medical department. Mother's expectations are raised to an even greater height this time.

Sissa and I never share confidences again nor do I mention her betrayal. I move from man to man the way some people weep.

AS JULIA WAS PUTTING TOGETHER A BOWL OF FRUIT AND A PLATTER of cheese, she told Daniel about her encounter with Gizi, how upsetting it had been. The woman is vile, she told him.

Don't take it so much to heart, no point making yourself sick over it, he said.

How can I not take it to heart? This is Lena we are talking about.

Yes. I know. But you can't get upset at every ignorant prejudice you encounter. How is Lena doing by the way?

Julia had gotten into the habit of keeping Daniel up to date on Lena's setbacks or recoveries. She's not doing badly these days. Still, I wish I could do more for her.

She isn't your responsibility, Julia, he shot back brusquely.

Daniel's irritation surprised her. I know she's not my responsibility, Daniel, but I do want to be there in case she needs me.

What a peculiar need Gentiles have, he said.

What do you mean?

I've seen it before. *Mea culpa* – retroactive guilt. The need to absolve yourselves.

His comment jolted her. What a peculiar thing to say to me, Daniel, she said. I am not trying to absolve myself and I do not feel guilty for what happened to Lena. Although I've often wondered if we couldn't have found out more about what was happening over there and if we couldn't have done something about it. The world had to know what was going on.

The world knew just enough to know that it didn't want to know more, he replied.

In view of the privileged life I've had, I probably don't feel guilty enough, Julia added. Don't you ever feel this way?

No. I sure don't.

You are right in saying we didn't want to know more. There were rumours. Reports. Boats filled with refugees turned away. Which I didn't learn until years later because no one ever talked about it. My mother thought it improper to discuss such things. Men's business, she used to say.

Daniel sighed. Yes, everyone should have done more, he said. Even people who were on the wrong side of the equation, like me.

You were younger, of course, but old enough to have heard the rumours, old enough to protest. But none of us did. It had nothing to do with us.

Oh, it had plenty to do with me. He looked at Julia and smiled.

It didn't have any more to do with you than the rest of us, Daniel.

It sure did. I'm Jewish, he stated, the laugh lines around his eyes deepening.

His statement took Julia aback. She suddenly felt uneasy and annoyed. Uneasy for fear she wasn't reacting the right way or saying the right thing, annoyed because he hadn't mentioned this before. She was experiencing the same reaction as when she first met Lena. It was ridiculous. She had never considered herself an anti-Semite, so why was she worrying about saying the wrong thing now? You're Jewish? she asked.

Daniel nodded.

Why haven't you said so before?

He shrugged. I guess for the same reason you never mentioned whatever it is you are.

It would never occur to me.

Well, it never occurred to me either. For your information, Jews don't go around thinking, we're Jews, look at me, I'm a Jew. We have you people doing it for us. He sounded weary.

You are being grossly unfair, Daniel. Those things never occur to me when I meet people.

Because you thought I was one of you.

Yes, old.

Now, now. You know what I mean.

Julia felt as if she had been duped and her irritation broke to the surface. In fact, I didn't think you were anything but a pompous mathematician, she said.

He chuckled and his voice softened. Yes, well, it isn't easy maintaining a balance between feeling superior and persecuted.

I don't think this is funny, Daniel.

Oh, don't take it all so seriously. I assumed you knew. Many people think all Jews look alike, that we all have telling characteristics. He smirked.

It was irritating to be classified as *many people*. Oh, stop it, Daniel. It simply never entered my mind. Also your name. It isn't Jewish.

No, my father changed our family name a long time ago.

It wasn't Browne?

Of course not. He grinned, hardly concealing the glee of what he was about to share. It was Greenberg. We changed our colours.

Greenberg? So why wasn't it simply shortened to Green?

Too obvious. There were already so many Greens, most of them Jewish.

It explained the G on the back of the worn silverware. But why? she asked.

We adapted. We had to. Practical matter of survival. My father needed to support his family and no one would hire him because he was a Jew. So he turned himself, the family, into one of you. It's not so unusual for immigrants to change their names, you know.

If you won't identify who you are, how do you expect other people to do so?

Why would people need to identify who I am? I'm Daniel Browne, a retired mathematics professor.

You could have changed it back to Greenberg. Your name doesn't present any danger now.

I grew up as Daniel Browne. This is who I am.

But what about your religion?

What about it? My family was never religious, hadn't been for generations. We were brought up in another tradition. We imagined ourselves the educated products of the Enlightenment, which had freed us from religion. We assumed we lived in a country without a history of pogroms and anti-Semitism. Until reality set in and my father became unemployable.

Was your own job ever threatened at the university?

Not me, personally. My name was Browne and no one identified me as a Jew. There had been so many restrictions, so many people turned down, some of them famous scholars. The reasons given for not hiring them are laughable now, but they were far from funny then. You had to be cautious if you were Jewish. I didn't talk about it until I was tenured and by that time things had eased up.

Some departments were hiring Jewish refugees immediately after the war. And there was a Jewish lecturer hired even before this, in 1930, I believe.

The fact you remember the year means they were few and far between. There were quotas and other excuses, stupid ones dating from way back. This one case, a brilliant Oxford mathematician, James Sylvester, was not hired because as a Jew he would not have subscribed to the doctrine of the Holy Trinity. This was the general level of enlightenment in those days.

As preposterous as it sounded, Julia had no reason to disbelieve him. Goodness, what does the Trinity have to do with mathematics? she asked. What mathematician would subscribe to it?

Daniel snickered and he continued bringing up anecdotes, each one more absurd than the last. Louis Namier, the ablest man Oxford ever had teaching economics and history, became world-renowned...

Also turned down? Julia volunteered before he could finish.

He nodded. You know why? Because of his accent.

But most of the faculty at the University of Toronto had English accents then.

Ah, but his wasn't English. He would have been a shoe-in if it had been. He was of Polish descent and a Jew. According to the president at the time, and I quote verbatim from one of the letters

I found in the archives, he had the Jewish characteristic of indistinct articulation. Can you imagine that? Indistinct articulation. The president was afraid the students wouldn't understand him. At least this was the excuse given in the letter I found.

Oh, dear. I taught an introductory ethics course which included Adam Smith who apparently suffered from a serious speech impediment. I guess they wouldn't have hired him either.

I suspect they would have made an exception for Adam Smith.

True. As a Protestant Scotsman born in the 1700s he would have been a contemporary of sort.

Daniel guffawed. Encouraged by Julia's comment and looking increasingly smug, he added, It gets better. In that same letter, the president wrote that he didn't like the idea of a Polish Jew interpreting history. Don't you love it? You can't have Jews interpreting history. God only knows what they'd dig up.

You are quite the detective, all this rummaging about.

It's a hobby of mine. Amazing what you come up with, he said. Julia didn't care how he stared at her.

Do you still think of yourself as Jewish? she asked.

Of course. People will always think of me as being Jewish. After my tenure, it was important to acknowledge it if only as a political fact. That's what being Jewish meant to me after the war, taking it on even if it wasn't at a religious level. Acknowledgment invokes a feeling of responsibility, I guess. I asked my father then if I should change my name and he said, Bah, don't bother, Greenberg wasn't our family name either. As it turned out, it had also been changed by an immigrant officer when my father entered the country. He said our name had been changed so often, he wasn't sure what it was originally, except he was pretty sure it started with a G.

It's so ironic, Daniel. I didn't know any Jewish people before I came here. Now the two people I spend most of my time with call themselves Jews and I'm still not sure what it means.

It means the two of us come from different traditions. It also means that people like yourself wouldn't have mixed with us back then.

Don't be ridiculous, Daniel. Not knowing Jewish people wasn't a conscious decision. It was how things were if you grew up in Wildwood Park.

Which makes it all the more dangerous. What about you? Were you brought up believing in anything? he asked.

You mean religion? Mother tried several, Anglican, Methodist, all Christian, of course. She wasn't particularly attracted to any of them, but she thought her daughters should be exposed to something spiritual, as she called it. She even tried Catholicism, but that was mainly because of piano lessons. She believed that particular people were best suited to teach particular subjects and piano lessons were best taught by nuns. She had heard a nun playing the organ at some event, a wedding or a funeral, and she decided only nuns knew how to convey the necessary emotions. She dragged us to Sunday mass at a chapel for several months. She loved the drama of it all—the black habits and crucifixes, the incense and music—although she refused to cross herself or to kneel. We found it rather exciting at first. There is nothing more jolting than the exuberance of an organ bellowing at 6:30 in the morning as a flock of black-clad women file into pews.

How long did you take lessons?

Nine years.

Daniel let out a low whistle. Impressive. You must have been quite good.

Adequate. The nuns thought it was darling to have twins playing duets or even the same piece simultaneously at the recitals every year. We hammed it up trying to outplay each other. The auditorium would vibrate with a barely synchronized rendition of Tchaikovsky's Military March. The audience was amused by it; mother, father, and the nuns beamed. The next thing we knew we were signed up for another year until we were old enough to object.

It must have paid off because I heard you play in the lounge a few days after I got here. One of the reasons I asked about you.

You asked about me?

A little. Haven't heard you play much lately.

My fingers aren't cooperating too well these days. Julia didn't tell him she could barely feel the keys anymore.

You continued playing when you went to university? After you married?

Oh yes, but mostly for my own benefit.

For your husband's too, I'm sure.

~22~

*FATHER OFTEN BRINGS CLIENTS TO THE HOUSE, ESPECIALLY THOSE
he considers friends with confidential business. One of the regulars
is a Frederick Blair, or as father calls him, Frederick Charles, using his two first names to emphasize the importance of Mr. Blair's
post as director of the Immigration Branch of the Department
of Mines and Resources. The two of them sit in the library, cigar
smoke hanging about their heads like halos.*

*The damn thing is, Harlan, the Jews don't know how to farm or
mine, Mr. Blair is saying. And the country hardly needs any more
businessmen or lawyers, does it?*

*Absolutely not, Frederick Charles. Absolutely not. Father's voice
has been made louder by the content of the flask he's been filling all
day. Enough competition in those areas already, I'd say, he adds.*

*I am missing Sissa lately. I hardly see her since she and Wilson
moved into their house on Kenilworth Crescent in the Beaches.
Since she told Wilson about my affairs. Perhaps once or twice a
month when they join us for Sunday dinner or if we are invited
to their house which isn't very often. Sometimes I wonder if Sissa
didn't move to the Beaches to get away from Wildwood Park.*

*On this one particular Sunday, Mother has prepared a roast
crown of mutton made up of twelve to fifteen ribs, its centre filled
with carrots, peas, and cauliflower, the ends of each rib sporting
festive paper frills. She refers to it as a crown of lamb, but the
length of the ribs and the time it takes to chew each mouthful
betrays the animal's years. As fond as I am of lamb, old mutton
to me tastes like wet wool and is as difficult to digest.*

I wish mother would serve my Sunday favourite more often,

brisket of beef with dumplings. I am grateful, however, that on this Sunday we are not having her most recent specialty, a bland mould of noodles filled with creamed chicken, carrots, and peas served with a jellied side dish, a green clot that invariably melts on our warm plates and oozes under the noodles and creamed bits of fowl.

Because father is too ill to join us—a euphemism for his drinking bouts that are becoming more frequent—Wilson assumes the seat at the head of the table and dutifully reports on the major events since he last visited.

The major bit of news on this Sunday is the appointment of a Jacob Finkelman as lecturer in law, the first Jew to win an appointment at the university.

Oh, this is good news. After all, they have their rights too, mother says, her remark an acknowledgment of her impartial largesse. Wilson's presence always has an uplifting effect on mother, so grateful is she to have one daughter married. Not married to just anyone but to a lawyer and professor.

Are you sure Finkelman was the first Jew to be hired? I ask Wilson. I distinctly remember hearing of a Hebrew tutor at King's College who lectured on Oriental languages.

Yes, a Hirshfelder. He was given the job quite a while ago and only after he converted to Christianity. Otherwise he would have remained a tutor or lost his post altogether. But people still remember him as the first Jew to have been hired.

Don't you find this odd? I ask. I'm teaching a Social Ethics course in which the history of the Hebrew people is discussed at great length, yet the university won't hire them. Doesn't anyone see any contradiction in this? Doesn't it strike anyone as unethical?

Wilson sighs. Well, we did just hire one. It's a slow process, but maybe it's for the best.

What's for the best? I ask.

We don't want too many at once. In their own best interest, of course. It would be hard for them to adjust to an unsympathetic environment.

Wouldn't the environment be less unsympathetic if there were

more Jews in it? What do you think? I ask mother and Sissa trying
to draw someone else into the conversation.
  *Perhaps it's best to stick to one's kind, mother says. Isn't that
so, Wilson?*
  Sometimes it is for the best, mother, he replies.
  Compromise is one of the characteristics I like the least about
Wilson. *He seldom commits to one point of view, always leaving
himself enough room to wriggle his way out or in.* As for Sissa,
as on most occasions when university matters come up, she defers
to Wilson who ignores her as if she weren't entitled to an opinion. What is even more annoying is his habit of looking to me to
validate almost everything he says. As if we were the only two
people knowledgeable enough to discuss what he understands to
be complex matters.
  So what do you think? I press Sissa, trying to get her to join in.
  About what? she asks as she gets up from the table. She goes to
the chair in the corner of the room like an animal trying to protect
itself. She picks up her knitting, a long empty needle stuck in a
woollen ball and another on which a nearly completed sweater front
hangs. It looks like the partial figure from a hangman's game.
  *About Jews not being allowed to teach at the university. Don't
you have an opinion?*
  *Oh, it's just another example of how knowledge is not always
of great service to men of knowledge, she* says and turns her attention to her knitting.
  I suppress a giggle while Wilson raises both eyebrows and fixes
her with one of his stares, the kind some people use to exercise
power over others. He interprets Sissa's response as personal
criticism, which I suppose it is. The most difficult aspect of these
Sunday dinners is how he goes out of his way to negate almost
everything Sissa does or says. She gave up becoming a teacher
to marry him and now she has to put up with his condescension
because she is only a wife and a mother.
  You must admit she has a point, I tell Wilson.
  His facial expression quickly shifts from condescension to so-
licitude.

Do wipe that patronizing smirk off your face, Wilson, I tell him. Mother intervenes. Now, now Sister, you are making mountains out of molehills. Mother credits the tension between Wilson and me as jealousy on my part. Because, as she puts it, Wilson chose Sissa over me. But I'm not to worry, my Prince Charming will come along eventually, she keeps telling me. Better late than never.

Wilson pats mother's hand. We're just stirring things to make the conversation a little livelier, mother.

No, Wilson, I want to shout at him, You don't stir things to make the conversation livelier, you put your wife down then patronize me to pit us against each other. Instead I look him straight on and say, Oh, Wilson knows how to make things livelier, don't you Wilson? We lock eyes. He knows what I am referring to—his letters left in my mailbox at school. Cornering me at every opportunity.

I have a lecture to prepare, I say as I get up from the table and start gathering the dirty dishes.

What's the paper on? Wilson wants to know, his mock interest another ploy to make us appear close, intimate.

On the instinct of sympathy. A subject about which you could be better informed, Wilson.

Now, now, Sister, mother chides.

As I leave the dining room Sissa continues knitting without looking up. I sometime understand Wilson's frustration with her. Why doesn't she stand up for herself? Her calculated impartiality infuriates me. She deserves Wilson. They deserve each other.

What is this instinct of sympathy on which I'm required to lecture? Is it the ability to imagine one's self in someone else's place? Is this ever possible? I used to think so, when Sissa and I were the primary actors in each other's lives and nothing came between us because there was no space between us. We understood each other better than anyone else then. I recognized myself through her. Through her I became a spectator to myself. Whatever path one took carried an element of recognition in the other. It should not have mattered if I chose a university degree over marriage and children. But it did matter. We were now using it against each other.

~23~

IT WAS A PARTICULARLY MILD DECEMBER WITHOUT SNOW OR ICE, allowing Julia and Daniel the occasional walk in the evening as long as she hung on to his arm and ignored her numbed feet. If she stumbled he did his best to make light of it: The old dogs asleep again, Julia?

Yes, they are very lazy these days.

Better the soles of the feet than the seat of the soul, he would say as he tightened his hold on Julia's arm. Bless him, she thought. Bless us old geezers for tripping the night fantastic at 8:00 p.m., she would say to herself.

There was excitement in being out when the streets and the restaurants were abuzz with activity, something Julia hadn't done for years. Decades, really. Diners sitting in large windows, sipping wine in full view, eating dinner so late, many of them dining alone. Young people scurrying about as if their day had just begun. Shoppers laden with Christmas bags and boxes.

This year would be the first time she wouldn't awaken in her own house on Christmas morning. Rachel and Adam suggested that she come a few days before Christmas and stay as long as she wanted, but she refused. She would only be in the way or, more accurately, they would be in hers. A few hours over a turkey dinner was all she could manage before yearning to get back to her friends, her suite, her bed. There was comfort in this.

The week before Christmas, Rachel brought a box of sugar cookies she had made from her grandmother's recipe, Julia's mother. To share with the residents, she said, but Julia knew she meant Lena and Daniel.

Biting into one conjured visions of crocheted angels and baskets

150

filled with candies on the Christmas tree. As Julia explained to Daniel, Mother preferred making presents to buying them, and for several weeks before Christmas she busied herself with sewing, knitting, and crocheting—doilies with wavy edges that stood up around lamp bases, lacy angels to hang in windows and baskets for favours on the tree. When she had finished crocheting the pieces she soaked them in a sugar solution to stiffen the thread and help them retain their shapes.

I guess you didn't celebrate Christmas, she told Daniel after she invited him to Rachel's for Christmas dinner and he declined the invitation. He would be going to his daughter's.

Of course we did. I grew up celebrating both Christian and Jewish holidays. Christian holidays so we wouldn't stand out too much in the community, and Jewish holidays on the quiet, mostly as excuses for family gatherings. My father sometimes read to us from the Talmud but it was in Hebrew or Armaic and we didn't understand a damn thing.

He didn't translate any of it for you?

Sometimes, when we'd start fidgeting and he realized he'd lost us, or when we made a mishmash of the basic prayers. He would then tell us about the funny parts of the Talmud, like the one about olives making you lose your memory. Do you know it?

No, I'm not familiar with any parts of the Talmud, Julia said and wondered why he would think she might.

Well, a Talmudist was dining at a rich man's house and he was gobbling up all the olives, which was really getting to the rich man. So he decided to reprimand his guest to teach him a lesson: Don't you know that eating olives will make you lose your memory, he said. And the Talmudist replied: Yes, I do. That's why I'm eating so many, so I won't remember how rich you are. Daniel's bellowing laugh rang out in the crisp, cool air and a few shoppers turned around and smiled.

I always loved Christmas, he went on. The turkey and the presents. Jesus was never the main focus. And I liked Hanukkah mainly because of the latkes. In our house, holidays were more gastronomical events than anything else. My father would try to casually remind us that Hanukkah was in celebration of the Jewish people's rightful return to Israel, but because he lived in constant fear of losing his job, the religious side was downplayed. For a long time I thought everyone celebrated both Christian and Jewish holidays.

Sounds like a good idea, actually, Julia said, then added, I think Lena feels let down by religion. She believes that God should have been there when her people needed Him.

Yeah, well, if you'll excuse my language, this really pisses me off. Turning the Holocaust into some metaphysical issue as if it were some avant-garde play on the existence or non-existence of God. The Holocaust should be a reminder of what people are capable of. After the war, some of my relatives rediscovered their Jewish soul. The Jews needed more soul, they said, as if the soul was a by-product of suffering. It pisses me off.

I can see how some people would become more spiritual after such an event.

More religious you mean. To tell you the truth, religion rooted in persecution scares the bejesus out of me. As terrible as I felt about what happened in the war, it didn't turn me or my family into believers. The more religious some of my relatives got, the more secular I became. Especially after I married. My wife wasn't Jewish.

Or religious?

No. She was the kind of person who let other people be. Other people's beliefs were fine by her as long as they didn't interfere with hers. We thought of giving the children religious education for a while, Jewish and Christian, to give them different points of reference and help them make up their own minds when they got older. My wife and I were very proud of ourselves for being so liberal. You know, like yourself, he said and gave Julia a slight elbow in the ribs. As it turned out, it was our children who changed our minds.

Why? What happened?

They came home one day arguing about which was the true religion and the true God. One son argued it was Judaism and the other argued it was Christianity. I remember thinking, we're breeding a microcosm of what's out there, creating divisions within our own family.

How did you solve it?

Our daughter did, actually. She was very quiet as she listened to her brothers' arguments, taking in every word. Until she finally said in that soft and composed voice of hers, Wouldn't God be a bigger God if there was only one religion for the whole world instead of lots of little gods for all the different religions? And it struck me. The kid was on to something.

From the mouths of babes, Julia said.

Exactly. I mean why would God constrict Himself to one people? Wouldn't this diminish Him? The only way religions can sustain themselves is by making their God smaller to make Him fit their own narrow definition.

Made even smaller now that He's become a political candidate, Julia added.

Daniel gave out one of his hearty laughs. You sure have a good head on your shoulders for an old broad, he said. He intertwined one of his arms around one of Julia's so he could hold her gloved hand.

Were you married a long time? Julia asked.

Fifty-five years. My wife died last year.

I'm sorry.

No need to be. They were good years, more than most people get.

What made them good years, Daniel?

What made them good years? We didn't get into each other's hair, for one thing. We let each other be. She was an independent sort. Liked things done her way and in her own time. She never interfered with my work or interests and I kept out of her way and didn't monopolize too much of her time. I was busy with my own stuff. School mainly.

Did any of your relatives change their names after the war?

Some.

To Greenberg?

Yes. Ironic in a way. My wife's maiden name was Granger and we had a good laugh when she inherited her parents' silverware. It was inscribed with a G. We decided to keep the Browne name because of the children mainly. The more stories we heard coming out of the war, the more my wife wanted to protect them. But we never made an issue of it. What's in a name? Who wrote that?

Shakespeare, I think. *Romeo and Juliet.*

Right. My wife and I liked going to Stratford, how about you and your husband?

My husband? No. The Stratford Festival didn't exist when he was alive. I went later with my daughter, then with her family.

What did your husband do?

A lawyer. He was on the faculty at Osgoode.

Really? Academics are like a pack of dogs, we sniff each other out, don't we? Were you well matched, if you don't mind my asking?

We might have been. Circumstances got in the way. And he died relatively young, at fifty-two, from a heart attack in the forties.

Julia felt she was explaining too much, providing unnecessary details, trying to round out history to make the story more credible although she had never really believed in well-rounded stories because she had never known well-rounded people. They only existed in fiction. She decided she'd said enough.

I'm guessing you're not comfortable talking about this, Daniel was saying.

You're guessing right, she replied.

Okay, let's change the subject then. You had a pretty good childhood? Before you married?

Oh yes. Other than father's nipping at the bottle which got worse after the war.

Daniel squeezed Julia's hand. She could at least still feel that much.

Is it me or are the cars multiplying at an alarming rate? she asked Daniel as they attempted to cross a busy street, Daniel holding on to her tightly.

Faster than bloody rabbits, he answered.

Above the traffic noise, a cloudless and glittering sky appeared higher and more silent than usual. Julia made some innocuous comment about the full moon and how strange it was to think of the clearly visible stars as having died billions of years ago. She'd recently read an article about atoms in human bodies being forms of matter created by exploding stars called supernovas and she wanted to impress Daniel. It might explain why my body feels so old, she added.

Yes, when it comes right down to it, we're just a handful of stardust, he said, glancing up. Did you know that if your twin sister had been put on a space ship travelling at a very high speed, then returned to earth, she would be younger than you are?

This must be why I always think of her as she was before she died, Julia said. In a way she did get on a space ship. Probably to spite me, she added.

He chuckled. Humour is a wonderful thing. I wish I'd had more of it myself. I was always so bloody busy and serious.

Do I detect regrets, Daniel?

A few, I guess. I might have been a little obsessed with my work. I was so sure that reason could be mastered, that it could make everything right with the world.

Oh, join the club. Pretty unreasonable when you think of it.

He chuckled again. Julia liked having someone laughing at her jokes.

I bit off more than I could chew, Daniel said, looking up at the vastness of a dark blue sky, stars shimmering as if they were trying to maintain a perpetual state of equilibrium, each one a blink of a cosmic eye.

Daniel Browne was not a casual stargazer. Most people looked to the stars to extract mythical models to justify their destinies. Daniel Browne was not one of those people. He did not see the Milky Way as a mystical road to an Underworld, or the seven stars of Ursula Major inhabited by spirits with human emotions. No, Daniel Browne looked to the heavens for equations rooted in clarity and certainty. While most of the philosophers Julia had studied reduced their scopes to the narrow field of human beings,

Daniel Browne searched for timeless answers that had little to do with the bewildering and ephemeral chaos of human affairs.

Oh, I doubt that you bit off more than you could chew, Daniel, Julia said as they neared Evenholme. I think you understand people far better than you give yourself credit for.

A CHRISTMAS MORNING AMONGST MANY, ALL OF THEM NOW *melding into one. Thomas and William, who have just learned to sit up by themselves, are playing on the Persian rug in front of the Christmas tree. They've pulled off the favour baskets from the bottom branches and are sucking on them to extract the sugar.*

Or a few years later when the two of them are pushing car toys around the tree, Tootsie toys mother bought because they are American made. Wilson, on the other hand, has gone out of his way to buy Dinky boats because the boys love anything to do with war and because they are British made, two claims he knows will chafe his mother-in-law.

Then another Christmas. And another, unchanged from year to year, except for the boys who are growing too fast. Anyone who didn't know they were twins would never suspect as much. William's hair has grown into blond curls and his eyes are deep brown, while Thomas's hair is dark and straight, his eyes an intense shade of blue. On this particular Christmas morning, they are wearing stout leather boots, the legs of their tweed trousers flapping at their knees above hand-knitted socks that won't stay put; stiff cotton shirts spill out from under cardigan jackets.

The floor is strewn with wrapping paper and comic books—Secret Agent X-9, Flash Gordon, Jungle Jim. The boys are lying on their stomachs, chin cupped in hands, their eyes jumping from one coloured square to the next as they hum to a popular song on the radio: The March of the Aviators in which human hearts are motors and arms are propellers. William dreams of becoming a pilot, Thomas, a sailor. Gripped by a child's innocence and curiosity, each one dreams of adventure, of treasures and exotic lands. Each one dreams of heroic battles and vanquishing bad guys. This is what children learn from these fanciful tales: good will always prevail over evil. Lessons that can never be unlearned.

My heart constricts at the thought of them growing up. I fear their fearlessness. Their eagerness to go on all the rides at Scarboro Beach Amusement Park. Because Sissa is afraid of heights, either Wilson and I accompany them on most of the rides although I refuse to go on the quarter-mile roller coaster. Sissa and I watch from the sidelines, the two of us weak-kneed as Billy and Tommy plunge down valleys and over hills until they disappear through caverns and tunnels and reappear grinning ear to ear.

Wilson agrees to go on the aerial swings with William if I agree to escort Thomas on Shoot the Chutes. Sissa, Thomas, and I watch and laugh as the swings revolve and lift Wilson and William up and out as on a gusty airplane ride. They then watch as Thomas and I climb into a small boat and are hauled up a steep incline to a high platform before being dropped at full blast into the waters of a lagoon below. To everyone's delight but mine, we emerge completely soaked.

Then the last Christmas we all spent together. The boys have now grown into young men and are developing too much interest in everything that has to do with war. And that delightful little girl, Rachel, the surprise child, wide-eyed, taking her first steps toward the Christmas tree.

~25~

AN OLD BROAD, DANIEL KEPT CALLING HER. SHE SHOULD NEVER HAVE told him she was older than he was. How much older he wanted to know, but she wouldn't tell him although she suspected he already knew. She suspected he already knew too much about her.

Does longevity run in your family? he once asked.

Not really. So far I seem to be the only one with the Methuselah gene. Father died relatively young, mainly because he never fully recovered from the war. And mother died of a broken heart.

Because of your father?

Yes, but also because my sister and I grew apart. She had predicted it would spell disaster and she was right. It did.

You and your sister had a falling out, did you?

I suppose that's what you'd call it. I'm grateful that mother died before my sister. She was at least spared that final injustice. All her life people thought mother was spoiled. A spoiled American, they called her, but she surprised everyone after father lost his leg. While he still gave the outward impression of being the head of the family and running a successful law firm, we knew he and mother had essentially exchanged roles. She nursed him, looked after every aspect of the household, covered up for him when he drank too much. She even managed to feign interest in his law practice when it was mainly the family's financial well-being she worried about. We always thought of her as young and active, until my father died and she grew old within a few months.

*

Mother is up in arms. Father has bought himself a fancy little sports car, a Stutz Bearcat. He can hardly walk any more, his lop-sided gait and jarring pounding have destroyed both hips and he is in constant pain. He has also developed nasty ulcers on his leg stump because of diabetes. Oh, Harlan not another automobeeele, she drawls in an accent evocative of the southern United States although she is originally from New York and has never been, as far as anyone knows, anywhere near the South. Accentuating the wrong syllable nevertheless to emphasize the foreignness of such a soulless machine. Surely, Harlan, one car is more than enough, she admonishes him as she changes the bandages on his stump. She seldom complains. She hates war, what it does to people, but she also admires the grand gestures that go with it. Having fulfilled his duty at such a personal cost makes father a hero in her eyes. They often argue about it. Hogwash, father, always replies.

Because it is now practically impossible for him to get around by foot, father has decided he would like to race about in a fancy little sports car and mother can hardly expect him to race about in a sedan, he says.

Even I who loves cars can clearly see the fault line of his argument.

You are not to race about in anything, period, mother scolds him. You will kill yourself, driving like a maniac with one leg. She has become very skilled at swaddling what is left of his leg. She twirls the white gauze over and around the stump a dozen times or so, splits two ends to tie and keep it in place without having to use tape.

Thank you dear, father tells her, placing his hand on the profes-sional-looking dressing. Then looks directly in her eyes: I don't care if it does kill me. The sooner the better.

It's a familiar argument. Mother knows she must reach further than his own self-interest. His family's safety is her trump card. The pollution you generate with those infernal machines will take us all with you, and the pond is threatening to turn into a lagoon again, she warns him. The pond mother is referring to is Taddle Creek, which originates a few yards from our house.

Within a few months of father buying the Stutz Bearcat, every-

thing starts to disintegrate at an even faster pace than before. Until late one night mother finds father slumped, passed out, behind the wheel. He barely managed to get home. She calls me to help her carry him in. Should I call Doctor Ferguson now or should we wait until morning? I ask assuming we will follow the usual routine—call Doctor Ferguson to help father get through the delirium tremens, then have him admitted to a private clinic where he will be intravenously fed for several days, then given light soups until he dries out. He stays sober for a few weeks, perhaps even a few months, but the dry spells, filled with shame and remorse, are becoming shorter, and the benders longer. He now weighs less than mother or myself, looks nothing like the man I remembered from my childhood.

No, mother says with steely calm, We are not going to call the doctor this time.

What do you mean? We have to. Doctor Ferguson is the only one who can get him into the clinic.

Yes, well, the last time your father came home from the clinic he made me promise that I wouldn't send him back there again. Your father is tired. Neither one of us can put up with this cycle anymore.

What are you saying? He could die.

Yes, he could, mother says with resignation.

I have always admired mother's composure under duress, but this unnerves me. It reminds me of the summer she decided to rid the garden of the toads. They had multiplied to the point where, as father had said, it was like the plague that befell Egypt. She devised traps and each morning she resolutely carried the grunting toads down the ravine. When she returned, the traps were empty. She was releasing the toads into the creek running through the bottom of the ravine, she said. The way she averted her eyes I suspected she was lying and I didn't dare imagine what she did to them.

If your father is strong enough he will recover on his own, she says.

And if he is not strong enough? I ask.

Then, I will respect his wish, I will keep my promise.

I am also tired of his drinking, yet I feel I should at least make an effort to protect him. It's not his fault, I tell her.

Nobody said it was his fault. It's the way things are. I made him a promise. And you must also promise not to call Doctor Ferguson until I say it's time. It's what Harlan wants. She usually refers to him as your father, but not this time. In referring to him by his first name she is letting me know that a decision has been reached between her and her husband. Oh, and one more thing, she adds, Whatever happens in the next few days should stay in this house. It would be better if you didn't call Sister. Sister won't understand, she won't see it the way we do.

It annoys me to think how easily I have become part of mother's conspiracy and her assumption that I can handle this kind of crisis better than Sissa. I also know that she's right. Sissa and Wilson don't seem to be getting along very well these days and she carries enough sadness for all of us.

We get father up the stairs and I help mother get him undressed and put him to bed in one of the guest rooms after which she resolutely shuts the door. Get some sleep she tells me. The next few days might be… she hesitates, then adds a word that is not normally part of her vocabulary: rough. The next few days will be rough, she repeats.

In the morning, when father calls her, she brings him thin gruel. From the hallway I hear muffled voices from the other side of the door. A few moments later, the door opens and mother emerges with the untouched bowl of gruel. She then goes to the cellar. She returns carrying a bottle of spirits. As she walks past me, she simply says, It's what he wants.

This routine is carried out over a period of ten days until it is time to call Doctor Ferguson, when we both know it is too late. Father's liver was not able to sustain the unrelenting assault from the excessive amounts of alcohol, the doctor tells us. Mother and I nod and say nothing. We understand the real assault on father—his inability to withstand the realities of the world outside Wildwood Park. In this he and mother had much in common.

Sissa has not been affected as badly by father's death as mother and I feared. It was his choice to drink himself to death, she simply says. After the funeral she keeps herself even busier than usual with her family.

Wilson also keeps busy. He is taking over father's law firm, an easy enough transition since he had been managing it mostly by himself for the last few years.

Mother hardly works in the garden anymore although she still wears the same version of her oversized gardening apron. Each morning, she pulls the neck loop over her head, reaches behind her back and ties the two sashes into a perfect bow, picks one of the many slim volumes of poetry she still reads and places it in the apron pocket. She collects several of the gardening tools from the shed, trims one or two plants, uproots a few weeds, then, providing the weather is warm enough, she sits on one of the benches by the high fence. She no longer gives the impression of a strong and determined woman. Father's death has drawn the last vestiges of vigour and independence from her. The defiance that used to define her is tenuous at best. She hardly shows any interest in her grandchildren anymore. She hardly pays attention to her little granddaughter, Rachel, blaming her advanced years when everyone suspects she disapproves of Rachel's birth. She disapproves of anyone having a child supposedly so late in life.

It is her promise to father that haunts her as she tries to reconcile the role she played in his death. Almost every conversation now begins with, It's what he wanted. He might as well have killed himself outright. Put a gun to his head. It was a miracle he didn't kill anyone, driving in his condition and on one leg. Hellish benders.

On warm days she sits on the stone bench by the fence and reads aloud from one of the books she extracts from her apron pockets:

"Old age is
a flight of small
cheeping birds
skimming

bare trees
above a snow glaze.
Gaining and failing
they are buffeted
by a dark wind—
But what?
On harsh weedstalks
the flock has rested,
the snow
is covered with broken
seedhusks
and the wind tempered
by a shrill
piping of plenty."

What was the name of the poem, again? Ah yes. *To Waken an Old Lady* by William Carlos Williams.

~26~

BECAUSE ADAM WASN'T ABLE TO MAKE IT TO THE LAST PRODUCTION of the regular opera season Thea agreed to go with Julia and Rachel instead. Everyone was apprehensive. The program consisted of two short operas, Bartok's melodramatic *Bluebeard's Castle* and Schoenberg's atonal *Erwartung*. Julia feared that Thea would hate them and cast a pall on the entire evening.

The unusual lighting effects—the program mentioned lasers—and the innovative staging by a playwright from Quebec, Robert Lepage, took the three women by surprise. It was like nothing they'd seen before and because of the unusual and original staging, the grand operatic themes of love, madness, and death were revitalized. Thea was especially impressed. That was so neat, she said after the performance..

So you liked this one then? a dubious Rachel asked.

Thea nodded. I loved it. The staging was amazing.

How was this not over the top? Rachel wanted to know. The singers were rising from rivers and walking through walls, for God's sake.

Sometimes you need to look at things in a new way, especially operas that have been performed thousands of times, Thea replied.

It was rather innovative, Julia conceded.

Rachel flashed Julia one of her give-me-a-break looks. It's change for the sake of change, she said.

Thea pounced. So what if it is? Isn't this what art should be about, change? Unless the old stories are re-imagined they end up as institutionalized culture, repeated over and over until they become meaningless. Opera needs a breath of fresh air. You and mom should keep an open mind.

You should keep an open mind too where your mother is concerned, Julia told Thea as the two of them waited for the night watchman to open the front door once they got to Evenholme.

*

When Rachel dropped by ten days later she was beaming with the pride of a mother whose child had just achieved a major milestone. Thea had a boyfriend. His name was Charlie. He was one of the reasons Thea hadn't come around since the night of the opera.

To counteract Rachel's immoderate enthusiasm Julia downplayed hers: I know how busy Thea is; her life doesn't have to stop because mine has.

Rachel groaned. Oh, stop it, mother.

Julia feigned ignorance. Stop what, dear?

This constant bellyaching about living so long. Should everyone be so lucky. Rachel's reply, swift and confident, reminded Julia of Thea. In this, mother and daughter were definitely alike, a couple of smart mouths.

You are too cheeky for your own good, Julia said. As miffed as she often pretended to be, she was rather pleased that neither Rachel nor Thea put up with her petty grievances. Condescension would have been infinitely more offensive. The three of them understood their peculiar way of displaying affection without resorting to sentimentality.

I wonder where I get it from, Rachel said. Anyway, I'm supposed to tell you that she will be here on Sunday and she's bringing Charlie.

Where did she meet this Charlie?

At school, in one of her classes, I think. They've been going out for a few months, but I've only met him recently. A nice enough young man, in spite of his appearance. Adam was impressed. Well, not at first, the shaved head threw him, but after they spoke a bit he was relieved.

A few months? Why haven't we met him?

She only brought him around last week. You know Thea, every

occasion is an opportunity for mutiny.

Is he in Cultural Studies too?

Rachel grimaced and shook her head. She and Adam were still waiting for Thea to discover her true calling. They had assumed that once her wanderlust had subsided she would settle into an honourable if not entirely traditional profession. But after nearly ten years of university interspersed with trips extending over several months, they were beginning to wonder if this Cultural Studies program would ever translate into anything. No, he's not, thank goodness. He's in Cognitive Science or something.

He must be the one who's interested in mirror neurons. Thea mentioned him a while back.

It's not easy getting information from either one of them. Everything comes to us in instalments. Did Thea tell you what she's planning for her doctoral thesis?

She told me she hadn't decided.

Well, she has. She's doing a thesis on comic books. Rachel rolled her eyes while Julia tried to maintain a measure of unbiased equanimity, at least outwardly.

Comic books?

Yes. Their historical, social, and cultural status. Can you believe it?

Oh. She hasn't said anything about this to me. Why would a university allow a postgraduate thesis on comic books, Julia wondered.

She's probably too embarrassed to tell you, Rachel added, trying to justify her own feeling of having been let down once again.

Julia decided to take the high road. Thea is patient, she said. We should be patient with her.

Oh, mother, she's not patient, she's indifferent.

Maybe she's patiently indifferent.

What is that supposed to mean?

Julia wasn't entirely sure what she meant. Maybe she's indifferent to what is available to her until something more appropriate comes along, she said.

And she's doing this through comic books? After ten years of going to school on again, off again?

She is very bright, she won't let you down.

We've always known that she's bright. This is why it's so puzzling. There's no depth to anything she and her friends do.

Oh, I don't know Rachel. Much of what was once considered profound turned out to be pretty disheartening.

Rachel sighed. This is exactly the kind of thing you shouldn't be saying to her. You encourage her.

Oh Rachel! It's the other way around. It's Thea who works her magic on me. The world needs more students like her. It wasn't so long ago when you were complaining how conservative students had become. At least Thea makes us think. Give her a little credit for goodness sake.

Julia had not expected what came next: And I suppose I don't, do I, mother?

You don't what, dear?

Make you think. I have never worked much magic on you, have I?

It shocked Julia to hear Rachel sound so tired and disillusioned. Oh, Rachel, how can you think this? It's not a competition. You grew up, had a family of your own. A successful career. I've always admired you for this. Enormously. Thea is still a puppy, like you used to be. We are very much alike, you and I, probably the reason we're always butting heads. You were always a perfect daughter, Rachel, my great success. When you were little, whenever you put your hand in mine, you drove away any loneliness or heartache I may have had. I lived in a small, claustrophobic world, but you drew me out of it, and out of myself. I couldn't have asked for more. Julia leaned over and took Rachel's hands in hers. She hadn't done this for a long time, too long, she now realized.

I often wondered, Rachel said.

Wondered what, exactly?

If, instead of staying home to look after me, you couldn't have done more with your life. If you hadn't had me.

Oh, Rachel. I assure you I did exactly what I wanted with my life. Exactly. So no more doubts, Julia said and squeezed Rachel's hands. Yes, Rachel had been her great success, but she often did wonder if she hadn't instilled in Rachel the values she thought were right for Rachel when they had, in fact, been right for Julia? Rachel had never questioned them. All Rachel had ever wanted was to please Julia.

*

Rachel is standing behind me on the narrow stairs leading to the attic. She is barely four years old. Mommy? she cries out. As calmly as I can I turn around and pick her up, pressing her head against my neck, leading us back down the stairs. Yes, mommy is here, Rachel. Mommy will always be here for you.

~27~

THEA BROUGHT CHARLIE ON THE FOLLOWING SUNDAY, A SIX-FOOT-five titan with a shaven head. He looked like a modern-day pirate with an earring in one ear and the largest sneakers Julia had ever seen on a pair of feet.

So, you're the new boyfriend, Julia said, looking him straight in the eye. He returned her glare, a wry smile on an appealing face in spite of the gleaming baldness.

Thea corrected her grandmother: Not a boyfriend, Nan, a friend who happens to be male. She turned to Charlie. My mother and grandmother see a potential husband in every man I speak to.

Charlie nodded and blinked indicating he understood perfectly. Nice to meet you. I've heard a lot about you, he said shaking Julia's hand vigorously.

I bet you have, Julia said. From the way he dressed Julia gathered he must have been one of those earnest political animals with far-left leanings. I suppose you're a radical? she blurted out.

He laughed. Why would you suppose that? he asked.

Julia shrugged. Young, bald, dressed in black. A Marxist maybe?

Behave yourself, Nan, Thea warned.

It's alright, Charlie said as he sat down. He lifted one foot to his opposing knee, stretched one arm along the back of the settee. Confident men always take so much space, Julia thought.

Charlie is not at all Marxist, on the contrary, Thea protested.

Not wanting anyone to speak for him, Charlie jumped in. Uh, uh, not me. Men with influential ideas should be held accountable. Marx should have practised what he preached.

Thea hardly gave him time to finish his sentence: Exactly. He couldn't even look after his own kids.

That's right, Charlie said. You can't go around preaching responsibility for mankind when you can't be responsible for your own children.

Julia hadn't expected such earnestness. At least not so soon into the visit. She should have known better than bringing up a subject she knew little about except that at one time she had thought Marx's ideas were at least hopeful. Until she read something he had written about philosophers interpreting the world while his ideas would change it. It was a notion that seldom left room for accommodation, tolerance, or compromise.

Where did the two of you meet? At school? Julia asked.

Thea made a point of responding first. In a bar, actually.

Charlie gave Thea a disapproving scowl. Come on, he admonished. He then turned to Julia. We recognized each other from one of our courses.

You're in Cultural Studies too? Julia remembered he wasn't but she wanted to give him the opportunity to take the conversation in whatever direction he wanted. She would learn more about him that way.

No, CogSci.

Which is?

Cognitive Science.

Which is?

It's interdisciplinary like Cultural Studies except the emphasis is on science. How the brain works. It integrates psychology, linguistics, computer science, the developmental sciences.

Ah, you must be the mirror neurons friend. It must be fascinating, the workings of the brain.

I was telling Charlie you should leave yours to science, Thea said as she gave two gentle taps to the top of Julia's head on her way to the kitchenette.

I'm still attached to it in case you hadn't noticed, Julia said. I doubt much could be learned from an old melon brain like mine. Old melon with the consistency of soft-boiled eggs. I wish I still had the ability to learn all these new things. The ability and the time.

There's a ninety-year-old man in one of my tutorials who just got a BA in Psychology and he's going for his Master's, Charlie said. His voice was unexpectedly quiet for a large man. It conveyed sensibility, but also control.

Thea had extracted from the plastic bags they'd brought an assortment of clear containers and was rummaging through cupboards for dishes in which to deposit a suspicious assortment of food. Julia hated eating anything she couldn't recognize. We could have had lunch in the dining room, she told them.

Charlie and I are not into those big mid-day meals. We thought this would be a nice change for you.

Julia wasn't up for change and would have preferred her normal diet, but she decided she should behave as she had been told. This was Thea's day and sabotaging it would serve no purpose. She turned to Charlie and more for something to say than anything else, she informed him that there was a resident at Evenholme who had a book on DNA that claimed that everyone was more or less the same.

Charlie nodded indicating he already knew. Yeah, the Human Genome Project. Yesterday's news. It's more complicated than that.

Oh, I'll have to tell my friend he's yesterday's news then. I guess everyone in here is.

How is your boyfriend these days? Thea asked as she set the table with brisk efficiency.

Feminism had accomplished at least this much. It was now possible for educated women to execute chores without their sense of self being threatened. Mom says it's a regular love fest, she added, and both she and Charlie laughed. It was a rare moment when Thea used Julia as the butt of a joke. Julia didn't like it, it felt like a defection on Thea's part.

He's not my boyfriend and it is far from being a love fest. We have tea and good conversations a couple of times a week, she explained to Charlie, somewhat put off at having to justify her friendship with Daniel. You are being impertinent, Thea.

We'll soon have drugs that can prevent, even reverse changes in the brain associated with aging, Charlie offered for no particular reason, at least none that Julia could understand.

Not in time to benefit me, thank God. Julia found it disconcerting listening to young people postulating on aging as if they knew more about it than the aged. She turned to Thea. Your mother said there was an accident at the race track. I saw it on the news, it looked awful. Cars bursting into flame.

It was terrible. The atmosphere's pretty gloomy over there.

Charlie nodded towards Thea. She was depressed for days, he said. It's time she quit working there, time to move on.

And what does Thea think? Julia asked.

I'm getting a little bored with it. I'm ready for something else.

That's good news. I've never understood what was so exciting about cars ploughing into each other and bouncing off walls. Scattering about like Dinky toys.

Charlie chuckled. Dinky toys? That's funny.

That's what it looked like on television. They said someone was killed.

Yeah, Thea said. One of the drivers died and another was badly burned. Poor guys.

It's hard for me to muster much sympathy for young men risking their lives to such a hare-brain sport, Julia said. She expected Thea to put up an argument, but she didn't.

My boss went to the funeral. He said there must have been over a thousand people there.

He was a draw to the finish then, Julia said.

Charlie chuckled again.

My boss said it was the tackiest thing he'd ever seen. The casket looked like a frigging car. Some kind of plastic. His red helmet and silver racing gloves were sitting on the hood.

I don't imagine the casket will deteriorate any time soon then, Julia said. I mean it's hardly ecological, filling cemeteries with indissoluble materials. I'm surprised it's allowed. The other day, Mrs. Thomson, the one with two artificial knees and hips, said she wanted to be cremated and I wondered at all the metal. Will it burn, do you think?

Charlie was laughing openly at the incongruous turn the conversation had taken until Thea also broke down and joined Charlie. Ah jeez, this is gruesome, Nan. God, you're the only one I know who finds humour in death.

You find humour anywhere you can around here and death happens to be handily close by. What happened to the other guy?

He was badly burned. Maybe he'll end up here.

Why here?

Wasn't there a woman who was badly burned sent here a few months ago?

Oh, her. She wasn't sent here to recover from the burns. She came later to recuperate from operations she underwent to prepare her hands for prostheses. Her hands had been destroyed in the fire, Julia explained to Charlie.

I wonder if she could be fitted with one of those Cybergrasps? Thea asked Charlie.

It depends how much of her hands are left, he said.

What are those ... cybergrasps? Julia asked.

Charlie has been experimenting with a glove that gives the wearer the impression of reaching into the computer and touching and feeling computer-generated objects, Thea explained.

A few guys I'm working with are trying to figure out how they can be used as prostheses, Charlie explained. It gives people the illusion of touching real things and real people.

Julia sighed. The illusion of touching real people wouldn't help this woman, I'm afraid.

Charlie thinks we'll soon be able to create the mind we want by choosing what we put in it. It was surprising to hear Thea quoting Charlie to such an extent, giving everything he said so much weight. Love's first flush.

Exactly how are we going to do this? Julia asked Charlie.

Different ways, Charlie said. Implanting studs into the brain and connecting them to a universal grid, for one.

Sounds a little Orwellian to me. What was so striking about this Gizi person was her lack of empathy.

It'll be possible to locate the part of the brain receptive to empathy, Charlie said. That's only one of the many things they're studying with mirror neurons.

There wouldn't be any need to study ethics or philosophy anymore? Julia asked.

Yes, but differently. The material will be deposited into the brain without having to memorize it. Although I doubt we'll have much use for philosophy by then.

I see. The geeks will make the Greeks obsolete, Julia said.

He grinned. Could be. The geeks are on the verge of inheriting the world.

Thea beamed with admiration. She had banked on Charlie to impress her grandmother and he was proving himself up to the task.

And love? Julia asked.

What about love? he asked, having suddenly lost the thread.

Will it be possible to deposit love into a person's brain? Make a person love another against the person's will?

So it was you he loved all along.

Wilson's heart failed, the doctor is saying, and I wonder if I am the only one who understands the irony of his statement. Wilson's heart failed the moment Sissa and I met him, the moment he imagined he loved one sister and married the other.

Or perhaps my own heart failed too when I rejected Wilson, when I let antagonism grow between us to attenuate the sting of that decision. As sad as I felt for Wilson and Sissa and the children, his death provided a clear boundary between what could have been and what was. I could now safely tell myself that I could never love anyone as much as she loved Wilson. Anyone, except Sissa.

Sure, but it won't be against anyone's will, Charlie replied. If people can choose what they put into their brain, they'll be able to choose who to love.

And hate?

Hatred, love, we'll be able to control them better.

Hasn't this gotten us in trouble before?

What do you mean? Charlie asked.

The need to control. Haven't we been down this road before?

This would be different. These studs implanted in the brain could teach us to control our own lives.

Oh, I'm sure someone will figure out how to use them to control others. What are these foods? Julia asked pointing to substances that reminded her of pre-digested food, one a bland creamy colour, another pink.

Greek, Thea said. Aren't they good?

And this? Julia pointed to a brown and purple concoction with seeds stuck to its slimy components.

Eggplant, Thea answered. She spooned large dollops from the three dishes onto Julia's plate. You eat them with pita bread, like this. She spread some of the pale goop on a triangle cut from round flat bread.

Julia nibbled at the pointed end of the bread. Whatever Thea had spread on it reeked of garlic. It would take her days to digest this.

Has Mom told you that Charlie and I are moving in together? Thea asked casually.

No, she hasn't. I must say, this is a surprise.

She would have preferred wedding bells, Charlie said.

What's wrong with wedding bells? Julia asked.

Moving in together is all we can handle right now, Thea replied.

All they could handle. Young people capable of thinking up outlandish ways of controlling hatred and love but incapable of handling a simple commitment. That's wonderful, Thea. Quite a few changes.

If it gets too claustrophobic, we'll get two apartments side-by-side when we make more money, Thea added offhandedly to lessen any starry-eyed impressions she may be conveying.

Not such a bad idea, Julia said.

Your mother mentioned something about your thesis. Why don't you tell me about it?

Oh, oh, Thea said with a smile that was more of a smirk. Don't you and mother have anything else to talk about? she asked. The two of you are such gossips and old artefacts.

Marginally better than a few weeks ago when you called me an old emission of wind.

She can't even say fart, Thea said to Charlie.

It annoyed Julia to hear Thea refer to her in the third person. Is it true? she asked. About the comic books?

Cultural Studies is the study of culture, and comic books are part of it.

They were never part of my culture.

Culture isn't only high-brow stuff, Nan. People read comic books before movies and television. Her tone suggested Julia had no knowledge of any of this.

I know about comic books, Thea. They are about the same age I am. It doesn't mean I read them. I liked movies and I still do occasionally, but I never read comic books.

Well, Billy and Tom certainly read them, Thea said. I'm using their collection for my research.

It was jarring to hear Thea mention William and Thomas. As direct as Thea was when it came to probing or confronting, she usually treaded carefully around topics she knew might upset her grandmother.

Mom was a little ticked off when we found them in the attic, Thea went on. She couldn't figure out why you wouldn't have given them to Andrew and Allan when they were boys.

They would have ended up in the garbage, Julia said. She had, in fact, thought of giving them away or throwing them out several times over the years, but could never bring herself to do so. It would have been too much like parting with what was left of the boys.

They are worth a fortune now.

Oh, Thea, not everything is about money. It was an unwarranted comment, the kind that stands in for another when it doesn't know how to express itself.

Do you want to know more about my thesis?

Of course. I wish you'd told me sooner.

I needed to think it through. I still haven't, not completely. I do much of the work on my own.

Thea is doing great, she's heading for a great career, Charlie said. He struck Julia as an honest young man, the kind who didn't need to ingratiate himself. Plus he was clearly smitten. They both were.

I wish Mom and Dad had half the confidence in me that you have, Thea said to Charlie. They think the best way to gain respect in a field is by narrowing it down as much as possible.

It's called specialization, Julia said. Your mother is very respected in her field.

Yeah. Studying the English novel from some narrow period in the nineteenth century then spending the rest of her life doing research, attending conferences, learning more and more about less and less. It's supposed to be intellectual but I find it kind of mindless, you know?

Charlie simply nodded. He thought it best not to implicate himself in a family matter, at least not in front of Julia.

Julia knew the argument well—a defiant young woman swerves away from parental expectations then tries to justify her decision by finding fault. Your choices are right for you and your mother's choices were right for her, Thea. Frankly, I'm surprised at how drastically you have narrowed her interests. She is involved in so much more. She's loved opera since she was eight years old. She's travelled more than anyone I know and she devoted more time to you and your brothers and your father than she ever did to her career. It seems to me, Thea, that your criticism stems from your own narrow perspective. It's not very elegant, especially at your age.

In a protective and supportive gesture Charlie reached across the table for Thea's hand, his eyebrows raised a good inch from where they were supposed to be, as if to say, Wow, where did this come from?

Thea was too astounded to speak.

So why don't you tell me about this thesis you're working on, Julia finally said.

Irritated and humiliated at having been upbraided in front of Charlie, Thea mumbled, Why bother, you'll hate it.

Can I be the judge of my own opinions? Julia countered.

I'm not so sure I want to hear your opinions, Thea said in retaliation.

Come on Thea, give it up, Charlie said. A smell of garlic lingered over the table.

Pulling her hands brusquely away from Charlie's and looking straight into his face as if she were refusing to address Julia, Thea said, It's on the History of the Comic Book. Its evolution into literature, into the graphic novel

What do you mean, graphic novel?

Novels done in comic-strip format. She was being purposely brief and evasive.

Which explains why I've never heard of it.

Contrary to what you may think, Nan, there's plenty out there you haven't heard of.

And why would anyone write a thesis on those?

Charlie thought it may be time to step in and help Thea. It's art. And witnesses to the past, he said.

They're comic books. For children, Julia protested.

Becoming a serious genre, Thea reiterated impatiently. I don't suppose you've ever heard of Art Spiegelman, she said enunciating each syllable as if speaking to a five-year-old.

No, should I have?

Again, Charlie took it upon himself to intervene. Graphic novels are more literary than the traditional super heroes or simple animal comics of the past, he said.

Literature is complex. Comic books have been distilled to the lowest common denominator.

Ah, jeez, here we go, Thea groaned. Good ole lowest denominator. That's a pre-fascist attitude, Nan. She glanced at Charlie and the two of them grinned. Approaching thirty, but children still. It wasn't so long ago when people this age were considered middle-aged, married with several children, owned their own homes, already established in careers or jobs.

What about this Spiegelman fellow? Julia asked. Why would he warrant a thesis?

Part of a thesis. I'm concluding the history of comics with the two volumes of his graphic novel, *Maus*.

Julia was trying to process what she was being told when something rang and startled her. She was about to get up to answer her telephone when she realized the ring was different, a familiar but distorted operatic air she didn't immediately identify. Was that the "Habanera" from *Carmen*? she asked.

Yes, Thea acknowledged with a triumphant grin.

Charlie reached into his pocket for one of those phones people carried around, robbing everyone in their proximity of tranquility and space. Excuse me, where can I take this? he asked.

Julia pointed him to the bedroom. She then turned to Thea. So this Art fellow has written a novel on a mouse? Like Mickey Mouse?

M-a-u-s. It's German, for mouse.

He's from Germany?

He's from New York, actually. His parents were from Poland, Auschwitz survivors. It's about what happened to his parents during the war.

Julia could sense Thea's growing apprehension as she reluctantly filled her in. What do you mean?

His graphic novels are about the Holocaust.

Julia flinched as her breath left her. Oh, Thea! How inappropriate! You can't be serious.

I am very serious and so is Art Spiegelman.

Why would he want to trivialize his parents' experience like this?

He's not trivializing, Nan. On the contrary, he wants to make his parents' ordeal accessible to more people, but not through conventional art or sentimentality. He didn't want to turn the Holocaust into some kind of elitist art form.

You're a post-graduate, Thea. You are an elitist no matter how you look at it, so don't pull this egalitarian nonsense on me. Who are the mice? The Germans?

No, they're vicious cats, but they look more human than the Jews who are the mice. That's how the Nazis thought of Jews, as vermin. The Poles are depicted as pigs and the Americans are goofy-looking dogs.

How stereotypically democratic. Isn't the plain truth disturbing enough?

Sometimes the historical truth isn't enough. When history stops speaking to us, or we stop listening because we've heard it so many times before, we have to find other ways of making ourselves heard. We have to make new connections.

You and your new connections. I don't know, Thea. This time I tend to agree with your mother. It sounds trendy.

Trends are part of the culture too. She paused for a while then added, You know, I never would have thought of doing this it if it hadn't been for what you told me about Lena and the comics I found in the attic. There's a link there.

No wonder your parents think I'm a bad influence. I don't know what Lena would make of this. I suspect she would say we should imagine ourselves as the human beings we really are. That's what good literature used to do, you know. And good movies. Not all, mind you, but movies where people pretended to be real people with real problems. Now everything has to be larger or smaller than life. We can't see ourselves anymore.

You'd love my post-graduate course on film, Thea said. She managed to sound tentative and hopeful at the same time.

You can get credits for going to the movies?

She nodded, Yes. You'd love it.

How education has changed.

You like movies? Charlie asked as he came out of the bedroom, checking his watch.

Another one who is always in a hurry, Julia thought. Little wonder he and Thea get along so well. I used to, she said. I thought good actors needed to have good insights into the characters they played. But I hardly watch them anymore. Television is pretty boring, especially those reality shows. The people always end up diminished somehow and I end up feeling embarrassed for them. They're the real cartoon characters. Maybe you're right, Thea. Maybe we're all becoming caricatures of ourselves.

That's radical, Nan, Thea said and looked to Charlie with a sardonic smile as if to say, See, told you I'd win her over.

Julia felt exhausted to the point of irascibility and she quickly rose from her chair. As she did so, her feet gave and she stumbled forward barely staying upright.

Thea and Charlie rushed to her, each one grabbing an arm, their youthful strength almost causing her to topple over completely.

Bit of a dizzy spell, Julia said. I'll just sit here until it passes. Her stomach was churning from the odd lunch she had eaten. It was her turn to check her watch. Don't bother with the dishes, Thea, the woman who tidies up will clean up tomorrow. To hasten the formalities, she steadied herself on the table as she got up, then walked over to Thea and kissed her on both cheeks. She backed away so she wouldn't have to do the same with Charlie. He wasn't family yet. It was wonderful meeting you, Charlie. I hope I'll see you again, she said.

He shook Julia's hand warmly then circled Thea's shoulders, his long arm dangling near her breast. I'm sure I will, he said. I'm not going anywhere anytime soon. He bent down and planted a kiss on top of Thea's head.

As they were heading out the door, Thea turned. Hey, Nan, do you know who my super hero is? she asked.

Who?

You.

That goes without saying, Julia said.

But it still needs to be said, Thea shot back and blew Julia a kiss.

Thea was finally shifting gears. While she still maintained a racer's strategy, she was also learning to negotiate the sharp turns she so often took. Was this the future then? Julia wondered. Was this what was in store for Thea and her Charlie? Two bright thirty-year-olds effortlessly discarding much of what had gone into shaping Julia's century, their idealism meshing into a whirlwind of uncompromising positions. So eager to hook themselves to contraptions like Cybergrasps because they had more faith in the artificial intelligence of machines than in the natural stupidity of men.

Julia wondered what Daniel was up to. What would he make of these newfangled contraptions such as studs implanted behind the ears? Would they make it possible for two people to enter each other's mind? Explore, as on a two-way highway, regions that were the same and regions that were different? Would a younger generation be able to exchange knowledge with an older generation and vice versa? Would a woman as old as herself be able to rediscover those images that come alive through the spontaneous and luminous details of a child's mind like the stick figures reaching out to one another in the drawings that Thomas and William so loved to make when they were children?

As Julia lay down on her bed she found herself wishing she could beam in Daniel so they could nap together. Had he also liked movies when he was young? The soft droning of a projector flickering in the dark, the hum of a fan as the acrid smell of heated celluloid spread throughout the theatre. Memories moving under Julia's eyelids as if on a movie screen.

~28~

THOMAS AND WILLIAM ARE SPENDING THE WEEKEND AT WILDWOOD *while Sissa and Wilson are away at some law society convention. A well-needed break, according to Sissa.*

The boys are sitting at the long table in the house library where an odour of pipe tobacco lingers. They are concentrating on drawings, holding on to crayons fatter than their five-year-old fingers. As each drawing is completed, William prints letters beside the shapes he has drawn: flr for three-petaled flowers in orange, purple, and red; hse for a blue house on a light green mountain; sn for a brilliant sun overlooking a dark green meadow. A figure with a round head and a round body and stick legs and arms has been assigned the two letters of a self-portrait: me. Thomas, who has recently learned to count is obsessed with numbers. At the top of each page of drawings he prints a number to indicate a proper order although the numbers are random and, most often than not, printed backward. He then passes the pages to me to sew to form a book. How many pages is that? he asks.

I think we have twelve, I reply.

He looks at his two hands. That's more than my fingers, he says. Can we make a book with one hundred pages? he wants to know. The magnitude of a number he can understand seems infinitely larger than some vague abstraction he can't fathom. You have fat books, he says scanning the shelves lining the walls of the library.

True, I have many fat books.

Can we see some of them? William asks.

Of course. I retrieve two collections of poems from the corner of a lower shelf where mother can readily retrieve her favourites.

Each boy stretches out his hands as if receiving an offering.

Thomas eyes the thinness of each book. These aren't very fat, he says, disappointed.

It isn't necessary to have lots of pages to say what you want to say, I tell him.

William opens the book and for a few seconds his eyes scan the letters aligned in their trimmed black lines. Who made this one? He wants to know.

A lady wrote it. Emily Dickinson.

What is it about?

I glance at the first line of the first stanza: All but Death, can be adjusted. It's about sadness, I tell him.

Is Emily old? Thomas asks. Is she one hundred?

Oh, no, not a hundred.

Older than grandma and grandpa?

She was younger than grandma and grandpa when she wrote the book, I tell him.

How old is Emily now? he finally asks.

She doesn't have an age now, Thomas, I say, already anticipating the next question.

Why not?

She's dead now. People don't have an age once they've died.

He ponders this for a few seconds then asks, Where is Emily dead?

I don't know where people go when they're dead, I tell Thomas while William skims the lines of the poetry book, pretending to read.

Is this book sad because there are no pictures in it? William asks, puzzled.

But there are pictures in it. They're made of words, I explain.

His eyes dart about the pages trying to extract patterns he can recognize. He shrugs and shakes his head. Do words have houses in them? he asks, then adds, And doorknobs? His voice betrays his scepticism.

Certainly, I tell him, remembering the out-of-scale knobs on the doors he draws, aware of the security that doors provide, but also the freedom that comes from being able to open or close them. Thomas, on the other hand, seldom draws doorknobs, his perfect geometric forms are the whitewashed cells of a closed intimacy. His yellow crayon stars in the sky glitter with the symmetry of perfectly superimposed triangles.

Do Emily's words have smoke coming out of her chimneys? William asks.

If there were chimneys in her poems, yes, I suppose they would have smoke coming out of them. I look at the white plumes and gray clouds above William's winter landscapes, an indication that it is warm and cosy in the shelters he inhabits when snow and wind lash at the outside world.

Because each twin invariably awakens the other's imagination, sometimes in opposition but more often in harmony, Thomas follows up William's question with his own. But why are Emily's poems sad and black then? he wants to know. There are no colours in her pictures.

I don't like these kinds of pictures very much, William finally declares as he returns to his crayons and a new blank page. Under his breath I hear him muttering, Emily should have borrowed my crayons.

I watch as he quickly executes one of his standard stick-arms and stick-legs figures with a round head and a round body. Tout rond, *all round, the French say of an innocent person whose images come alive through spontaneous and luminous details, the pure products of an absolute imagination.*

This time he adds another figure, one sporting luscious red lips and yellow Rapunzel hair, one stick arm extended toward the other figure so they hold hands.

What a beautiful picture, I tell him. Who are those people?

It's me and Emily, William replies without hesitation.

JULIA DEBATED WHETHER TO TELL LENA ABOUT THEA'S THESIS AND decided against it. A doctoral thesis required its own language, which would be too removed from the story of the two Nalis.

Their story had been related to Julia in brief, spontaneous phrases, outbursts that had either lost their way or could no longer be contained. *Did they shave your head? They don't put bromide in your food here.* On a few occasions, depending on Lena's mood or state of mind, there had been longer and more vivid accounts, but these were rare. Once, in the middle of a gin game, Lena had suddenly placed her hands over her ears as if trying to filter out noise.

What's the matter, Lena? Is there something wrong?

The babies are crying. The babies in the village, they are crying.

There are no babies here, Lena. You are travelling again. Travelling had become Julia's euphemism for when Lena's mind tried to escape the present.

Of course, of course. Lena stared at Julia. Gin, she said and laid her cards on the table.

As good a player as she normally was, hardly any of her cards matched or were in the proper order. She had been discarding and picking up mechanically, randomly, not paying any attention to the game.

There you go beating me again, Julia said as she swept up the cards. I can't bear to lose one more game, Lena, so why don't we go for a short walk in the garden. Time for fresh air.

Once outside Julia asked Lena if she could still hear the babies.

No. Lena paused. I thought I could hear them, she offered as an explanation.

It happens to me too, Julia reassured her. I'm sure I'm hearing something before I realize it's only a residue in my head. Annoying, isn't it? We are like old records you and I. Grooves so worn the needle gets stuck. Why do you think you could hear babies crying?

Lena pressed a gloved hand to her throat. In those few weeks before they came to deport us, all the babies in the village were crying. They knew.

What did they know?

That something was going to happen.

You mean the babies sensed it?

Yes. They felt fear from their parents, in the arms that held them. They heard it in their fathers' voices and drank it in their mothers' milk. She relayed this with such certainty there was no reason for Julia to doubt her.

Did people know what was going on beyond the village?

They heard things, but they didn't believe what they heard. These things couldn't happen. God would not let such things happen to his people. But something was wrong. It was in the air. We could breathe it. The babies could feel it. The babies' instincts were better than their parents'. Their instincts had not yet been replaced by doctors.

Doctors? What do you mean?

No, no, not doctors. She waved her hands to erase what she'd just said. I mean those things to believe in. Like religion.

Like religion? I don't understand. Oh, you mean doctrines?

Doctrines, yes, yes, doctrines. Like Dobermans. *Dobos torten.* Whatever. She put her hand to her mouth to stifle a giggle.

Dobos what?

Torten. Dobos torten.

What are those? Julia asked.

Hungarian cakes. She pursed her lips trying to compose herself. Lena Kohn was out of the woods once again.

There was so much Julia wanted to ask but didn't dare, her

questions held hostage by the flagrancy of Lena's answers.

Julia was familiar with many of the gruesome details of Lena's past. She had read accounts, seen photographs and films, the historical documentation. But because of Lena, facts now sprang from their historical and abstract contexts and translated themselves into the vivid experience of a friend who also happened to be a twin. Their backgrounds were different, but Lena and Lili had not suffered their fate only because they were Jewish, but because they were twins. This fact kept haunting Julia.

On a few occasions, Julia dared to delve a little further than she should have, especially on days when Lena was in one of her chattier moods: There's one thing I am curious about, Lena. About your sister, Julia said, trying to sound casual. But I wouldn't want to bring back painful memories.

Oh, they come back anyway. The ones to forget are the ones to never go away.

You said that you and Lili were identical.

Yes. So were you and your twin, weren't you?

Yes, we looked exactly alike. But we were also different in many ways. It's those differences I cherish the most. But I used to fear them too.

Lena nodded. Only mama and papa, my brother and sister could tell us apart. And later, Uncle Pepi. But only because of what he did. She pointed to her cloudy eye. Because of what he did to my sister. He destroyed both her eyes. We each had a brown and a blue eye but they were... She crossed her wrists into an X.

Cross-eyed?

She giggled. No. My sister's left eye was brown and her right eye was blue. But with me it was the other way around.

Oh, the colours were reversed.

Yes. My brown eye used to be browner. It was not damaged like now, she added.

There was no need to ask how Lena's or her sister's eyes had been destroyed. In any case, Lena would tell Julia if or when she was ready to. My sister and I shared a similar thing, Julia said. Except it wasn't as obvious as the eyes. Everyone thought I was right-handed and she was left-handed, although I discovered later that I was ambidextrous.

What does this mean?

Ambidextrous? I can write or handle things with either my right or left hand. I think my sister might have been able to do the same, but she never tried it. By the time I realized I could do this, she was gone. I've read this is common with identical twins. It's called reversed physical characteristics.

Like my eyes and Lili's?

Yes. I once read that some left-handed people might have been part of an early set of embryonic twins even if there was only one baby at birth. The lost twin syndrome. A twin disappears in the womb, absorbed by the other twin. But I think it happens in life too.

How? What do you mean?

I think one twin can absorb the other. Be absorbed by the other.

I don't understand this.

I can't explain it, Lena. To tell you the truth I'm not even sure what I mean. I once read that it's possible for a twin to stop growing inside the womb in order to save the other twin if it becomes impossible for both to survive. One will be sacrificed for the other. Maybe it happens in life too. Maybe this is how true love begins.

Lena shook her head. It is nature. Biology. It has nothing to do with love.

Biology has everything to do with love, Lena.

This is too complicated to think about. Mama said our lives would be different, my sister's and mine. That our lives might be different from hers but also from each other. But those are not the words she used.

What words did she use? Do you remember?

A story. She liked to explain things with stories. There was one story about why we were twins and why we wouldn't always want the same things. Mama said we had different destinies. One was to open doors and the other was to close them.

I don't understand.

We didn't always listen to Mama's stories very carefully, but after Lili died I remembered this one about twins who looked so much alike people could only tell them apart by the way they touched doors. One twin opened doors by touching them with her right hand while the other twin closed them by touching them with her left. Mama said every door carries a two-way fate and only twins know about them because they have a special gift.

What kind of fate?

Those qualities that people have. You know, like too much humility or too much pride. These are dangerous, mama warned us, but twins can help each other open and close those doors so there is not too much humility or too much pride. Never too much laughter or tears.

Which one are you? Julia asked. Which one was I? she wondered.

Oh, who knows. It's only a story, Julia. Lena dismissed what she had just told Julia with a shrug and a wave of her hand.

It's a beautiful story. Let's pretend it's possible.

If it be possible, then Lili's destiny was to close doors. She was not a dreamer like me. Not so gully... How do you say this word that sounds like a bird, a gull?

Gully? Oh, gullible.

Yes, she was not so gullible. She knew how to shut doors when the time came. When the sadness was too much to bear. Then she closed the door. Lena made a loud clapping sound with both hands.

What about your door, did it ever open?

Yes.

Onto what? Julia asked between breaths, part of her wanting to hear more while another part wanted to veer the conversation in a different direction. Why was she pursuing this?

Evil, Lena declared, emphasizing the two syllables. My door opened on a world of evil and Lili and I woke up from the dream we were living with mama and papa.

Where was this dream you were living before the door opened?

On a farm in northern Hungary. It was called Transylvania then. Our house had no electricity or running water and we worked hard, but it didn't matter because we didn't know about electricity and running water and we thought hard work was normal. There wasn't time to think about anything else. We were together, mama, papa, Lili and me, my little brother and sister. The vegetable garden was big enough to feed an army. It probably did after we left. There was a flower garden and a fruit garden with trees. Every year, mama made jars of jellies and jams that sparkled red, blue, and purple on the shelves. Stewed tomatoes and pickles. We complained about having to do this every year, all the peeling and the chopping and the boiling. It took hours. Days. But we must have been happy because we never thought we weren't. We never thought about it because we were too busy picking vegetables and fruits and milking cows. We made our own cheese. You never tasted such cheese. And Papa and the rabbi butchered a few animals every year.

Lena suddenly stopped walking. She had been transported to a world when life made sense. Where nothing existed beyond gardens and orchards, beyond family and farm animals. In a barely audible voice she added, God was good then.

Yes, Julia wanted to say. Confined within the borders of a farm or a village, God is usually good. Instead, she asked, Did you and Lili go to school?

We were no longer in school when we left, but my little brother and sister were. Everyone in the village went to the same school— Jewish, a few Catholics, and other non-Jewish people. No one thought anything about it. The village was made up of different people. We thought this was how it was everywhere. We didn't know the rest of the world wasn't like us.

A rude awakening, Julia thought. The inward glow of a secluded farm oblivious to the darkness surrounding it. The inward glow of Wildwood Park.

Lena went on talking in no particular order of events before and after the intrusion, as she referred to their deportation. She talked of what she missed most about the farm after they left, especially when she got hungry in the camps—the glistening jars of jams and jellies, stewed tomatoes, and pickles.

Do you know what happened to the farm? Julia asked.

Lena shrugged. Probably a collective after the Communists came. Like all the other farms.

Where did you go after the camps?

The Americans sent us to other camps to get better. I thought I was lucky at first, but it was Lili who was lucky.

Why?

She died. I read later that more than three thousand twins went to the camps and only one hundred and forty survived. I was surprised.

That so few survived?

No. That there were only three thousand twins. I thought there were more. So many were disappearing every day.

Three thousand people is a large number to a child.

Lena nodded and shrugged. Yes, more people than in my village.

Numbers hardly mattered to Lena now. In concentration camps, comparatives were as irrelevant as the different levels of cruelty that took place there.

But you survived, Julia offered and realized how callous it sounded as soon as she'd said it.

Oh, Julia, Lena said, followed by a word Julia didn't understand.

I beg your pardon?

Csirkesazr, Lena repeated.

What does this mean?

Chicken shit.

What's chicken shit?

What you said. I survived. It's crap. Chicken shit.

It was always strange to hear Lena use this kind of language in her Eastern European accent. But why? Julia asked.

I don't know how many times I hear this. You survived. You are a survivor. Crap, crap, crap. Being a survivor means it is over. For me, it is never over. I survived and for what? To wait for another salvation like a good girl? I am not a survivor, I am a left-over.

You shouldn't say that.

Oh, what do you know? You don't know. This is what it feels like. All my life, to feel like a left-over.

Lena spoke with the resignation of a person who has nothing left to lose, a shrunken heart abandoned to itself. It struck Julia then how utterly alone Lena was in her knowledge, in spite of visits from family and friends. Her fate had created an impenetrable distance between herself and the rest of the world. Yes, Lena had survived, yet life was not sufficient compensation for what she and her sister had witnessed.

Foolishly, mainly because there was so little for Julia to add, or perhaps to absolve herself for having nothing more to say, she asked, Is there any place for forgiveness in all of this, Lena? Can you ever forgive?

Lena looked at Julia in disbelief. What forgiveness? To forgive who?

I don't know. The people who did those things to you and your sister. If only for yourself.

For what? To make me feel better?

I don't know, maybe it would help heal...

Heal? Forgiveness to set me free? You don't know what you're talking about, Julia.

I just thought...

This is not some feel good schmancy television show. Forgiveness is useless when what happened can't be fixed. How to forgive evil? Do you think Uncle Pepi asked for forgiveness when he ran like a coward to South America? He went to confession maybe, got down on his knees and asked God to forgive him? *Csirkeszar*, she repeated once again.

Lena was right, of course, Julia didn't know what she was talking about. And Lena certainly had every right to be angry. The air was particularly cheerful and chatty with birdsong and Julia wondered if there had been birds singing around the camps. What happened to the choir of sparrows at dusk if they landed on one of the electrified fences?

194

Sensing Julia's uneasiness, in a voice spuriously light-hearted in her effort to change the mood, Lena asked, Did you know what they called the place where the victims' suitcases and belongings were left before they were exterminated?

No, Julia said. It was astounding how easily such words as exterminated could be spoken.

Canada, Lena said.

Canada? Why?

The mountain of suitcases left behind was a gold mine, she said. Those who were lucky enough to search the suitcases and packages always found something in them to help them survive a little longer. Food or valuables to exchange for food.

Why Canada over any other place?

Some people heard about gold mines in Canada, a land of hope and freedom. Some even called Canada the new land of milk and honey and dreamed of coming here.

Was Canada finally a land of hope and freedom for you, Lena? Julia asked, the question incongruous, silly, even.

To hope, for my children and grandchildren, maybe. But this can never be taken for granted. Never. When I came here, to this place of real gold mines, I heard things. Jewish children refugees turned away. Nine or ten thousand of them. They could have been saved. She hesitated before adding, But they weren't. What hope is there in this?

~30~

OF COURSE NOT, FREDERICK, FATHER IS SAYING TO THE DIRECTOR of Immigration. You can't let too many in if they don't know how to farm or mine.

There have been reports in the local newspapers, not only of the rising popularity of Hitler in Germany but of what is happening here in Toronto: LEAGUE FOR THE DEFENCE OF JEWISH RIGHTS THINKS CITY WILL BE REPORTED ABROAD AS CENTRE OF HITLER-ISM, the headline instigated by events in the Beaches where Sissa and Wilson live. Sissa said they were barely aware of the confrontations or what they were about although the Jews were known to litter. She hadn't seen it herself, but that's what she'd heard.

As for those of us living in Wildwood, the newspaper reports might have been taking place in a foreign country or on another planet. We don't know any Jewish people, except for the owner of a chaotic hardware store just outside Wildwood Park. I did ask myself why everyone referred to him as the Jewish hardware store owner when other proprietors in the neighbourhood were never identified by race, religion, or country of origin. Well, except for the Italian grocer directly across the street from the Jewish hardware store.

At first, the confrontations in the Beaches seem to be the high-jinxed escapades between one gang who wears sweatshirts stamped with swastikas and another gang who wears shirts bearing maple leaves. Until articles in the two major newspapers, The Evening Telegram *and* The Globe *make it clear that the Swastika Club has been organized for the main purpose of driving away "aliens" and "obnoxious visitors," euphemisms for members of the Hebrew faith. According to the "Swasis" it is time to let aliens know they* can no longer ignore the rights of long-established citizens living in the area. It is the Swasis' right to say so. SWASTIKA BEACH CAMPAIGN WITHIN THE LAW.

The mayor urges Jewish citizens to remain calm and not make trouble. The most effective response to outbursts of anti-Semitism is to avoid provocation, he warns. It is best to place one's faith in the power of the deeply-rooted British traditions of the country, he is quoted as telling the crowd who breaks into song: White Canada Forever.

Ah! mother exclaims, pointing an accusing finger to the offensive article. They are hiding behind British traditions again.

Except for a comment in passing now and then, no one in the neighbourhood gives the clashes at Kew Beach much thought. At the university where concepts of free speech and equal rights are right-minded ideas wearing their own lustrous halos, there is talk of organizing demonstrations to support the Jews, but nothing comes of it.

One evening, as I relate my scepticism of anyone seriously wanting to help to Andersen Biggs he grows exasperated with me. His exasperation is not new. He has tried to convince me to marry him for a few years now and, not having succeeded, I suspect he's trying to find a way out, a reason to end our relationship, which we both know has lasted far too long.

Don't tell me you like Jews? he bluntly asks.

The vehemence of his question takes me aback and I can't think of anything to reply except, Well, I don't know, Andersen. I don't know any Jews.

It is the wrong answer.

IT TOOK SO LONG TO LEARN THE RIGHT ANSWER TO A WRONG question, Julia thought as she lay in bed, reluctant to get up. Each wrong answer bringing with it its own dulling of conscience.

There were too many mornings now when her body was but a blueprint of aches and pains. She had never planned to get this old. It wasn't so long ago when old age was but a concept, an undesirable condition from which she intended to exempt herself if only through sheer will. Now she was one of them, an old woman, her past eclipsed by those with a future.

At the bakery a few days before, while paying for cookies she bought for her visit with Thea and Charlie, she had confused those new one- and two-dollar coins. It took several seconds to figure out the right amount and she could hear a woman behind her sighing and fidgeting until she finally complained that there should be a special line for the old. Her words paralyzed Julia for a second, but only for a second. She spun around. The woman was barely in her thirties, but old enough to know better.

And there should be a special line for despicable loud-mouths like you, Julia told her. Thankfully, a few people in the line applauded and Julia felt justified.

The truth was as clear as the wrinkles on Julia's face. She would have to face the fact that she could not go out on her own anymore. It wasn't the first time she'd had trouble with money and a series of other embarrassing incidents. A month ago, when she was still able to get to the library on her own, she had noticed people doing double-takes as they walked by her, until she realized she was wearing her linen jacket inside out. Pockets and labels flapping for the world to see. When she stopped to take it off, a young woman offered to help, which made Julia feel even more demeaned.

You're unusually quiet today, Daniel remarked when he dropped by Julia's suite for their tea.

I'm feeling a little under the weather today. Would you mind making the tea, Daniel?

No, of course not. He worried about her. She hadn't been her usual cheerful self lately. Everything alright?

I think Lena might be transferred. Her confusion is getting worse.

What is she doing now?

She's collecting pieces of crayons. She goes around asking people if they have left-over crayon stubs she can have. When they tell her they haven't, she tells them to ask the children or to look in the children's pockets. I hear she's also tearing sheets of paper off the nurses' clipboards if she gets the chance.

What for? What does she do with them?

She draws on them with the crayons. Childish pictures of houses and farms. Animals.

It sounds like it might be better if she were transferred. She probably shouldn't have come here in the first place. A little too far gone already.

But she can be so clear minded at times. What harm is there in collecting pieces of crayons?

I'm sure the doctors know what's best for her. Whatever happens, I'm sure she'll be in good hands. Daniel was trying to put a positive spin on a hopeless situation for Julia's sake.

This morning at breakfast she confused me with her sister. She kept calling me Lili.

We'll go and see her as often as you want, he said as he opened the refrigerator door to retrieve milk for the tea. I think something might have died in your fridge, he said as he took out a bowl with the purplish brown concoction.

Sunday's lunch, would you believe?

It looks pretty nasty, he said wrinkling up his nose. Should I throw it out?

Yes. Surprisingly it didn't taste as bad as it looks. Julia tried to suppress a cough she'd been struggling with for a few days.

Is that chest cold of yours still hanging on?

A little. She then told Daniel about the incident at the bakery, how it had rattled her. You usually don't let incidents like this bother you, he said.

The less strength I have, the less indignation I seem able to muster to push me forward, she said.

He placed a hand on her forehead. When was the last time you saw Doctor Wyman?

I can't remember. I forget my appointments.

He shook his head. Yeah, on purpose. You're impossible. He has office hours tomorrow. I'll take you there myself.

I know I shouldn't let people get the best of me. I finally faced up to being old in here. I can hold my own in here. Out there I feel vulnerable.

This is why we are in here, Julia, because we are vulnerable out there. I thought you had this figured out. I overheard you lecturing someone specifically along those lines just a few weeks ago.

It's easier to recognize in others what you can't change in yourself.

Spoken like a true philosopher, he said.

Haven't been a true philosopher for some time now.

Who was your favourite?

She suspected he was trying to get her mind off what had happened at the bakery or her cough. Oh, I don't know. I'm on to you.

What do you mean?

You're trying to distract me.

Maybe. But I'm also curious. Did you have a favourite?

I don't remember. It was too long ago.

When you were studying, you must have preferred one or two over the others.

I preferred philosophers who thought happiness should be the main purpose in life. They were more benevolent than those who were always aiming for something higher. They were usually motivated by power or cruelty. But in the end, I became disillusioned with the lot of them.

Was this why you gave up teaching?

Partly. A professor professes to tell the truth, but so many of the so-called truths I was teaching weren't mine and I was beginning to doubt their veracity. I also wanted to look after Rachel. We were being hit by so many tragedies and I needed to reconsider how I was going to live my life. Refocus, Thea would call it.

About the time your sister died?

Yes.

It must have been hard, losing a twin sister.

It was.

Did your sister study philosophy too? Daniel asked.

What?

Your sister, did she study philosophy?

No. She started teachers' college, but she quit after a few months to get married.

Didn't you say she had taken a few philosophy courses?

Did I? She might have. It was a long time ago.

Did you know that the philosophy department is now housed in a dingy administration building on Huron Street?

Julia wondered why he would know this, what he was driving at. Yes, she said, I have always suspected that philosophers thrive better in inelegant surroundings.

Daniel gave out a loud laugh and shook his head. Oh, Julia, you are one wonderful old bird. He then looked away and said nothing for a few seconds.

You seem uncomfortable, Daniel.

It's nothing. Just wondering.

About what?

Your sister's name. You said it was Jane? Jane Crane?

What was he getting at? Yes.

And she quit school to get married? But you went on with your studies in philosophy?

Something was wrong. He sounded different, his tone calculated, as if he might be trying to sound casual. Why all these questions, Daniel?

Just curious. He reached for a biscuit but didn't look up.

I don't like this, Daniel. My relationship with my sister is none of your business.

Why would a few questions bother you so? I just want to know more about the woman I've been spending most of my time with this last year.

But it's my sister you're asking about. It's rather strange to be curious about whether my sister took courses in philosophy. You know the old saying: Familiarity breeds contempt. Julia knew she sounded ridiculous, spouting off old clichés to avoid giving Daniel straight answers.

Contempt is the last thing I want from you, Julia. I assumed we were friends.

Familiarity has never advanced the cause of friendship, Julia said. It's best to keep a little distance.

I see. Even after so many months? So many afternoons spent together?

Especially after so many months and afternoons. You are taking liberties.

If that's how you see it, we'll maintain a distance then. But since you're so fond of maxims, I have one of my own: To find a friend, you must close one eye, but to keep her, you might have to close both. Something like that. He waved his tea-soaked biscuit in the air and a piece fell to the floor.

The jig was up. He knew about her. You've been roaming the university archives again, haven't you? Julia asked.

Yes.

Digging into my past.

Yes, but...

It's contemptible. You once told me I could trust you.

You can trust me. I didn't do this recently, Julia. It was several months ago, shortly after I moved in. I saw you and asked about you. Everyone described you as this smart old broad...

Oh, stop referring to me as an old broad. Or an old bird. I've already heard too many references to my age recently.

Sorry. Everyone said you were an intelligent woman who still read a lot and took an interest in things. Then I heard you play the piano. And I heard you had taught at the university and I was excited about all this. You must admit it's a little depressing when you first move in here. Realizing that most of the people here have left their interests behind. You were different. Someone said you were feisty.

Who did?

Never mind.

Dogs are feisty, not old broads.

Sorry. You see, I missed these qualities in my wife and....

I am not a replacement for your wife, Daniel.

I know, Julia. I was looking for someone with whom I could talk, that's all. I couldn't bear listening to any more war stories or about Dominick Ridley's haemorrhoids. I swear the man's got his head stuck up his ass. I'm not the easiest person to talk to. People think I'm weird because I taught mathematics and physics.

Julia was reminded of the mathematician joke. Ah, you don't know the half of it, she said.

Oh, I heard about it, what you said. It made me laugh. Made me want to know more about you. It had been a long time since I felt curious enough to want to learn about someone beside myself. Between you and me, I was getting a little bored doing mathematics all day.

How flattering, a replacement for mathematics.

You know what I mean.

So, you went snooping. What did you discover? Julia could feel herself shivering and she could hardly control her voice. Her past was about to catch up with her, take over the present.

Don't be angry.

Stop stalling. What did you discover?

He fidgeted with his cup, was about to get up but sat down again. Well, I didn't find a Julia Brannon anywhere. Or a Julia Crane. Either as a philosophy student or a lecturer.

Maybe I changed my name. It's been known to happen.

You told me once your sister's name was Jane and your maiden name was Crane. A Jane Crane did graduate in philosophy and subsequently obtained a graduate degree in Philosophy and Literature. She also lectured at University College.

Strangely, the anger and apprehension of a few moments ago began to dissipate and a wave of relief washed over Julia. You were very thorough, Daniel, she said. Funny, I always assumed it would be Thea who would discover this little secret of mine.

So it is a secret? You never studied philosophy?

Of course I did. I studied philosophy and literature. And I lectured at University College.

Then what's the story here?

Julia didn't know if the pressure in her chest was due to her cold or to what she was about to reveal to Daniel. She took two or three deep breaths. I'm amazed I got away with it for so long, she said. Especially after I moved here and started to talk so openly about having studied philosophy. I hadn't done so before then, you know. Never. But once I settled in, I wanted to live the time I had left as myself. So I started to tell the truth about studying philosophy and teaching at University College. Rachel heard about it. The doctors and nurses told her that my interest in philosophy and literature had a very positive effect and kept me sharp and all that nonsense. At first she assumed it was a mistake, then she wondered if I wasn't becoming disoriented, confusing myself with her Aunt Jane who had studied philosophy and taught at University College. I think she began to entertain the idea that I was truly getting senile.

Daniel was staring at Julia as if an alien had landed in the room. Jesus Christ, what are you saying?

Julia continued. When Rachel first broached the subject, I dismissed it. Made up some story that I had also taken courses in philosophy. She and Thea must have discussed it because Thea was suddenly showing great interest in my twin sister. She wanted to know more about the two of us. She thought if I wrote about it I'd be able to sort it out. Or she and Rachel would.

I'm confused. Is your name Julia?

Well, it has been for more than fifty years. I have lived longer as Julia than I did as Jane. Oh my, this is strange. My name used to be Jane. I was Jane Crane until my sister killed herself. I then took on her name, her identity, if you will. Julia Brannon was my sister. She's the one who married Wilson Brannon.

Holy Christ! You've pretended to be Julia Brannon all these years? You were never married to the Brannon lawyer?

I don't know if you would call it pretending. My sister might as well have killed me too that day.

But why? Why would you do such a thing?

It was spontaneous, really. There wasn't time to think it through, not at first. It happened on the spur of the moment. Who knows, I might have been in a state of shock. Later, when I let myself think about it and I began asking myself why, I realized I might have felt responsible for her death.

But why would you?

From the moment I saw her lying there I wanted it to be me. What could I do to take her place? What could I have done to prevent this? Why hadn't I guessed beforehand? There must have been warnings, clear signs, I kept telling myself. How could my intuition have failed me to such an extent? I knew she was depressed, despondent, but I assumed she would recover. I would see to it that she recovered. We were the Crane girls, determined and obstinate, both of us. We always carried on regardless. Plus Rachel kept calling me mother. It was the strangest thing. Almost immediately after they moved in with me, after Julia learned of her sons' deaths, Rachel started to call me mother. She intuitively knew who to turn to when her mother couldn't take care of her. It all came back to me when I wrote about it a few days ago. I could see it all as clearly as if it had happened yesterday. Only clearer.

So let me get this straight, Daniel was saying for the third or fourth time. You're not Julia Brannon.

Not originally, no. Julia Brannon was my sister. She killed herself. How strange it was to hear herself admitting this after all these years.

You're Jane Crane?

I was Jane Crane, yes.

Jesus Christ, how did you pull this off? There was stunned disbelief in his voice but not the disapproval Julia had expected, for which she was grateful.

It was easier than you might think. Quite easy, in fact. I imagined I was Julia. I imagined that Rachel was my daughter. And the first thing I knew, I was Julia and Rachel was my daughter. Part of who we are is how we are seen and everyone had always confused my sister and me. We shared everything, looks, mannerisms. Except she was left-handed. After her death I started to write with my left hand and discovered, to my amazement, that I was ambidextrous.

You sound so matter-of-fact about this, as if it were normal, Daniel said.

It isn't as if it happened yesterday, Daniel. I have lived with this for a long time. Oh, I wept bitterly at first. For having lost Julia, but also for myself. Until one day, I decided it was time to move on. I packed everything from my previous life and stored it away in the attic. Like I did before moving in here. The rest was easy, much easier than I had anticipated. There wasn't any need for me to be as assertive anymore. I no longer needed to win every point because there was nothing left to prove. I devoted much of my time to Rachel. We travelled a great deal, an excuse not to see the people I had known, or the people Julia had known. The married couples Julia and Wilson associated with hadn't kept in touch with Julia after Wilson died. Married couples don't have much to do with widows. Some people did try to contact Julia after word got out that Thomas and William had been killed and that one of the Crane girls had committed suicide, but it was mainly out of curiosity. When I didn't return calls or didn't show up for dinners and parties that Julia was invited to they assumed she had gone a little eccentric due to everything she'd gone through. Even the best of friends will desist in times of crisis.

Not all friends, Julia. I don't believe that.

Most, although I might have been to blame. I also discovered something else, something astonishing, really. I'd gone into philosophy to discover who I was, who I could be without my sister. But philosophy and academic life create their own social requirements, which didn't get me any closer to who I was, not really. Ironically, I came closer to this by becoming my sister.

This is the damnedest thing I have ever heard. What about Rachel? You never told her?

No, I never did.

She never figured it out?

She would sometimes look at photographs of me and my sister, stare at them for the longest time and after a while she'd say, I can't tell the two of you apart, either one of you could be my mother. Thea has said the same thing. Either one of you could have been my grandmother.

But why would you do this, for Christ's sake. Why?

Oh, I don't know, Daniel. As I've said, I did it without thinking. For my sister. I wanted to give Julia her life back, any life, and it was the only one I had. But mostly I did it for Rachel. How could I let this little girl go through life wondering why her mother had abandoned her like this? A child wouldn't understand. She wouldn't know how crazed a mother can become at losing two sons. She would assume that her brothers meant more to her mother than she did. What would this do to a child? Or she might have thought she had done something to drive her mother to kill herself. Children do this. Their fragile and self-centred egos assume they are to blame for all sorts of things—divorce, drink, suicide, abuse. She might have understood eventually that it isn't so, but I couldn't take the chance, not at the beginning. Then it just grew into this secret I had to protect because of the bond it had created between me and Rachel. After a while, I almost never thought about it. It just was.

Someone must have suspected.

I don't think so. Wildwood is a small world of its own. It turned out to be the perfect hideout. Rachel and I were safe there. I've always marvelled at how easily children can enter fictional spaces as if they were real, like those drawings on the wall over there. My pretence also became real. I was Julia. Rachel was my daughter. The world was restored to me simply through a different name.

What about your work, didn't you miss it?

To tell you the truth, I was fed up with teaching. When so much happens to you, once you have lost so much, the need for philosophy is not as urgent as when you have everything. My sister once said that knowledge wasn't always of great use to men of knowledge. I mulled this over for a long time until I realized how many people I worked with only related to others through their narrow perspectives, which became utterly useless to me.

Your sister must have been in a desperate state to have done such a thing. Leave her daughter like that.

So much had been taken from her. She knew I would take care of Rachel. As it turned out she was a wonderful little companion, ready to follow me everywhere.

What did you do for money, if you don't mind my asking?

Financially, I was very fortunate. The house in Wildwood was paid for by the time my parents died. There was Wilson's insurance. The law firm wasn't worth much but I was able to sell what was left of it. Wilson and Sissa's house in Balmy Beach. But it was my grandparents' summer house in Hayground Cove that made the difference. It had been left to my mother and although it had fallen into disrepair she could never bring herself to sell it. It wasn't worth anything, but the acreage around it was. The Hamptons were replacing the Riviera as the international playground of the rich and climbing. The sale provided me with a tidy sum. I guess there are situations where family tradition comes in handy after all. Julia marvelled at how easily she was able to look back and laugh, how comfortable she felt talking about this to Daniel. She felt closer to him because of it.

Christ, he said, What do I call you now?

Julia. Just as everyone calls you Daniel Browne.

I guess we're just a couple of old fakes you and I, he said, shaking his head.

Fakes who are true to themselves, Julia said.

Are you going to say anything about this to your daughter? he asked.

I don't know. As I said, I've been writing about it, intending to give what I've written to either Rachel or Thea. In case it did matter, but it hardly seems to anymore.

It does matter. Your daughter should know what you did for her.

Oh, I did it mostly for myself, Daniel.

It's hard to believe she never suspected anything.

Sometimes I think she does suspect but doesn't bring it up—to protect me as much as I tried to protect her. Sharing secrets, especially unspoken ones, is perhaps what deep attachments are made of.

This is different, Julia.

We'll see. What about you? If you suspected something for several months, why did you wait until now to bring it up?

He pondered this for a few seconds. I couldn't be sure, of course. I kept going back and forth. You had either gone to university using another name for some reason, or you were pretending to have gone. After a while, it didn't matter. I liked you either way. It's like you said, unspoken secrets are what attachments are made of. Plus I didn't want to upset you, for the same reasons Rachel wouldn't want to either.

Why now?

Well, I'm not sure. I was still curious, of course. I wanted to… he hesitated for a moment as if he were about to add something then decided against it.

You wanted to be sure before it's too late?

It's never too late to decide who you'll be, he chuckled.

The irony is I have been rather happy as my sister. I reconnected to something I'd lost. Not so much because of the life she lead, it was pretty ordinary, but in having to duplicate it so carefully. I became more mindful of her life than I'd been of my own.

It doesn't make sense, giving up your life like that.

I'd already lived that life. For more than forty years I lived my first life, then I had a second one. I've spent the last few years reconciling the two.

This is extraordinary. Your daughter and granddaughter should know about this.

Perhaps I'll tell them soon, Julia repeated.

Yes, she would tell them soon, Julia thought. Thea was right, there was hope in a life's story even if it wasn't always entirely one's own. It was the reason Julia went to the lounge several afternoons a week. In an environment where death whirred under a thin membrane of a few remaining weeks or months, people wanted to remember. The essence of memory resided primarily in gathering facts that had scattered over the years and organizing them into a story, each fact an element, an atom consisting of a small nucleus that grew into various tales, sometimes tall, sometimes complex, sometimes simple. It was in this that bonds were formed and new attachments were made. As long as someone listened and remembered, a person's life stabilized into clarity. As Thea had once said, new connections were made.

I would like you to do me a favour, Daniel, Julia said.

Of course, anything you want.

I would like Rachel and Thea to have what I've written, but only after I've gone. If I'm transferred, would you retrieve the laptop and keep it until everything's over? You can give it to them then.

Sure. If I outlive you, which I probably won't. I don't see why you wouldn't want them to know before though.

I don't want to have to deal with their endless questions and explanations, only what's on the computer. I've thought it all out, this is what I'm leaving them. My house, what's left of my money, and my story, the way I want to tell it. It's enough.

They sat in silence for a while, until Daniel nodded toward Thomas and William's crayon drawings. So your boys made those?

My sister's boys, Julia reminded him.

Right, your sister's. He smiled, his first relaxed smile of the afternoon. It's going to take some getting used to, he said.

There's no need to, Julia said.

He stared at the two framed drawings, each one different in its childish execution, each one of a house exploring a different perspective, each one strengthening the other.

Those stars they drew in the sky, did you know they were Stars of David? he asked.

Oh, so they are, Julia said. I never thought of them as Stars of

David, I just assumed they were easier to draw than five-pointed stars.

They would be. They're perfect hexagrams. One triangle pointing up, the other pointing down. Do you know what the symbol meant, originally?

No, I don't.

The reconciliation of opposites. There are excavations of ruins in ancient Israel dating back to pre-medieval times where walls are inscribed with hexagrams alongside swastikas. Ironic, isn't it?

Julia nodded to the drawings. I simply thought of those stars as superimposed triangles perfectly executed by my nephews.

Daniel laughed. You would. You know, I've been one lucky bastard, he said.

In what way? Julia asked.

I've had the fortune of hooking up with the most amazing women, he said as he reached across the table. He took Julia's hands in his and brought them to his mouth. For a split second she was sure she had felt his lips brushing against her numbed and wrinkled hands. For a split second, her senses were restored.

~32~

SISSA HAS NOT BEEN TO THE HOUSE IN MORE THAN TWO YEARS AND *my first reaction is amazement when I see her running toward the house with two unopened envelopes fluttering like trapped birds in her hands. You have to open these, she shouts as she bursts into the house. Oh, God. Oh, God, she keeps screaming between sobs.*

Surely, these are not the infamous telegrams that everyone has been talking about. Thomas and William are barely eighteen years old. No one would send them on a dangerous mission at eighteen. And why are there two envelopes? The Navy wouldn't put them on the same boat. Surely not both of them. But then why wouldn't they? William and Thomas would never agree to being separated. I seize both envelopes from Sissa's hands and tear the first one open: Deeply regret OS Brannon, W. missing at sea as a result of the sinking of HMCS Athabaskan in the English Channel. Letter follows.

I keep my eyes on the telegrams so I won't have to face Sissa. My hands shake uncontrollably as I tear open the second envelope: Deeply regret OS Brannon, T. missing at sea as a result of the sinking of HMCS Athabaskan in the English Channel. Letter follows.

OS. They couldn't take the time or space to write out their rank of Ordinary Seamen. Untrained boys too young to know better. W. and T. They couldn't even write out their full names.

For the next few months, Sissa can hardly care for herself let alone Rachel. I insist that she stay with me. In spite of my own grief, this will be an opportunity to right everything that went wrong between us. I will keep the rest of the world at bay. I will comfort her when she awakens from vigilant nightmares where Thomas and William's cradles give way to a liquid gravity that fills their eyes, mouths, lungs with water so briny it sears away all flesh and turns them into skeletons. In time, we will somehow work our way through this and rebuild our lives together, I will see to it.

Days, weeks go by when Sissa hardly gets out of bed. When, finally and gradually, she begins staying up for longer periods, a quiet compliance settles over her, a silent grace. Everyone who drops by marvels at how well she is coping. It is because of Rachel, they whisper. Rachel will save her.

I agree. It was her children who gave her the strength to cope with Wilson's death, and now her little daughter will do so again.

What about you? they ask. Are you getting enough rest? You're looking awfully tired. And thin. Shouldn't you be eating more?

I'm fine. We'll both be fine, I assure everyone.

The truth is I worry about Sissa. Her marriage had vindicated her as a woman. Her children had proved right her choice of not going on to teachers' college. She believed she had found in Wilson and in her children the love everyone craves for.

Now, the lenses through which her life filtered were being removed one by one. Father. Mother. Wilson. Her two sons.

The news of William and Thomas's disappearance at sea magnified a hundredfold the pain of losing her husband. Not only losing him from a heart attack but what followed after he died. The discovery of our letters, Wilson's and mine. Why had I not destroyed his letters instead of returning them to him? Was it reluctance to destroy the triumph of my rejection? Why had he stored them away in his desk for so many years? Was it an unwillingness to give in to defeat?

So it was you he loved all along, Sissa said when I found her sitting on the floor of his office, the letters scattered around her. She had been to his office to retrieve his things, found the letters filed away and read every one of them.

Sissa, I said and rushed to her, but she pushed me away.

Her face was so completely rearranged by what she was feeling that I hardly recognized her. He told me, you know. He told me it was you he loved, she said. A few years after we were married.

When he made love to me, he pretended he was making love to you. But it hardly mattered, I'm the one who got him, it was me he married, not you.

I didn't love him, Sissa.

It doesn't matter whether you loved him or not. He loved you and I kept him away from you.

After this, I didn't see Sissa for two years.

After the telegrams, sensing her mother's preoccupation and grief, relying on her instinct to bond with someone on whom she can count, Rachel spends every second of her waking hours with me. She follows me around as if she were tied to me, and although she goes to sleep in her own bed at night, I find her nestled beside me in the morning. Gradually, she begins confusing me with her mother and referring to Sissa, to my sister, Julia, as Auntie Jane. These are the only occasions, since the telegrams, that Sissa smiles, a sad, wry grin that, in hindsight, should have alerted me. But then everything in hindsight seems a signal.

On that fateful morning, I decide to go out in Julia's station wagon for groceries and to run errands that I've I neglected since the world came to a standstill. She has left an old sweater she often wears on the newel post and I grab it as Rachel and I rush out the door. A few neighbours I meet smile at Rachel, stop to chat. How sorry they are to hear about the dreadful events. Their eyes search the ground in order to avoid mine, then look deeply into mine, an indication of their sincerity as they tell me how delighted they are to see I am recovering and doing so well. I realize then, probably because of Rachel, the station wagon, and the sweater, that they think I am Sissa. For some reason, I go along with it. It's too much to explain, plus I don't feel like speaking to anyone. It is Sissa I want to be talking to as when we were girls, as when before everything changed. As I drive back to the house I begin to feel I might be able to laugh again and can hardly wait to share this prank with Sissa. They thought I was you, Julia, I'll say, and we'll both fall on the bed laughing like we used to.

All is quiet when I enter the house and I assume she is sleeping. I don't call her name right away. It is a beautiful day and I will insist she get up so the three of us can eat lunch on the porch or in the garden. It is a little cool, but I will wrap her with her sweater and my body warmth.

I open a tin of the tomato soup that she likes to eat with a dab of sour cream floating on top. I make a few cucumber sandwiches. When the soup is ready, I call her. No answer. As I make my way up the stairs, I call her again. Sissa? Are you up there? Rachel follows me, calling: Get up, Auntie Jane, get up sleepy head.

Her bed is empty and there is no one in the bedroom. I check the bathroom and when I turn, I see the attic door ajar at the top of the narrow stairs. There is a note pinned to the door. Sissa, are you up there? I shout. Are you up there, Auntie Jane? Rachel echoes behind me.

I climb the narrow stairs and unpin the note while pushing open the attic door. I glance at the note: Do not let Rachel in, it says. Where is Auntie Jane? Rachel asks behind me. I know I must not scream. I know instantly what Julia has done.

Go back, Rachel, I tell her doing my utmost to stay calm. Go back down the stairs. I peer into the attic and I see my sister on the floor, a dark red halo around her head. I quickly shut the attic door and rush down to pick up Rachel, gently pushing her head against my neck as if to protect her from the scene she might imagine behind the door.

She senses my panic and searches my face to decipher what is going on. Mama? she says. Who is she referring to, I wonder? Is she asking where her mama is, what has happened to her, or is she confusing me with her mother as she has been doing for the last few weeks?

It's okay, Mama is here, Rachel. Mama will always be here for you.

Is this your sister? the policeman asks.
Yes.
Her name?

Sissa.

I beg your pardon?

I hesitate, but only for a second. I think of Rachel calling me Mama. For the last few weeks she has called her own mother, Aunt Jane, and she has called me Mama. My sister's name is Jane, I tell the police officer. My name is Julia. The transition is so easy it doesn't feel as if I were lying at all. I am Julia Brannon.

You twins? he asks. You two look awfully alike.

Yes, we are twins, I reply.

Married? Husband? Children?

Who?

Your sister. Did she have a husband? Children?

No, I lie. She never married. She taught at the university. Philosophy.

You her only next-of-kin?

Yes, I'm her only next-of-kin. I'm about to add, except for her daughter, but I catch myself. Rachel is Julia's daughter and I am Julia now. I wonder how long it will be before I no longer need to catch myself. Before I am able to move freely within this emptiness. How long will it be before Jane Crane no longer exists and I become Julia Brannon?

I'll be darned, the policeman is saying. A Colt automatic. Anyone living here in the first war?

Yes, my father. He's dead.

Quite a few of 'em still around. The government smuggled thousands from the States during the Great War. This here's an officer's model. He turns the pistol around. A Slimline, beautiful, he whispers with admiration. He then points to the rifle lying beside the trunk.

And this here's a Mark III Ross. Damn things jammed so badly, they killed as many soldiers behind it as they did in front of it. He looks at me staring at him and remembers why he has been called to the house and he blushes.

I must reclaim her from this suicide, I keep telling myself. I request that her death be recorded as accidental. There is such stigma attached to this murder of the self, a crime if the attempt fails, an act of lunacy if it succeeds. Theories born out of superstition.

I'm afraid that's not possible ma'am, the policeman tells me. We have to enter the right cause of death on the certificate. It's the law. Any idea why she would have done this?

I can't bring myself to tell him about Thomas and William. Wilson. Our estrangement. There have been enough invasions. Enough death.

The officer senses my hesitation and assumes it is his duty to help me fill in the blanks. A love affair gone sour, maybe? A broken heart? That's what's usually at the bottom of these things.

I suppose you could call it that, I tell the officer.

Yup, that's usually the root of the problem, he answers. Love gone wrong.

Everyone at school is in a state of shock. It's beyond comprehension, one professor writes in a note of condolence. Jane Crane was always so confident, the last person who would do such a thing. You sound just like her, a voice says over the telephone.

A transposed murder, a man who drops by tells me. He teaches psychology and claims to have known Jane Crane, but I don't remember ever meeting him. Why would he maintain that he knew me? I wonder. Suicide is hostility turned from the real object of hatred on to the self, he says with authority. I am witnessing my own death.

Assuming the psychology professor is right, who was the object of Julia's hatred? Against whom did she wage this disguised act of war. Against Wilson? Myself? Against war itself?

At her funeral, I feel little. This is what irreparable loss is, the absence of feeling. The world as I once knew it is no longer there. I am no longer there. At the grave site, Rachel and I are suspended between earth and an abysmally high and clear blue sky. Holding on tightly to my hand, she keeps asking questions. Why is aunt Jane in a box? Why is she dead? Why does she want to rest in the ground? Won't she be cold there? Will she ever come back? The questions persisted for several months then stopped abruptly as if she too wanted to tuck away the past.

Oh, Sissa, will I ever learn to be you? How to be a mother. How to write with my left hand. How to love. There was a time when you and I shared a solitude until the world and its expectations intruded and took that solitude away. This is how it's going to be again, Sissa, only this time it will be between your daughter and me. We will live as a couple of solitary beings until the world intrudes and Rachel chooses a different path, as we did. But this time, I will not let a space grow and widen between us, a devil's playground, as mother used to call it.

LENA HAD BEEN TRANSFERRED AND JULIA WAS NOT FEELING STRONG enough, physically or mentally, to visit her. She sent Daniel instead, but Lena had not recognized him. She was locked inside some other place, confined to a windowless concentration camp of then. Nothing else existed for her now.

Julia had known her little more than a year, yet she couldn't stop thinking of her. There was so much more she needed to know about Lena and her sister. Had Lili stopped eating to save Lena? Had Julia given up her own life for her sister or was it the other way around? Had Sissa given up her life for the other Sissa?

Julia wanted to know more about this man Lena referred to as Uncle Pepi. Her only recourse now were books and since it was impossible to get to the library on her own anymore she solicited Daniel's help. He flatly refused: This is becoming an obsession, Julia. Forget about this.

I can't. I keep thinking about it.

Then start eating more olives, he said.

It's not funny, Daniel.

No it certainly isn't funny. Another reason why you should be looking after yourself instead of trying to understand. Let it go. It's not your story.

I'm not trying to understand, Daniel. I'm sure I won't. And I disagree with you that this isn't my story. It's everybody's story.

I can't help you with this.

You mean you won't.

No, I mean I can't. I can't take it. The thought of you cooped up in here, reading that stuff. It drives me crazy. I won't let you do it.

Had Julia felt more like her old self she might have told him it wasn't up to him. There was, however, little point in arguing plus his concern moved her. It's okay Daniel, she said. You're probably right, these events are past and I shouldn't spend so much time dwelling on them.

The next day, she turned to René who was still dispensing, along with the usual prescribed medications, his generous doses of tactful understanding. Their paths seldom crossed and they never spoke again at any length as they had done a few days before Mr. Wilkes was transferred. If they met in hallways or in the lounge they greeted each other long enough to maintain a link, the kind that didn't require a large investment of time or emotion. They shared a running joke, a newly made up Cartesian cogito misquote of some sort.

How are you today, Mrs. Brannon?

Oh, I think I'm fine therefore I must be fine.

A few weeks ago, as he was rushing down the hall, he took the time to congratulate Julia on her ninety-eighth birthday.

Kind of makes you think, doesn't it? she called back.

It also makes me want to live to ninety-eight, he replied.

Bless him, she thought. The simple experience of dealing with the day-to-day always prevailed for Evenholme's Descartes.

I have a favour to ask of you, she said to him the day after Daniel turned down her request to retrieve books she had on reserve at the library.

Certainly, he said, as Julia expected. What can I do for you?

She gave him a list on which she had written the names of several books. It shocked her to see how shaky her handwriting had become. Would you pick these up from the reserve shelves at the library? she asked.

No problem, he said, but when he saw the titles—*Mengele: The Complete Story; The Nazi Doctors; Auschwitz*; he paused, perplexed: Are you sure you should be reading these?

I see no reason why not, she replied.

Don't you already know enough about this nasty business?

No. I need to learn more.

Surely Mrs. Kohn told you as much as you want to know?

It's not a matter of wanting to know. I would, in fact, rather not know.

What exactly do you want to find out? asked René.

Many things. Why the children called him uncle, for one.

It's normal for children to try to get closer to those who hold their lives in their hands. Not only children, he added and turned his head to one side. His averted gaze conveyed what he already knew of love motivated by fear.

Yes. I realize this. I also believe there are people who have gone further into human nature than others. You told me once how you had learned something from one of the nurses who treated the residents badly. It changed you and changed how you relate to the residents here. I feel I've also learned something from Lena. Something I should have known a long time ago. I need to look into it further.

He shook his ahead in disagreement. If this is what you want... But I don't approve.

Most of the next few weeks were spent reading with hardly a break to meet with Daniel, which made him uncharacteristically grumpy. You're reading that stuff, aren't you? You went ahead and got the books anyway. You stubborn old broad. How many have you read?

One or two.

I can't stand it, fooling yourself into thinking you'll understand any of it.

Oh, the more I read the less I understand. But at least, now I know more than I did.

So, you know more, big deal.

Yes, Julia knew more and it was a big deal, bigger than she had ever imagined. Alone in her room at night, with no sound other than the occasional footstep trekking the hallway, she fought off sleep and kept reading. Daniel was right, the more grisly the details, the less she could wrap her mind around them. As much as she tried to find a place in which to put this new knowledge, she couldn't find one. She pored over the details of Uncle Pepi's cruelty to children hoping that any new knowledge would shed light on the questions they raised, but there was no garden, as her mother's, no philosophy or theory, no language or doctoral thesis that could illuminate the facts as they appeared on the pages of these books. Instead, she was plunged deeper into incomprehension. Yet it felt right that she should know about this. It felt right that she should endure this knowledge in the hope that something could come from knowing.

The only light in the suite came from a full moon flooding it from wall to wall like a projector catching objects in its path—family photographs; children's drawings; her mother's framed combs; the vase with the mice that Rachel finally retrieved from the attic. A beam travelling at the speed of time as it moved from the past through the present towards the future. Julia knew this light. It was the indelible, immemorial light as the one captured in Stieglitz's photograph of the Flatiron Building with the small patch of snow caught between two branches, the kind of light the eye holds on to when everything around it begins to fade.

Julia raised herself from the settee and walked to the desk on which the laptop was sitting. She felt shaky, but there was one more thing she wanted to add to what she'd written for Rachel and Thea. Something that felt as real as if she'd lived it, something relating to what Lena told her when she said, Try to imagine walking in my shoes.

It was almost impossible to write. Her eyes burned with fever and the keys on the keyboard kept blurring and moving. *From childhood you move into memory, from memory you move into imagination*, she wrote. As she doggedly pecked at each key she realized this may well be her last entry.

~34~

THERE WAS MOVEMENT IN THE ROOM, RUSTLING, AND VOICES. Julia had entered some remote region where mornings and afternoons reconstituted themselves as daydreams while nights never reached the labyrinth of deep sleep. She was suspended between reality and dream.

She woke up with a start. Rachel! Thea! Have you been here long? I must have dozed off.

You've been sleeping all afternoon, Nan. Thea wiped Julia's forehead with a damp cloth.

Do I have a temperature?

A little. The nurse says it's because of the pneumonia.

Rachel and Thea looked at each other. Like most people with years still ahead of them, they had not yet learned to concede to the inevitable.

Where am I? Where are my things? Julia asked.

You're in the hospital. You'll stay here until you get better.

Get better at what? Dying?

Don't be silly mother, Rachel said, trying to feel her way around what Julia should or should not know.

The poor dear, Julia thought, she looked as if she were about to pass out. It doesn't matter, Rachel, nothing can hurt us now, Julia said. Except for this damnable mattress. It won't mould itself to what's left of my spine and hips. Whose bed is this?

It's the hospital bed, mother.

Does this contraption roll up?

I'm not sure you should sit up. We should probably ask the nurse. Thea reached for a cable pinned to the side of Julia's bed.

Oh, just roll the damn thing up. I doubt I'll die this very minute.

Although it would hardly matter, I'm more than ready.

Are we ever ready, mother? Rachel asked, her eyes wide with apprehension, like the time when she called her Aunt Jane Mama on the attic stairs.

Rachel, my little daughter, Julia thought. Better prepared than you'd think, she said. Especially people like me who are under the illusion of having led fruitful lives.

Old cynic to the... Thea was about to say Old cynic to the end, but caught herself. Always the old cynic, she chided instead.

Don't knock it. It's what's kept me going all these years. I was having the strangest dream just now.

What about?

Dark shapes falling off buildings, flitting about like birds or bats.

You're probably thinking of the disaster in New York last week, Rachel, said.

There was a disaster?

We saw it on TV, remember? Two planes flew into the twin towers in New York and people were falling and throwing themselves out of windows.

No, no, my dream wasn't on television, it was real. It actually happened. A woman threw herself off The Flatiron. Poor thing. She so wanted to die and I've kept her up on that ledge all those years. I guess I can finally let her go now. With all the others. I can finally let them go.

Rachel and Thea, noticeably uncomfortable, kept giving each other significant looks.

Oh, do stop looking at each other that way. The two of you are so transparent, it's pathetic. So, I'm not likely to make a hundred after all.

You can recoup from the pneumonia, Nan. Your mind is too sharp to give up yet.

Hmm, it must have improved from a few minutes ago because I didn't know where I was then.

You have to hang in there, Rachel said.

Whatever for, Rachel?

For us. For Daniel. And Lena. She needs you to visit her.

No, no. It was me who needed them. Lena lives mostly in the past now, she thinks I'm her sister. Her son arranged for a psychiatrist or a therapist to see her a few times a week, as if what is happening to her could be worked out in therapy.

I think this may have been a while back, Rachel said. Before she was transferred.

Oh. She's been transferred too, has she?

Yes.

And Daniel? Has he been transferred?

No, he's still at Evenholme. He's been here to see you several times.

Has he? I must have been dozing. Too busy to wait around for me to wake up, I suppose. Probably rushes back to his equations where everything makes sense. Oh yes, I left something with him. My laptop. I told him to take it out of my room if I was taken to the hospital, or that other place. Julia raised her eyes to the ceiling.

Rachel groaned. Oh mother, please.

Let me finish, Rachel. I told him to give it to either one of you, but you should probably read it first, Rachel. Snippets I wrote now and then like you asked me, Thea. Enough to make up a story, a history, if you wish.

That's great, Nan. Julia was surprised that she could feel Thea squeezing her hand.

But spare me the embarrassment and wait 'till I've died.

What would they make of the facts they were about to learn, Julia wondered? The confirmation that Julia was not their biological mother and grandmother. How would Rachel react upon learning that her biological mother put a gun to her head? Unlike her grandfather who had the courage to turn the gun against others but not against himself? Passing on the responsibility to his wife. Would Rachel hate her for not telling her sooner, or would she hate her for not carrying it to her grave? She, the replacement, the substitute filling in for everyone who had died. Now, it was her turn at last.

As if burdened by everything they had witnessed for almost a century, it was impossible for her eyes to stay open. As she closed them, Julia felt herself being carried away as when love propels you forward.

~35~

IT IS COLD. WAR WEATHER. SISSA AND I ARE GETTING OFF A TRAIN *and follow mother and father and hundreds of people down a ramp, women and children pushing against each other to avoid being separated. Several men in uniform wait at the bottom of the ramp. One of them, a man with movie-star good looks, with medals and an Iron Cross pinned to his chest, is whistling something classical. The adagio from Bach's Violin Concerto in E. Unlike the other men, his uniform is clean, neatly pressed, and his boots highly polished. Mother is relieved. We will be safe in the hands of a man who is so highly decorated and with such refined taste. The handsome doctor carries a riding crop in his white-gloved hands, what a child would call a horse stick.*

It will be all right, mother keeps saying as guards push everyone towards the men in uniforms. I put my hands over my ears trying to block the horrendous screams as children are taken from their mothers. The screams are like nothing I've heard before.

It will be alright, mother insists. Nothing will happen as long as we stay together. Above the screams of children and mothers, guards are calling a foreign name: Zwillinge. Mother raises her hand. What does it mean, zwillinge? It means twins. Is this good to have twins? she asks. The guard nods, yes.

We've heard that twins were given special treatment in the work camps; the reason mother and father didn't leave us at the convent like my brother and sister. The nuns couldn't take us all and they had heard that twins received special treatment. We were the lucky ones, the nuns said.

My daughters, they are twins, mother shouts at the guard. See how alike they are. No one can tell them apart.

Other mothers with children of different ages and sizes put up their hands trying to pass their children as twins or even triplets.

As soon as the man with the horse stick spots Sissa and me, he pushes through the crowd. He stops whistling as he studies our faces, his own face flushed with anticipation. He keeps staring at our eyes, sees himself reflected there, one brown eye, the other blue. He has never seen such a phenomenon. I can smell his cologne. It masks the smell of shit, vomit, and that other strange smell from when we got off the train. From now on, at every opportunity, I will try to move closer to him. To smell his cologne.

He points to me and Sissa to join unusual looking people forming a line to the left—Gypsies, dwarfs, hunchbacks, but also twins. Also a few people who look German, but who have yellow stars sewn to their clothes. Mother and father join a longer line to the right and disappear. I turn to Sissa and I am surprised to discover that she no longer looks like me. We are no longer images of each other. She reminds me of someone else. She looks like Lena.

On the first day, the boy and men twins are separated from the girls and the women, except for very young boys and girls who are allowed to stay together in the girls' barracks where Sissa and I are. It is called The Zoo. It is next to a building with chimneys and plumes of white smoke billowing into the sky and we wonder why this particular building has so much heating when ours has so little.

Because we are a special group, one of the women guards tells us, because we are Doctor Mengele's children and he is a special uncle, the children are to call him Uncle Pepi and the older twins are to call him Uncle Mengele. It must be strange for the older twins, those who look older than mother and father to have an uncle.

The next day we are taken to Uncle Pepi's work place, the laboratory. Some people call it the hospital. We are told to take off our clothes, but because we are special our clothes will be returned to us. Our heads will not be shaven unless we have lice. We wait for a long time, sitting on a wooden bench, shivering with cold, until we are weighed and Uncle Pepi takes measurements of our heads and different parts of our bodies. We are cold and hungry and now we understand. As important as we are to Uncle Pepi and his work, our discomfort is of no consequence to him. His research is more important than we are. We mean everything to him, he tells us, but we know it is the other way around. He is the one who will mean everything to us. Everything.

After he finishes weighing and taking measurements he brings out colourful silk dresses for the girls and white pantaloons for the boys. He pats the little ones on the head and awkwardly hugs the older twins and gives us all chocolate and candy.

He then takes us outside and organizes a soccer game with each twin on an opposite team. On one team, the girls wear blue silk dresses and the boys wear white pantaloons with blue ribbons, while on the other team the silk dresses and the ribbons are red. Each twin is required to play against his or her twin brother or sister while Uncle Pepi writes down notes on a clipboard.

On other days, instead of playing soccer, silk scarves are tied against our eyes and we play a game Sissa and I often played with other children when we were girls, Blind Man's Bluff. Sissa and I were very good at it. The object of Uncle Pepi's game is for the twins to identify each other by touch, an easy enough task at first, but it becomes more difficult as some of the twins are being physically altered by Uncle Pepi's experiments. It becomes even more difficult for the hands to feel any difference between the taut skin of children's faces as everyone becomes thinner.

I like this game, the silk scarves soothe the burning from the chemicals Uncle Pepi has been injecting into one of my eyes. Each pair of twins has a special purpose in Uncle Pepi's research. With Sissa and me it is our eyes. He is haunted by them. They hold a mystery, a riddle he is determined to solve. If we are very good and very lucky, he tells us, he will turn each brown eye blue. Wouldn't this be wonderful? Think how beautiful we would be. Think of the distinctions he would receive if he could turn his own brown eyes or, for that matter, the Führer's, blue.

There is another pair of twins who haunts him almost as much as Sissa and me. They look very different from one another. They are fraternal twins. One is small with dark hair and, like most children, he could be from any ethnic background but because he has a Star of David sewn to his clothes, no one questions that he is Jewish. The other twin is tall and blond and he also has the Star sewn to his clothes in spite of being the ideal Aryan type the Germans are so proud of. Uncle Pepi can't understand how someone Jewish could look so German, especially a twin. Every day he draws blood from the blond boy and transfuses it to the dark-haired boy in the hope he will develop Aryan features. He bleeds the blond boy so badly that the veins in his arms and legs dry up as he wastes away. The other boy also dies from the transfusions because of his brother's different blood type. Their names were William and Thomas—Villem and Tomas.

Uncle Pepi has given me a piece of red crayon, a reward he sometimes gives children when they behave the way he wants them to. He keeps the crayons in a jar on shelves with other jars in which he saves strange things that look like pieces of meat suspended in liquid. Most of the crayons were brought into the camp by the children. This is what is most often found in their pockets when they are searched. Pieces of crayons, chalks, and coloured pencils. Only those who are sent to the twin barracks are allowed to keep them. Sometimes I retrieve these pieces when they are left behind, when the children get too sick to draw or when Uncle Pepi takes them for a walk to the place where there is smoke rising above the chimneys. I now have red, yellow, blue, and black pieces of crayons in various sizes, and one small yellow one.

When I have been especially good and have not whimpered or complained, I ask Uncle Pepi for a piece of paper from his clipboard. I like drawing houses with yellow lights in the windows, houses on the look-out throughout the night. It is always warm inside my houses with smoke rising in gray rings above the roof. I especially like to draw large doorknobs that will allow Sissa and me to open doors and walk out into a luminous and boundless space.

Nan?

Acknowledgements

My deep appreciation to my first readers, Lisa Tostevin and Jerry Tostevin for their editorial advice and to Peter Tostevin.

Thank you to CANDLES Inc. who provided me with material including the biographical *Echoes From Auschwitz, The Story of Eva and Miriam Mozes*, Eva Mozes Kor as told to Mary Wright (CANDLES Inc., Terre Haute, Indiana). My thanks also to the following publications: *The University of Toronto: A History*, Martin L. Friedland (University of Toronto Press, Toronto). *Distant Thunder*, Joyce M. Kennedy (Sunflower University Press, Manhattan, Kansas). *The Valour and the Horror*, Merrily Weisbord and Merilyn Simonds Mohr, based on a television series by Brian McKenna and Terence McKenna (Harper Collins Publishers Ltd., Toronto). *The Canadian Naval Chronicle*, Fraser McKee and Robert Darlington (Vanwell Publishing Ltd., St. Catharines). Newspapers from the thirties and the forties, *The Evening Telegram* and *The Globe*.

Thanks to Scott Drewery for his advice on stereographic images. And to Susan Kalman for her personal story.

I am grateful to Luciana Ricciutelli at Inanna Publications and Education Inc. for her commitment to women writers, and to the Ontario Arts Council's Writers' Reserve Program.

This novel is a work of fiction. Although it reflects elements of historical accuracy, resemblances to actual persons living or dead are coincidental.

Photo: Jerry Tostevin

Lola Lemire Tostevin was born into a French-speaking family in Northern Ontario (Timmins) although she writes mainly in English. She has published seven collections of poetry, one collection of literary essays and two novels, *Frog Moon* (1994) and *The Jasmine Man* (2004). Her work has been translated into French and Italian. She has also taught creative writing at York University in the 1980s and '90s and was writer-in-residence at the University of Western Ontario during the 2004-05 academic year. Her work has been the subject of several graduate and post-graduate theses. She currently devotes most of her time to writing. She lives in Toronto with her family.